She felt his fi...
lifting it so she would meet his
gaze.

"I didn't realise how much I'd missed you," he whispered.

"Well, that's one of us," she said, thinking she'd realised how much she'd missed him every waking minute since they'd broken up.

"I really shouldn't kiss you," he said.

"That's right."

"We're both going to have to keep our relationship professional. We can't let what happened last year happen again," he told her.

"I agree," she said firmly. "So stop looking at me like you want to make love to me against that door."

Taking Care of Business
by Brenda Jackson

ᗨ᙭ᙀᗧ

HAS THE ELUSIVE TAG ELLIOTT FINALLY BEEN CAUGHT?

While matriarch Karen Elliott recuperates at the family's estate in the Hamptons, youngest son Tag is apparently getting down to more than business with his mother's social worker here in NYC.

Seen together strolling through Village galleries, sipping coffees at a Tribeca café and cruising the Hudson, Tag and Renee Wiliams became the city's hottest couple when they appeared together at a benefit gala last night.

Dubbed the city's "Catch of the Day", handsome Tag was unavailable for comment. Apparently the magazine editor is more comfortable writing the news than making it.

But with their relationship causing quite a stir around town, Tag's grandfather, publishing magnate Patrick Elliott, will no doubt have a lot to say when he returns to town in a few days. Stay tuned!

Available in January 2007
from Silhouette Desire

The Forbidden Affair
by Peggy Moreland
&
Tempt Me
by Caroline Cross

☙ ❧ ☙ ❧

The Elliotts
Billionaire's Proposition
by Leanne Banks
&
Taking Care of Business
by Brenda Jackson

☙ ❧ ☙ ❧

Craving Beauty
by Nalini Singh
&
His Wedding-Night Wager
by Katherine Garbera
(What Happens in Vegas...)

Billionaire's Proposition
LEANNE BANKS

Taking Care of Business
BRENDA JACKSON

SILHOUETTE®

Desire™

*Silhouette, Silhouette Desire and Colophon are registered
trademarks of Harlequin Books S.A., used under licence.*

*First published in Great Britain 2007
Silhouette Books, Eton House, 18-24 Paradise Road,
Richmond, Surrey TW9 1SR*

The publisher acknowledges the copyright holders of the
individual works as follows:

Billionaire's Proposition © Harlequin Books S.A. 2006
Taking Care of Business © Harlequin Books S.A. 2006

*Special thanks and acknowledgment are given to Leanne Banks and
Brenda Jackson for their contribution to THE ELLIOTTS series.*

*ISBN-13: 978 0 373 40224 3
ISBN-10: 0 373 40224 4*

51-0107

*Printed and bound in Spain
by Litografia Rosés S.A., Barcelona*

BILLIONAIRE'S PROPOSITION

by
Leanne Banks

LEANNE BANKS,

a *USA TODAY* bestselling author of romance and 2002 winner of the prestigious Booksellers' Best Award, lives in her native Virginia with her husband, son and daughter. Recognised for both her sensual and humorous writing with two Career Achievement Awards from *Romantic Times BOOKclub*, Leanne likes creating a story with a few grins, a generous kick of sensuality and characters that hang around after the book is finished. Leanne believes romance readers are the best readers in the world because they understand that love is the greatest miracle of all. Contact Leanne online at leannebbb@aol. com or write to her at PO Box 1442, Midlothian, VA 23113, USA. An SAE (with return postage) for a reply would be greatly appreciated.

THE ELLIOTTS

Patrick m. Maeve O'Grady

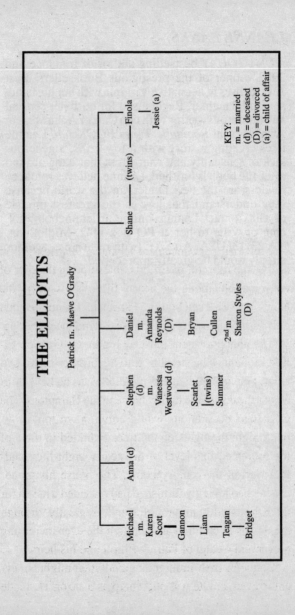

Michael
m.
Karen
Scott
— Gannon
— Liam
— Teagan
— Bridget

Anna (d)

Stephen (d)
m.
Vanessa
Westwood (d)
— Scarlet
|(twins)
— Summer

Daniel
m.
Amanda
Reynolds
(D)
— Bryan
— Cullen
2nd m
Sharon Styles
(D)

Shane —— (twins)

Finola
— Jessie (a)

KEY:
m. = married
(d) = deceased
(D) = divorced
(a) = child of affair

One

"**I** have an announcement to make," Patrick Elliott said to the roomful of Elliotts, interrupting the roar of conversation among the nearly fifteen present for the New Year's Eve celebration. Patrick had stipulated that only family members and spouses attend the gathering.

The announcement must be big news, Gannon Elliott thought as he stood next to his brother Liam. Curious, Gannon studied his grandfather as he held court across the den of the family home in the Hamptons. The Christmas decorations would come down tomorrow, but tonight the lights on the trees twinkled in three of the rooms on this level of the nearly eight-thousand-foot turn-of-the-century home. The house his grandmother had lovingly furnished had provided a haven for the Elliotts through the births and, tragically, through the deaths of children and through the ever-increasing power and wealth of Patrick Elliott and his heirs.

Gannon's Irish-immigrant grandfather might be seventy-seven, but he was still sharp as a razor. He made dominating the magazine-publishing world look like a piece of cake, with magazines that covered everything from serious news to celebrity watching, showbiz and fashion.

"But it's not midnight," cracked Bridget, Gannon's younger sister, in response to their grandfather. "You have the night off, Grandfather. Did you forget it's New Year's Eve?"

Patrick's eyes sparkled as he wagged his finger at her. "How could I forget with you here to remind me?"

Grinning, Bridget dipped her head and lifted her glass in response. Gannon shook his head and took a swallow of whiskey. His brash sister always seemed to be stirring the pot when it came to their grandfather.

Pausing for a moment, Patrick glanced at Maeve, his petite wife of more than fifty years. Patrick might be the workaholic lion who had built a publishing empire, but Maeve was the one woman who could soothe the savage beast.

The love and commitment emanating from both their gazes never failed to humble Gannon, arousing a gnawing sensation in his stomach, a vague dissatisfaction that he refused to explore. He mentally slammed the door on the feeling and watched his grandmother Maeve, love shining in her eyes as she nodded at his grandfather.

Patrick looked back at the family assembled by his invitation. "I've decided to retire."

Gannon nearly dropped his glass of whiskey. He'd

figured the old man was so wedded to his conglomerate that he would spend his last moments on earth making another deal. Murmurs and whispers skittered
through the room like mice.

"Holy—"

"Oh my God."

"Do you think he's sick?"

Patrick shook his head and lifted his hand in a qui-
eting motion. "I'm not sick. It's just time. I have to
choose a successor, and because all of you have per-
formed so well with the various magazines, the choice
is difficult. I've decided the only fair way to choose is
to give each of you an opportunity to prove yourself."

"What on earth is he doing now?" Bridget whispered.

"Do you know anything about this?" Gannon asked
his brother Liam, who worked for the conglomerate
rather than one of the individual magazines. Everyone
knew Liam was the closest of any grandchild to Patrick.

Liam shook his head, looking just as stunned as
everyone else in the room. "Not a clue."

Like the rest of the family, Gannon knew that the
four top magazines were headed by Patrick's sons and
daughter. Gannon's own father, Michael, was editor in
chief of *Pulse* magazine, a publication known for cut-
ting-edge serious news.

"I will choose from the editors in chief of our most
successful magazines. Whichever magazine makes the
largest profit proportionally will see its editor in chief
take over the reins of Elliott Publication Holdings."

Complete silence followed. A bomb wouldn't have been more effective.

Three seconds passed, and Gannon saw shock cross the faces of his uncles and cousins. He looked across the room at his father, who looked as if he'd been hit on the head with a two-by-four.

Bridget gave a sound of disgust. "This is insane. How can it work? Do you realize that since I work for *Charisma* I'll be working against my own father?"

Liam shrugged. "Is that any worse than pitting brother against brother, brother against sister?"

"Shane against Finola?" Bridget added in disbelief about their aunt and uncle. "They're twins, for Pete's sake. Someone has to talk to Grandfather and make him see reason."

Finola stepped next to Bridget and shook her head at her father. "He won't be changing his mind. He's got that 'till hell freezes over' expression on his face. I've seen it before," she said with a trace of bitterness.

"It's not fair," Bridget said.

Finola had a faraway look in her eyes. "He has his own definition of fairness," she said softly, then seemed to shake out of her split-second reverie. She smiled at Bridget. "I'm glad I have you on my team."

Gannon had never been one to shirk a tough fight and he wouldn't shrink from this one either. "May the best Elliott win," he said to Finola, although he knew the stakes were damn high. "Talk to you later," he said to Bridget, Liam and Finola, then moved toward his father, immediately confident that he would do anything to help his father make their magazine, *Pulse,* the top dog at EPH.

He was an Elliott, born and bred to compete, excel and win. Every Elliott in the room had been raised with the same genes and high expectations. It was in their blood to fight and win. Shrewd as always, his grandfather had known that fact when he'd issued the challenge, Gannon thought. Regardless of who won—and Gannon was damn determined to make sure his father was the winner—Patrick had just assured a banner year of earnings for each magazine and Elliott Publication Holdings.

His uncle Daniel stopped him on the way to his father. "You look like a man with a mission."

"I think we all are," Gannon said wryly and squeezed his uncle's shoulder. "The least he could have done was pass out a year's supply of antacid with this kind of news."

Daniel chuckled and shook his head. "Good luck."

"Same to you," Gannon said and walked the few feet to where his father and mother stood.

Twirling his glass of brandy, his father met Gannon's gaze. "I should have known this earthquake was coming."

"Who could have predicted this?" his mother, the most easygoing person he knew, asked. She met Gannon's gaze and smiled. "I see you've already recovered and are ready for the game."

"It's in my genes," Gannon said with a nod to his father.

"You have some ideas already?" his father asked, clearly pleased.

"Sure do." Gannon knew the first person he wanted on the *Pulse* team: Erika Layven, the woman he broke up with over a year ago.

Erika Layven reviewed the layout for the April issue of *HomeStyle* magazine with a critical eye as she took another sip of instant hot chocolate with marshmallows. Wiggling her sock-clad feet beneath her desk, she studied the spring-flower theme of multicolored roses, sprigs of lavender and cheery pansies. A huge contrast from the gray, bitter-cold January late afternoon she glimpsed outside her fifteenth-story window in Manhattan.

The weather made her feel cold and old. The recent report from her doctor hadn't helped much either. Add to that the New Year's Eve party she'd attended with a forgettable man and the more forgettable kiss at midnight and she could feel downright morose.

If not for the pansies, she told herself and straightened in her chair. She had a bunch of reasons to feel good. As managing editor of Elliott Publication Holdings' new magazine *HomeStyle,* she had the opportunity to help create a vision and make it come true. She had power. She had influence. She had a dream job. If she felt herself missing the rush she'd felt when she'd worked for *Pulse,* she pushed it aside. This was better, she told herself. In this world, she ruled.

A knock sounded at her door and she glanced at the frog clock on her desk. It was after five-thirty on Thursday night. Most employees had left for happy hour.

"Yes?" she called.

"It's Gannon," he said, then unnecessarily added, "Gannon Elliott."

Erika's stomach jumped into her throat and she took a full moment to catch her breath. What did *he* want? Pushing her curly hair from her face, she pulled together her composure. "Come in," she said in as cool a voice as she could manage.

The door opened and Gannon—six-foot-two, black hair, green eyes and killer body—filled the doorway, filled the room. She steeled herself against him and strictly instructed her hormones to behave, her palms to stop sweating and her heart to stop racing.

Idly wishing she'd kept on her boots so she could meet him *almost* eye to eye, she stood in her sock feet behind her desk. "Gannon, what a surprise. What brings you here?"

"Hadn't seen you in a while."

Your choice, she thought but took a different tack. "I've been very busy with *HomeStyle.*"

"So I hear. You're doing a fabulous job."

"Thank you," she said, unable to fight a sliver of gratification. Gannon was tough. He'd never been given to flattery. "It looks like *Pulse* is full of excitement as always."

He nodded. "What did you think of the series we ran on fighting Internet viruses?"

"Excellent," she said. "I loved the day spent with an Internet security soldier. Fascinating." She paused a half beat. "I would have added a fraction more human interest."

His mouth lifted in a half grin. "That's one of the things I always admired about you. You see the good in an article but are always looking for a way to make it better."

"Thank you again," she said, feeling curious. "You still haven't told me why you're here."

He glanced at her bookcase and tilted his head sideways to read a few titles. "How much do you like it here?"

Confused by his attitude, she studied him carefully as he lifted her frog clock from her desk. He wasn't acting normal. Although she wasn't sure what normal was for Gannon. Their relationship had clouded her instincts where he was concerned.

"What's not to like? I get to help rule," she said and smiled.

He glanced up and met her gaze and she felt a mini *kaboom* go off inside her. He chuckled. "That's one way of looking at it." He returned her frog clock to her desk and reached for her mug, lifting it to just below his nose. He smiled. "Hot chocolate with marshmallows. You must not want to stay up tonight."

Erika's stomach twisted and she felt her sense of humor wane. Gannon possessed all kinds of insider information on her because they'd been lovers. A fact she had tried hard to forget during the past year. "A good night's sleep keeps me sharp."

He nodded and paused thoughtfully. "Do you miss *Pulse* at all?"

The blunt question surprised her. "Of course I do," she said. "The fast pace, always being on the cutting edge. There was an adrenaline rush every day."

"And you don't get that here," he concluded.

"*HomeStyle* provides a different kind of satisfaction."

"What if you were given the opportunity to come back to *Pulse* with a promotion and salary increase over last time?" he asked.

Erika was taken off guard again. The prospect of being inside the best newsmagazine in the world provided a potent lure. There was nothing laid-back about *Pulse*. Working for that magazine had demanded the best of her mental and creative energy. It had forced her to grow. She'd been surrounded by brilliant, ambitious people.

And she'd gotten involved with a man who had ruined her for other relationships.

She pushed her hair behind her ear and looked outside the window as she tried to form a response. "It's tempting," she admitted.

"I want you back on the *Pulse* team," Gannon said.

"Tell me what it would take for you to make the move and I'll make it happen."

Erika gaped at him in shock. When the faintest gossip had surfaced about her relationship with Gannon, he'd stopped everything between them cold and had begun to treat her as if she were just another team member. His behavior had knocked her sideways enough that she'd known she couldn't work with him anymore. The position at *HomeStyle* had offered a haven from him, and she was slowly getting over him.

"I need to think about this," she finally managed.

He blinked in surprise and she felt a sliver of satisfaction. Gannon was accustomed to hearing yes, not maybe. She saw his jaw clench and felt another dart of surprise. *What* was going on here?

"That's fair enough. I'll drop by to talk with you tomorrow after work."

"Sorry. Can't do," Erika said. "I have an appointment out of the office at four-thirty. I'm not coming back in."

He gave a slow nod, as if she were trying his patience. "Okay, are you working this weekend?"

"From home." She glanced at her calendar. "Tuesday would be best."

"Monday, after work," he said in a brusque voice that had frightened the life out of more than one intern.

The tone unsettled her enough not to push further. "Monday after work," she confirmed.

"Good. See you then," he said, holding her gaze for a couple of seconds too long. A couple of seconds that sucked the oxygen from her lungs before he turned around and left her office.

Erika immediately sank into her chair and covered her face with her hands. "Damn him," she whispered. He still knocked her sideways. She scowled. She didn't like it. Didn't like it at all.

But part of her response was understandable, she told herself. Preparation was key with Gannon. She absolutely couldn't fly by the seat of her pants with that man.

Erika rubbed her knees and paused for a breath after ten games of one-on-one. She'd had her lunch handed to her during the last six games. Looking at the fourteen-year-old responsible for pounding the living daylights out of her via a basketball, Erika shook her head. "You could show a little pity for the elderly."

Tia Rogers, the pretty but lanky girl with chocolate-brown eyes who Erika was mentoring, shrugged as she walked to the side of the basketball court Erika had reserved for their use. Since she'd been promoted, she got dibs on the EPH gym.

"You ain't old. You just sit on your butt too much in that fancy high-rise office."

"Aren't old," Erika automatically corrected, though at the moment thirty-two seemed over the hill. "Getting paid to sit on your butt isn't all that bad. And I don't just sit on my butt," Erika said. "By the way, how's algebra?"

Tia made a face. "I don't like it."

"What'd you get on your last test?"

"B minus," Tia said.

"It's going up. That's the right direction." Erika patted the girl on the shoulder and scooped up both their coats from the bleachers. A group of men immediately took their place on the basketball court. Erika led the way to the elevator. Tia was quiet on the ride down.

"I need an A," Tia finally said in a glum voice. "I need all As if I'm going to get a scholarship to college."

"You'll get a scholarship," Erika said, waving at the security guard before the two of them stepped out into the cold night.

Tia swore and spit as she stepped outside. "How do you know?"

Erika swallowed a wince. She was supposed to inspire Tia and help polish her mentee's rough edges. Tia, who lived with her aunt because her mother was in prison for repeated drug violations, had been chosen for the mentor program because she worked on the school newspaper. "Ditch the spitting and swearing."

"Everyone else swears and spits," Tia said in a challenging voice.

"Everyone else isn't you. You're different. You have talent, brains, common sense and, most importantly, you have drive."

Tia met her gaze with wide brown eyes filled with hope but tempered with skepticism. It was Erika's job to help give the hope and drive she glimpsed in the young teen a bigger edge in the battle.

"Is that what got you your fancy job in the office you showed me a couple weeks ago? I hear you always need a connection."

Erika exhaled and her breath created a visible vapor trail. "I'm working for a company where most of the executives are related and I'm not part of the family."

Tia smiled. "So you've had to kick some butt, too."

"Metaphorically speaking," she said as an image of Gannon's backside slithered across Erika's brain. She'd had a tough time totally banishing him from her mind since his surprise visit yesterday. She still didn't know what she was going to do about *Pulse*. She lifted her hand to hail a taxi.

"My aunt keeps asking me why you don't have no man."

"Why I don't have a man," Erika corrected.

"S'what I said," Tia said and climbed into the taxi that stopped by the curb.

Erika climbed in beside her and gave the taxi Tia's address. "I don't have a man because—" She broke off. Why didn't she have a man? Because Gannon had ruined her for other men. "Because I fell for someone and he dumped me."

"Wow," Tia said. "Why'd he do that? You're pretty for an older lady. You got it going on."

Erika groaned at the reference to age. "Thanks, I think. Why'd he dump me? I guess he didn't think I was the right woman for him."

Tia swore again. "You should teach him a lesson. Go get you another man. A better man."

"Yeah," Erika said, thinking she'd been trying to do that for a year now.

An hour later Erika walked into the Park Slope brownstone she owned and immediately stepped out of her shoes and into her bunny slippers. She looked down at the pink furry footwear and smiled. They always made her smile.

Making a mental promise to wash the clothes in her gym bag, she left the bag in the hallway and headed for the kitchen as she glanced through her mail. Bills, bills... She paused at the postcard that featured a Caribbean cruise and felt a longing for hot weather, sunshine, an icy margarita and the sound of steel-drum music.

Sighing, she dismissed the mini fantasy and used her remote to turn on the sound of Alicia Keys while she poured herself a glass of red wine. She picked up her phone and listened to her messages.

The first was from one of her best friends, inviting her to visit a trendy new bar. The second was her mother checking on her. Erika bit her lip in response to that. Her mother had called her at a weak moment and Erika had told her too much about the results of her doctor's visit. The third message was from Doug. *Doug the dud,* she added. A nice enough guy. He was just so boring.

The call-waiting beeped as she listened to his message and she automatically picked up. "Hello?"

"Erika, I wondered when I would hear your live voice again. How are you, sweetheart?"

Her mother. Erika winced. "I'm sorry, Mom. I've been very busy at work and I took on a mentoring project with an inner-city teenager. How are you? How's bridge?"

"Your father and I came in second last night. We host tomorrow night. What is this about mentoring an inner-city teenager? Darling, you don't really think that will take the place of having your own child, do you?"

Erika's chest twisted. "No, but it's a good use of my energy right now."

"Honey, if you would just make a little effort and be more open-minded, I know you could find a man in no time. Then you could have both the husband and the baby you want."

Erika squeezed her forehead. "I'll make a deal with you, Mom. I'll go out with two men next week if you stop asking me about this for the next week."

"I'm just thinking of your well-being. You've always wanted children."

"I know."

"You just kept putting it off," her mother added.

"Mom," she said, and Erika couldn't keep the warning note from seeping into her voice.

Her mother sighed. "Okay. Two dates, two men next week. I'll say a prayer and make a wish on a star."

Erika felt her heart soften. Her mother did love her. She just felt the need to interfere sometimes. "I love you. Have fun tomorrow night."

Clicking off the phone, she set it down and smiled, picturing her parents and the house in Indiana she'd left behind when she moved to attend college in the East.

The town of her childhood had often felt sleepy to her, the pace hadn't been fast enough. She'd wanted more excitement, more action, more challenge.

She remembered the smell of the cholesterol-laden, but delicious home-cooked meals that had greeted her every time she returned home, and the scent of chocolate chip cookies every time she left again.

She remembered making crafts with her mother on rainy days and the countless times her mother had sat with Erika while she'd done her homework. Her father had taught her to play basketball and encouraged her to relish her height instead of being afraid of it.

She'd always known she had the best parents in the world. She'd also always known that she would need to leave in order to really fly.

And she'd certainly learned to fly. At least professionally. In the back of her mind, she'd had a mental plan. Graduate from college, get on a career track that would take her to the top and along the way she would squeeze in finding a husband and having a baby.

Before she'd even graduated from college, Erika had wanted a child, but she'd told herself not to get caught in the trap of getting married and having a baby before establishing her career. It was all about discipline, she'd said, but many times she felt a strong longing on rainy days to make crafts with a child of her own, to nurture and love a human being and experience the wonder of helping a little someone become the very best person they could be.

Her work was exciting and rewarding, but part of her remained untouched. Part of her longed for something that work couldn't fulfill.

Sighing, she opened her eyes and pulled a sheet of paper from the wooden file she kept for mail. She glanced at the medical report again and sighed. Endometriosis. That was why she'd had such terrible cramps. That was why her fertility was headed into the toilet. That was why she would consider having a baby without a husband.

Two

At precisely five thirty-one in the afternoon, Erika heard a knock at her office door. Her stomach dipped, but she ignored the sensation. Today she hadn't kicked off her shoes below her desk. Nope, today she wore high-heel boots that brashly flaunted her five-foot-nine-inch height and a black suit with a crisp white blouse. Today she was prepared.

She strode to her door and opened it, spotting Gannon lifting his hand for another knock. He was still too damn tall. She would need stilts to meet him eye to eye. Dressed in a black wool suit with a faint blue stripe, he would leave quivering females in his wake wherever he went—the elevator, his office, the street. Erika imagined women all over the office melting into the carpet.

His green gaze flicked over her, then he looked into her eyes for an assessing second. When he'd taken the time, he'd always been able to read her. Better not to let him see too much, she thought.

"Come in," she said and returned to stand behind her

desk. She liked having a large wooden object between her and Gannon. At that moment she wished her desk was a little bigger, perhaps boat-sized. "How are you?"

"Fine, and you?" he asked, moving the folder he held into his other hand.

"Good, thank you." Pleasantries over. "I've thought about your offer. I loved working at *Pulse*. It was the most challenging and creative job I've ever had. I loved the fast pace. I loved working with such sharp minds." She paused and took a quick breath and reminded herself she was doing this for her sanity. "But I'm very happy and productive where I am right now. I have an excellent rapport with everyone who works for me. It's a warm atmosphere and it works for me."

He remained silent.

Poo. He was going to force her to say *the words*. She would have much preferred doing this via e-mail or fax. "So thank you very much for your wonderful offer. While I'm tempted, I'm going to decline."

He looked at her for a long moment and gave a slow nod. He moved closer to the desk and picked up her half-full mug. "The job you have at *HomeStyle* is like hot chocolate with marshmallows. It's nice. It's comfortable. A few challenges every now and then. You have to choose whether to feature needlepoint or knitting, find new crafts for Valentine's Day, a decor for spring."

Erika felt defensive. "You're right. Making marshmallow bunnies isn't going to rock the world. It's just going to make it a little nicer, a little more comforting."

"As I said, this job is hot chocolate. The problem, Erika, is you had the best whiskey in the world at *Pulse.* You know what it's like to come to work knowing you'll get an adrenaline rush. That the story you tell and the way you tell it *could* rock the world. Underneath the hot chocolate with marshmallows and bunny slippers is a world-rocker. You can fight it all you want, but you and I both know it's in you."

The challenge in his eyes made something inside her sizzle and pop. She hated that he knew her so well. She hated that he'd known her so well and left her so completely, but she wouldn't tell him that was the reason she wouldn't return to *Pulse.*

"I want you to reconsider," he said.

She swallowed a groan. She'd really had to pump herself up for this. "I've given your offer a lot of consideration. You have my answer."

His lips turned up slightly in a grin she'd seen before. A grin that signaled Gannon was in for a battle, determined to win. A grin that scared the life out of her. "Your answer isn't acceptable to me. I want you to reconsider. My father does, too."

Oh great, she thought wryly. Two Elliotts teaming up against her. "I'm very happy here."

"We'll make sure you're happy at *Pulse.*" He laid the folder he'd held during their discussion on the desk and flipped it open. "How would you like to do this story?"

Erika saw photos of babies and her heart stopped.

She bent down to look at the copy. "Making the Perfect Baby: The New World of Genetic Manipulation," she read and looked at him.

He smiled. "I knew that would get your attention. You always loved the combination of science and human interest. Cover story with your name on the front. That's the kind of story that could win awards. Rock the world."

Gazing at the photos of the beautiful sweet faces of the babies, she swallowed over the lump in her throat. Did he know how much she wanted a baby? How could he know? They'd never discussed it.

She took a shallow breath and forced herself to smile. "Very tempting, but I've given you my answer."

He paused just a second, as if she'd surprised him. "Okay. You don't mind looking over the story and giving me your thoughts, do you? Think about it and I'll drop by on Wednesday."

The trendy new cocktail bar, the Randy Martini, was packed with twenty- and thirty-something Manhattanites testing the wild, extensive menu of over a hundred martinis. It took two and a half martinis for Erika's best friends, Jessica and Paula, to get Erika to confess what had her so distracted. "I want to have a baby and my gynecologist told me I need to do it soon or maybe not at all."

"That stinks," Jessica said and patted Erika's hand.

"Maybe you could get a dog or a cat," Paula suggested.

Erika shook her head. "I want a baby, not a canine or feline."

Paula lifted her own martini in salute. "You might change your mind when the kid hits puberty or when you start shelling out the green for college."

Erika shook her head again. "Even though I've been career-oriented, I always knew I wanted to have a child."

"You could wait until you find Mr. Right and try adopting, although I hear that can take forever," Jessica said. "Any Mr. Rights on the horizon?"

An image of Gannon slipped into her mind. She immediately stamped it out. "No."

Jessica made a face. "I guess you could go the insemination route."

Paula looked horrified. "Get pregnant without being able to blame it on a man for the rest of your life?"

"It could be fun," Jessica said.

"For whom?" Paula asked. "Erika grows to the size of a beached whale, then gives birth to something that looks like a screaming pink alien."

"You have no maternal instincts," Jessica said. "It could be fun for you and me. We could throw her a shower and go to those labor classes with her. We could even go in the delivery room with her."

"Speak for yourself," Paula said.

"And we could be aunties," Jessica said with a smile. "I'm liking this idea. I'll even go with you to a sperm clinic, Erika."

"I hadn't considered anonymous insemination," Erika said. "I have this fear that they would give me the wrong vial and I'd end up with a crazy man's sperm."

"They probably toss the crazy sperm," Jessica said.

"But how do you know what you're getting?" Erika mused.

"You don't," Paula said. "Unless you do a genetic study or at least get a look at all the guy's siblings and parents...and aunts and uncles and cousins and grandparents."

Erika thought of the Elliotts. Now that was an awesome gene pool. "It would be great if I could choose."

"Yeah," Jessica said as she sipped her drink. "We could start with that blond guy by the bar with the buff bod."

"And what if he's dumb as a bag of hair?" Paula asked.

"We can put intelligence on the list, but that guy looks good enough that he could make millions by being a model and then retire in leisure."

"What list?" Erika asked, feeling a little blurry from the alcohol.

"We're making a list of sperm-donor requirements. Play along," Jessica said firmly. She pulled a pen from her purse and shook the dampness out of a cocktail napkin. "We're doing this for the sake of your future child."

"I would want intelligence," Erika said, allowing herself to be drawn into the ridiculous discussion. "Good looks aren't enough."

"I agree," Paula said. "And no terrible diseases or addictions."

"Excellent points," Erika said.

"You've already got the height factor covered," Jessica said.

"No shrimps," Paula interjected. "He doesn't need to be the height of a pro basketball player, but definitely over six feet, right?"

"Right," Erika agreed. "And a sense of humor. Is that genetic?"

"Lack of it can be," Paula said and waved for the waiter. "Three death-by-chocolate martinis."

"Chocolate?" Erika echoed. "I'm on my third."

"No meal is complete without chocolate," Paula said.

"I didn't think martinis constituted a meal," Erika said.

"Sure they do," she said, pointing to her glass. "Celery's a vegetable, isn't it? Cream cheese inside the olive counts as protein, and appletini provides the fruit."

"Back to the list," Jessica prompted. "Do you have a strong preference for hair or eye color?"

"No back hair," Paula said.

"I'll second that," Erika said, amazed at how much this ridiculous conversation was reducing her stress level. "I prefer dark hair."

"Eye color?"

"Green, if possible." Why not go for the whole she-bang, she thought.

"Okay," Jessica said and nodded at the waiter as he delivered their chocolate martinis. "We have our assignment now. Each of us is to keep our eyes open for a father for Erika's baby. A tall, intelligent man with dark hair and green eyes. Healthy, no addictions. He must have a sense of humor."

"And what are we supposed to do once we find this specimen?" Paula asked.

"That's easy," Jessica said with a scoff. "Ask him to donate some sperm to Erika."

Erika choked on her sip of chocolate martini. "He'll think you're crazy."

Jessica shook her head. "That's why he needs a sense of humor."

The following morning Erika awakened late, feeling as if a truck had run over her. Thank goodness she didn't have any appointments this morning. She couldn't remember the last time she'd had a hangover. Oh, wait, yes she could. It was last year when Gannon had broken up with her. The bad thing about having a mad, passionate affair with her boss was that she hadn't been able to tell a soul, not even Paula or Jessica.

Keeping the secret had intensified everything about her relationship with Gannon. The highs, the lows, the ending. She kept telling herself that if she'd been able to talk with her friends about him, he wouldn't have affected her so much. Unfortunately part of her remained unconvinced.

Her phone rang, the sound of it reverberating pain-fully in her brain. She snatched it from the cradle. "Hello."

"Erika, this is Cammie. Are you okay?"

"I'm fine," she reassured her. "Since I didn't have any appointments scheduled this morning, I decided to come in a little later."

"That's fine," Cammie said. "Except Gannon Elliott has called twice asking for you."

Darn. "Just tell him I'll get back to him this after-noon."

"I think he wanted you to sit in on a luncheon meet-ing."

"For what?" Erika asked, immediately feeling sus-picious.

"He didn't tell me."

Erika sighed. "I'll call him in a few minutes." Frown-ing, she turned on her coffeemaker while she jumped in the shower. Skipping the blow-dry, she smoothed on some hair-wax stuff her stylist had given her and pulled her hair into a low ponytail. She applied some makeup, pulled on a don't-mess-with-me black trouser suit and a pair of boots, grabbed her coffee and coat and walked out her door, glowering as she hailed a cab.

As she scooted into the taxi, she called his office number by rote. One more thing to irritate her. She needed to forget him. "Erika Layven, returning Gannon Elliott's call," she said to his assistant.

"I'll put you right through."

"Hello, Erika. I wondered where you were," Gannon said in a deep voice that slid through her like warm whiskey.

"I understand you wanted me to attend a luncheon appointment. My afternoon is crammed. What did you have in mind?"

"We're having a luncheon meeting at *Pulse*. The subject for the article I gave you is on the agenda. Love to have you there. I think your input would be invaluable."

Erika thought again of the article outline he'd left for her. The subject fascinated her. She'd peeked at it at least a half dozen times after he'd left her office. Temptation slid through her like an evil serpent. "I don't know. Like I said, I'm very busy this afternoon."

"You could scoot out after the discussion about the article," he suggested.

He made it too easy. "Okay. As long as you understand that I'm staying at *HomeStyle*."

"Great. I'll see you at noon," he told her.

Erika walked into the *Pulse* meeting room a few minutes early. Furnished with a large wooden table set with seven lunch boxes from a local deli-bakery, the room emitted a let's-get-busy feeling.

"Very nice choice, Lena," Erika said to Gannon's assistant.

Lena, a young married woman who was the mother of twins, beamed. "When Gannon told me you were coming, I made sure there was decent food. Inside the box there's a chicken-salad sandwich, spicy vegetable soup, a fruit cup and a slice of lemon pound cake."

"You're a woman after my own heart. Wouldn't you rather work for me?" Erika joked. "I'm so much easier to please than he is. And I don't bark."

"Who says I bark?" Gannon asked from behind Erika.

She cringed at being caught talking about him at the same time she felt a shot of adrenaline at the sound of his voice. His voice had always affected her that way, sent her heart and hormones off to the races. She definitely needed to rein in her response to him. "Coffee, please," she mouthed to Lena, then turned to face Gannon. "Good morning. Your assistant has arranged a lovely spread for the meeting."

His killer Irish eyes were a bit too sharp for her taste this morning. And why did she always forget how broad his shoulders were?

He glanced at the table, then returned his gaze to Erika. "Yes, she has. She resisted fast food when I told her you were coming."

"Bless you, Lena," Erika said and accepted the piping-hot coffee Gannon's assistant offered her.

"You weren't trying to steal her away from me, were you?"

"Just making her aware of her options," Erika said with a smile.

"Who says I bark?"

"Everyone," she said without batting an eye.

He glanced at her coffee. "Black?"

She nodded and took a sip.

"Hmm. Black coffee…coming in late this morning… Did you have a late night last night?"

"Nope." That was true. She'd come home early and fallen into bed as a result of one too many martinis.

"Out with the deadly duo?" he quizzed, speaking of Jessica and Paula.

She'd revealed far too much of her personal life to him during their affair and she didn't like his reminders. "As a matter of fact, yes. How's your family?" she asked, turning the personal questions on him.

He paused and shook his head. "Same as ever."

"That's about as vague as you can get," she said, studying him.

He leaned closer to her, making her heart jump. "You'll learn more if you rejoin the *Pulse* team," he told her in a low voice as four more people entered the room.

Michael Elliott, editor in chief of *Pulse* and Gannon's father, entered the room and extended his hand to Erika. "Good to have you back. We've missed you."

"It's good to see you, too, Mr. Elliott," she said as she shook his hand.

"Erika, glad you're back," Jim Hensley, chief copy editor, said as he entered with the rest of the department heads.

"Great to see you," Barb said.

Howard gave her a thumbs-up.

The greetings felt good. A couple of minutes passed while Lena provided everyone with coffee and a bottle of water.

Michael called the meeting to order. "Let's get to business. Gannon, you go first."

"I'd like to start with the baby story since Erika tells me she'll need to cut out early. Erika, what are your thoughts?"

"I suggest incorporating several points of view. A scientist, a couple who have chosen their baby's sex, outlining the procedures and costs involved, and a couple who considered choosing their baby's sex but changed their minds. It would be interesting to learn which sex is chosen most frequently. And at-home techniques that do or don't work."

"I like it all," Michael Elliott said. "And you're the one to do it."

Erika blinked. "Excuse me?"

"Since you're moving back to *Pulse*," Gannon's father said, "you should take the lead on this. It's going to be a major story with possibilities for awards. You're perfect for it."

Erika tossed a questioning glare at Gannon.

"That's exactly what I thought," he said. "We have a contact for the scientist, but knowing you, you have your own. You always found the most amazing contacts and got the best quotes."

"Hey," Barb said, "if you keep talking about Erika

like she walks on water, you're going to make the rest of us feel like hacks."

"She does walk on water, doesn't she?" Howard said, wearing a deadpan expression.

Erika glanced at Gannon and felt a sliver of suspicion. This meeting was way more warm and fuzzy than the meetings she remembered from a year ago, and while Michael Elliott gave the occasional pat on the back, he'd never been one for effusive praise.

If Gannon had pulled his father and three of *Pulse*'s top power brokers in on seducing her back to the team, something had to be up. Something she hadn't been told. Something big.

"You guys are too good to me." She glanced at her watch. "Time for me to go back to *HomeStyle* land. It was great seeing all of you."

Gannon stood. "I need a quick word with Erika. How about if everyone starts on lunch?"

"No problem," his father said. "Don't take too long."

Lena handed Erika's lunch box to her. "Don't forget your lunch."

Erika couldn't prevent a smile. "Spoken like a true mom. Thanks." She walked out the door, feeling Gannon directly behind her.

He pulled the door closed and she rounded on him. "There seems to be some confusion."

"What confusion?" he asked, his face revealing nothing.

"Your father, along with other staff members, appears to have the false impression that I'm rejoining *Pulse*."

"Admit it, Erika. You can't resist the baby story. You want to be back on *Pulse* so bad you can taste it."

"The baby story interests me, but it's not enough to bring me back to *Pulse*."

"Then what is?" he asked, surprising her again with his wide-open offer. "We need you on the team more than ever. Name your price."

Three

Gannon allowed Erika thirty hours to think about what he could do to bring her back to *Pulse*. The negotiation process was turning out to be tougher than he'd planned. In the past, although he'd appreciated Erika's originality and adventurous attitude on the professional end, he'd always thought of her as cooperative.

Even at the end of their affair, she hadn't fought him when he'd abruptly broken off with her. He still felt a twinge about it. He'd always been scrupulous in avoiding office affairs. Lord knew his grandfather frowned on anything that bore even a hint of scandal. Gannon knew the reason he'd risen to his present position so quickly was because he'd embraced the Elliott family work ethic by skipping vacation for two years and because he'd built a reputation of integrity.

Erika had been his one slip. Her combination of natural beauty and willingness to take chances and succeed had caught his attention. He'd never met a woman he could talk with more easily. At the same time, he knew about the kick of fire beneath her black suits and businesslike attitude. He'd seen her naked, felt her body against his, felt himself sink inside her, into an oblivion of pleasure.

He felt himself harden at the memory and swore under his breath. He adjusted his tie and opened his office door to find his father on the other side.

His father looked at him quizzically. "Bad time? You headed somewhere?"

"Just wrapping up a little negotiation. What do you need?"

His father gave a short laugh. "Funny. You looked like you were gearing up for battle."

"Nothing I can't handle," Gannon said and shook off a ripple of discomfort.

"I'm knocking off early to take your mother to dinner."

Gannon did a quick mental calculation. "Let's see, it's not your anniversary, her birthday or your birthday. What's the occasion?"

His father frowned at him. "No need for a special occasion," he said but pointed to the slight bulge at his middle. "She's trying to get me to cut out some of my takeout." He lifted his eyebrows. "Having a wife wouldn't be a bad idea for you either."

Gannon shook his head. "I'm married to my job. I'm married to winning the competition so you'll be the new CEO of EPH."

His father smiled and squeezed Gannon's shoulder.

"You're a formidable opponent, Gannon. I'm glad you're on my team."

Even though Gannon was thirty-three years old, he still appreciated a pat on the back from his father. "Wouldn't have it any other way."

"Okay. Don't stay too late or your mother will fuss at me."

"Enjoy your meal and give Mom a hug from me," Gannon said and headed toward the elevators. "Good night." He stepped inside and punched the button for Erika's floor. Seconds later the doors whooshed open and he walked to her office.

Her assistant had already left, so he knocked lightly on her door.

"Come in," she called.

Gannon stepped inside her office and watched her hold up one finger as she talked on the phone. He nodded and pulled the door shut behind him. He approved of the comfortable but businesslike room. Erika's touches of individuality made it interesting without being fussy.

Down deep Gannon felt the drag of fascination with her. She was perfectly groomed, with curves in all the right places. Unashamed of her height, she wore heels without batting an eye. She rarely attempted to tame her riot of long brown curls. Her hair suggested a wild streak, one which he'd experienced intimately.

She hung up the phone and met his gaze. "Sorry. That was the nervous producer of a new decorator makeover show we're featuring."

"You reassured him," Gannon said.

She nodded and lifted her wrist to look pointedly at her watch. "He should be good for fourteen hours. Have a seat."

Good sign, he thought. At least she was willing to talk this time. Unbuttoning his jacket, he pulled the chair closer to her desk and sat down. "What do you want?"

She met his gaze for a long, level moment that ricocheted through his system. "First, what is behind your determination to get me back at *Pulse?* I've been at *HomeStyle* for a year. You didn't make a peep when I left. Why the big rush now?"

"Circumstances have changed. I can tell you why, but I'll need you to keep it confidential," he said.

"Of course," she said.

He knew firsthand that Erika could keep a secret. She'd been as discreet as he had been when they'd been involved. "My grandfather has decided to step down and he has chosen an odd way of determining his successor. The four top magazines of EPH will compete against each other during the next year. The editor in chief of the magazine with the highest increase in sales proportionally will become the new CEO of EPH."

Erika stared at him speechless for a long moment. "Wow," she finally managed and nodded. "So you, of course, are determined to see your father be CEO."

"That's why I'm willing to give you a raise, a promotion and whatever else I'm capable of giving to get you on our team."

She gave a half smile and glanced away. "In that case, this is what I want," she said and opened the folder to the photos for the baby article he'd shared with her days ago.

She wanted the article? This was too easy, he thought with a surge of victory. He leaned back in his seat and waved his hand toward the folder. "We have a deal. The article's all yours."

"I'm not talking about just the article, Gannon. Yes, I want the article. I also want a baby."

Gannon stared at her in confusion. He shook his head. "I couldn't have heard you correctly. You said you wanted a baby?"

"You heard me. I want a baby."

"What does that have to do with me?"

Erika stood. "You have excellent genes. I want them for my child."

The woman had gone insane. Totally, he thought. He shook his head and opened his mouth to tell her she was crazy, but she raised her hand to stop him.

"Just listen. It really won't be that difficult for you. We can sign an agreement. I won't expect financial or any other kind of support. All I want is your sperm. We don't even have to go to bed. You can donate it at a laboratory. I'll even buy the girlie magazine. All I want is your sperm," she repeated.

He gaped at her for a moment of intense silence, then

stood. "You've lost your mind. Why do you want me? Why don't you find some other guy? Get married?" he asked, although the prospect of Erika getting married didn't sit well.

"I told you. You're tall, intelligent, no diseases. Great genes. If I'm going to have a baby, I need to get pregnant soon."

"Why? Plenty of women wait until late in their thirties to get pregnant."

"I can't," she said, and he saw the edge of desperation in her eyes. "My doctor told me I have a condition that affects my fertility and the longer I wait to conceive, the less likely I'll be able to. I've always wanted a child, so I need to do this now."

The strain in her voice made his gut knot. "What about adoption?" he asked.

"I looked into it. It's expensive and takes forever."

Of all the requests he'd expected when he walked into Erika's office, this one didn't even come close. He raked his hand through his hair. "I don't see how—" He broke off when he saw the combination of stubborn determination and desperation on her face. "I'm going to have to think about this."

She nodded. "I understand. Let me know when you decide."

"Would you consider working part-time for *Pulse* while I decide about—" he cleared his throat "—donating my sperm?"

She looked at him for three seconds. "No."

"But I can guarantee an increase in your salary, a promotion over your last tenure with the magazine, increased visibility. How can you turn that down?"

"I want a baby. You won't have to do that much to help me. Your donation is a deal breaker. And I want a contract."

Gannon swallowed an oath. What had happened to sweet Erika during the last year? She'd grown a spine of steel. Lord help him. "I'll get back to you," he said shortly and turned toward the door.

"Thanks, and good night to you, too," she murmured from behind him.

He strode to the elevator, mentally swearing every other step of the way. He punched the elevator button and shook his head. How in hell could he make this kind of deal? He could see the discussion he would hold with his attorney now. If he found out, his grandfather would have a cow.

Gannon had been told by both his father and grandfather that he needed to set an example of unimpeachable discretion and integrity. How could he possibly explain this to his family, let alone the rest of the world? He walked out of the elevator and headed for his office, giving a distracted nod in response to a copy editor's greeting.

Entering his office, he closed the door behind him and loosened his tie as he walked to the window. Staring down at the city lights, he rested his hands on his hips, his mind sorting through a dozen possibilities.

Just because Erika had made a bizarre request didn't mean he didn't still want her on the *Pulse* team. There had to be a way around this.

Seemed like old times, Erika thought as she walked into the quiet cocktail bar miles from the office. She and Gannon had met in countless bars just like this one during their affair. Far from the office, quiet, not trendy. Something inside her twisted at the memory, but she ignored it. She hoped this place made good martinis.

Glancing around, she caught sight of Gannon standing as he waved her toward his booth. She walked toward him feeling a slight jump in her stomach at the sight of him. It was a sin the way the man looked just as good at the end of the day as he did at the beginning. His clean-shaven jaw and the scent of cologne had made her dizzy in morning meetings. She'd found his five-o'clock shadow ruggedly sexy during the evenings they'd worked late. After the first time he'd left her breasts red from the friction of his jaw against her skin, he'd made a point to shave. She remembered how having his passion directed solely at her had made her giddy.

She told herself not to feel that way.

"Thanks for coming," he said, motioning her to the other side of the booth. Ever the gentleman, he took his seat after she did. "How was the traffic?"

"Busy as always. I'm glad I caught my cab before it started to sprinkle."

"I have a hired car tonight. I can give you a ride home if you like."

"I may take you up on that."

"Would you like dinner?" he asked, giving her a menu.

"Maybe an appetizer and a drink," she replied, eyeing the shrimp.

"Appletini still your favorite?" he asked with a grin that was a little too sexy and knowing for her comfort.

She shook her head. "Peach with champagne on top."

He raised his eyebrows. "A change?"

"I've found I like a little fizz," she said.

The waiter approached the table and Gannon gave her order, then his own. "Whiskey," he said. "And buffalo wings. Hot," he added.

"Hope you've got your antacid handy," she said, unable to prevent a grin. "I hear that as people age their stomachs become more sensitive."

He stared at her for a long moment. "Are you suggesting that I'm getting old?"

She shrugged. "None of us is getting younger," she said and switched the subject. "So tell me why you wanted to meet with me."

"I've thought about your requests and I think we can work something out. It may require some modification," he said.

"Such as?" she prompted, her heart picking up. She couldn't believe Gannon would agree to her demand.

After he'd left her office the other day, she'd wondered
if she'd been half-crazy to make such a request. But one
thing she'd learned was that if a girl didn't ask, a girl
wouldn't get.

"Within two weeks I can get a contract from our
legal department with the terms of your employment,
including your position and the increase in your salary."

"And an office with a window and a door that can
be closed," she added.

He gave her a half smile. "My, my, you've gotten
much more demanding during the last year."

"It's been a learning year," she told him. A year of
learning, hurting and getting over him. She was still
working on that last part.

"Good for you." He paused while the waiter served
the drinks, then he took a long draw from his whiskey.

Erika took a tiny sip from her martini and told herself
there was no reason for her to feel nervous. None at all.
She had a perfectly wonderful position and she would be
perfectly fine to stay where she was at *HomeStyle*. *Pulse*
would be more hectic, more exciting and, with Gannon
always around, much more distracting and disturbing.

"Regarding the other matter," he said vaguely in a
low voice.

"The donation of your sperm," she clarified.

He took another drink of whiskey. "Yes. I'll have to
do that through my personal attorney. My grandfather
would implode if he saw anything like this on a company contract."

So Gannon was actually considering her request. She couldn't believe it.

"This would require secrecy. Not discretion. Complete secrecy. I'm sure my attorney can do it, but it won't be done overnight because he's out of the country."

"When is he due to return?" she asked with healthy skepticism.

"Two weeks. He's on a Mediterranean cruise celebrating a second honeymoon."

She took a breath. "So how would we work this? I would start at *Pulse* after he returns?"

Gannon shook his head. "No. I told you *Pulse* is under the gun. I want you to start immediately."

She laughed. "I don't see how. *HomeStyle* will need some sort of transition."

"I've already suggested that Donna Timoni could take your place. You can start work at *Pulse* by the beginning of next week."

Erika blinked at him. Although she agreed that Donna Timoni would be her ideal successor, she wasn't ready to hand over the reins this second. "This is fast."

"Have you forgotten?" he asked with more than a hint of daring in his green eyes. "At *Pulse* the only speeds are fast, faster and fastest."

She nodded, remembering the magazine's mantra. "We don't leave them laughing. We leave them in the dust." She paused and took a sip of her martini. "What about the contracts?"

"Like I said, I can have the company contract for you within a week or two. The personal contract will take a little longer."

"Okay. There's only one other part to this agreement. I can go back anytime."

"It's a deal," he said and met her gaze. "You won't want to go back, Erika. If you're honest with yourself, you'll admit you've missed *Pulse*."

His instincts about her had always gotten under her skin. No man had known her better. No man had been more intuitive about her. In bed or out. She swallowed a sigh. Just because she was getting his sperm didn't mean she was getting his heart or his mind. Or even his body, if he made his deposit at a lab.

Working with him every day would probably drive her mad. She would use all that excess energy to keep looking for the man who could top Gannon Elliott.

The appetizers arrived and they naturally changed the topic of conversation. While she shared her shrimp with Gannon, she asked about his grandmother, Maeve Elliott.

"I've always been fascinated by the story of how your grandfather and grandmother got together," she said.

He offered her a buffalo wing and she shook her head. "The seamstress and the tycoon who stole her away from Ireland."

"How has she put up with your grandfather all these years?"

"He adores her," Gannon said. "And she's a saint. You can't help but love her. She makes up for all the affection Grandfather has such a tough time giving."

"She's the one member of your family I always wanted to meet," Erika said, then quickly realized she should have kept that confession to herself. "It would have been a great feature for *HomeStyle*. Tea with Maeve Elliott."

"Not a bad idea for *Pulse* for a personality-slash-human interest story."

"You're a total thief," she accused.

"Put your loyalties in the right place, Erika. You're on my team now."

His possessive tone sent a shiver of pleasure through her. She remembered when he had made her feel as if she were the most important woman in the world. He tried again, unsuccessfully, to tempt her to eat a buffalo wing and asked about her best girlfriends. He knew about them, but they didn't know about him.

They finished the appetizers and another drink, and Erika glanced at her watch. "Oh my goodness. It's ten o'clock."

He grabbed her wrist. "Nah. Your watch must be wrong."

"Check yours," she said. "Where did the time go?"

He looked at his watch and swore, then met her gaze and held it for a long moment. "We never had any trouble filling the moments."

Her stomach tightened at his reference to their past relationship. She shook her head. "No. We didn't."

His gaze held hers for another moment before he looked away and sighed. It was probably her imagination, but she would have sworn there was just a little longing in that sigh.

"You want a ride?" he asked.

"That would be nice."

After calling for the car, he paid the check and ushered her outside. "There it is," he said, pointing to a black Town Car. "I'll get it," he said to the driver as the man stepped out of the car. He held the door open and Erika slid across the leather bench seat. Gannon followed, closing the door behind him.

"Still in Park Slope?" he asked.

"Yes," she said, immediately aware of his closeness. She smelled a hint of aftershave mixed with whiskey and the combined scents of Italian leather and fine wool. As he gave her Brooklyn address to the driver, she glanced down at his long legs. She knew he'd played soccer in college, but she'd always wanted to play one-on-one with him. She knew he was a ferocious competitor no matter the game.

He touched her shoulder and she looked at him. "Yes?"

"I said you should buckle up," he told her, reaching over her shoulder to pull the strap across her. "Didn't you hear me?"

She smiled. "That second martini must have hit me."

The car swerved, throwing Erika against Gannon's chest. His arms closed around her.

The driver slammed on his brakes and swore. "Sorry, folks," he said.

Her face inches from Gannon's, Erika stared into his green eyes, holding her breath. She felt his gaze move to her lips, burning her with the imprint from his eyes.

"Once for old time's sake?" he asked in a low voice, sliding his hand behind her neck. "We need to get this out of our systems, don't we?"

She could have pulled away. He would have allowed her to refuse.

But she didn't.

Four

Erika held her breath. Her heart seemed to pause, too, as if she'd been waiting for this, for him, for such a long time. Microseconds lasted forever.

Finally his lips touched hers. He increased the pressure and she sighed. He rubbed his mouth sensually over hers and she allowed herself the guilty pleasure of sinking into him. He slid his tongue past her lips and she tasted the cool peppermint candy the waiter had left with the bill.

As he massaged the back of her neck, she leaned into him, wanting more. The sensitive tips of her breasts grazed his hard chest and she swallowed a moan. She hadn't known her body had responded to his so quickly. She was so wrapped up in how he felt that she forgot how he affected her.

He lowered one of his hands to the side of her breast, and her heart stuttered. She wanted him to caress and squeeze her. She wanted his bare hand on her bare breast. An intimate image seared her mind of the two of them, tangled together as close as a man and woman could get.

Gannon deepened the kiss and Erika felt her mind turn like a kaleidoscope. With each turn she grew more dizzy.

The sound of a cough penetrated the roar of arousal in her ears. The cough sounded again. Gannon reluctantly pulled away, his eyes dark, mirroring the same passion that kicked through Erika.

"Uh, excuse me, Mr. Elliott," the driver said. "I didn't want to interrupt, but we've been parked for three minutes now and that policeman across the street keeps pointing at his watch."

Arousal and embarrassment warred for domination inside her. Erika licked her lips, tasting Gannon all over again. Swallowing a groan, she glanced away and covered her eyes to compose herself. She could just guess how worked up she looked. She probably looked as if she would have been willing for Gannon to take her in the backseat, heedless of the driver's presence or the anal policeman across the street.

She adjusted her hair and pulled her coat around her more securely. "Well, thank you for the ride. It was fun catching up over cocktails. I guess I'll be seeing you in the office."

"I'll walk you to the door," he said.

"Not necessary," she said, needing to get away from him so her brain cells would begin working properly. "I don't want you to get a ticket."

"Carl, go ahead and drive around the block once. I'll

be here when you get back," Gannon said and helped her out of the car.

He escorted her to the door, and when they stopped, Erika was reluctant to look at him. She didn't want him to see what she knew was written on her face. "Thanks ag—"

She broke off when she felt his fingers on her chin, lifting it so she would meet his gaze.

"I didn't realize how much I'd missed you," he whispered.

"Well, that's one of us," she said, thinking she'd realized how much she'd missed him every waking minute since they'd broken up.

"I really shouldn't kiss you," he said.

"That's right."

"We're both going to have to keep our relationship professional. We can't let what happened last year happen again," he told her.

"I agree," she said firmly. "So stop looking at me like you want to make love to me against that door."

He sucked in a sharp breath and leaned against her, nudging her against the building. "As long as you stop looking at me like you want me to take you against that door."

"No problem for me," she whispered, her heart pounding in her ears.

"Or me." Immediately he made liars of both of them when he took her mouth again and gave her a kiss that screamed *sex*.

* * *

Four days later Erika sipped another cup of coffee halfway through another fourteen-hour day as she joined the *Pulse* staff meeting.

Michael Elliott sat at the head of the table with Gannon to his right and Teagan, also known as Tag, Michael's youngest son, to his left. Erika gave a quick nod to Gannon but purposely didn't meet his eyes.

After going at it with him in front of her Brooklyn brownstone, she'd decided she needed a strategy if she was going to work for *Pulse*. Number one on the list was to avoid Gannon. Number two was the two-foot rule. Always keep two feet between herself and Gannon.

In this instance, number two was easy to keep because she chose to sit on the opposite side of the room.

"Hi, Erika. Good to see you," Michael said.

"Thank you, Mr. Elliott. Good to see you, too," she said.

"How much longer do you think you'll be dividing your time between *Pulse* and *HomeStyle?*" he asked, ever the hard-edged businessman. "We'd like all your attention here."

"I appreciate that, Mr. Elliott, and trust me, I'll be happy when I can stop bouncing back and forth between the fifteenth and twentieth floors."

Teagan smiled in sympathy. "Feel like a yo-yo?"

"A little, but that will change soon enough."

"When?" Gannon asked.

Erika tensed. She didn't like being put on the spot. Plus Gannon had made it clear that she would be working for his father, not him. Barely glancing at Gannon, she looked at Michael. "I hope to wrap up most of my pressing business with *HomeStyle* within two weeks."

"Good," Michael said, then his lips twitched with humor. "We're just greedy for the edge you're going to give us."

Erika smiled. "You flatter me. Thank you."

"Not really," Teagan said. "If you've got a magic wand in your purse, we'll take that, too."

"We won't need magic," Gannon said.

"As if you wouldn't use it if you had it," Tag retorted. "Everyone knows us Elliotts are a bloodthirsty, competitive lot. You think Liam has forgotten when Bryan broke Liam's arm during a touch football game at the Tides?"

Erika knew that Liam was Tag and Gannon's other brother and that Bryan was one of their many cousins.

"It was an accident," Michael said.

A knock sounded at the door and Michael frowned in displeasure. "Who is it?" he barked.

The door cracked open and Bridget, Michael's daughter, stepped just inside the room. "Sheesh, what a face," Bridget said to her father. "You'd think I interrupted a discussion on the fate of the country." She gave a quick glance around the room and her gaze paused on Erika. Realization crossed Bridget's face. "Oh, not the fate of the country," she corrected. "The fate of EPH. How sneaky that you pulled in Erika Layven. We were looking at her for *Charisma*. Finola will be disappointed. I hope they promised you the moon, Erika, because you're worth it."

Erika couldn't help smiling at Bridget's smart humor. Finola was Michael's sister and she was editor in chief of *Charisma*. Finola also employed Bridget as her photo editor. It must cause Michael endless heartburn knowing his own daughter was working against him. "Close," Erika said, referring to the moon. "Please tell Finola thanks for thinking of me."

Gannon cleared his throat. "Dear sister, what are you doing here?"

Bridget batted her eyes. "You're not happy to see me?"

"Bridget," her father said, clearly ready for the nonsense to end.

"I just wanted to tell you personally that I can't come to dinner tonight. Please tell Mom I'm sorry. Finola wants me to stay late."

Michael nodded. "Your mother will be disappointed," he said.

"I know." She threw him a kiss. "I'll make it up to both of you." She threw a saucy smile at the group. "Good luck."

Michael cracked a smile, pride beaming through his usual hard-nosed attitude. Bridget closed the door behind her and Michael cleared his throat. "Okay, back to work."

An hour later the meeting ended and Erika headed

for the elevator. Just as she hit the button for the fifteenth floor, Gannon appeared and slid inside. "You want to go up to the executive dining hall so we can talk about your story more? I had an idea—"

Erika shook her head. "I can't afford the time right now. I need to look over photos from a shoot of comfortable European homes." She sighed. "That's the closest I'll get to Europe for a while."

"Maybe you can dream up a feature set in Europe," Gannon said.

"No time," Erika said again and shrugged. "It's just cabin fever. I get it every January. The cold temperatures, the gray sky, always having to be inside." She smiled. "I get anxious for recess."

The elevator doors whooshed open and Gannon followed her to her office. Erika felt a sliver of irritation. He was distracting and she had no time for distractions at the moment. She stepped behind her desk. "I wish I could talk with you right now, but I really can't."

"Okay. You want to meet for a drink after—"

"No," she said and added, "thank you."

He looked at her for a long moment. "Is this about what happened the other night?"

"You mean the foreplay on my front doorstep?" she asked, her edginess growing. "You and I have an agreement about your contribution to my little personal project, but we can't let that interfere with our jobs."

"No chance," he said in a chilly voice.

Easy for him, she thought and bit back a scowl. "I

do better with boundaries. Since your father is my superior, it shouldn't be difficult for you and me to limit our interaction."

"That's gonna be tough," he said skeptically. "We're on the same team, and the atmosphere at *Pulse* is intense."

"I know," she said. "But there's always e-mail."

Gannon laughed. "Erika, a big part of the reason I insisted that you join *Pulse* was because of the dynamic you bring to every discussion even if it's not your assigned area. I'm counting on you for that." He stepped closer to her desk and Erika felt her heart rate speed up. "Yes, there's chemistry between us. But it's nothing you and I can't handle."

She bit the inside of her cheek. He made it sound so easy, but for Erika it was the hardest thing in the world not to turn into some sappy puddle of willing woman whenever he looked at her. "Fine," she said. "Limit your time alone with me and always keep two feet away and I think we'll be fine."

"Two feet?" he echoed, staring at her in surprise.

"Minimum," she said crisply. "I'm glad you find it easy to keep business and emotion—or in this case perhaps I should say hormones—separate. But unlike you, I'm mere mortal, carbon-based, and boundaries help me immensely."

"And what about when the time comes for me to make my *contribution* to your little personal project?"

"I thought we agreed you would do that in a lab."

"If you don't change your mind," he said, his mouth stretching upward in a sexual grin that unfairly threatened her knees. And her spine.

"That's pretty arrogant," she told him.

"We'll see. Since you're busy now, I'll stop by tomorrow night," he said and strolled out of the room.

Erika bared her teeth and gave a low growl. The man was so aggravating. What made it worse was that he was right. She hated that. He tempted her, always had. She wished she possessed the magic antidote for his effect on her.

The following day she dropped Gannon a quick e-mail telling him she couldn't meet him due to a mentor meeting, which was the truth. Tia had asked to rearrange their meeting because of a conflicting basketball game.

Erika arranged for a taxi to pick Tia up and met her for a quick bite to eat. Afterward she brought Tia upstairs to the nearly deserted office to show her some of the inner workings of *HomeStyle* magazine.

"It's cool and pretty, but it's kinda boring. I'd rather write an article about something more important than arranging flowers," Tia said.

Erika secretly agreed, but she knew she needed to provide perspective. "Yes, but I've gained new skills by taking this job. I've been one of the top people, so I've learned to make decisions quickly when necessary. It's also given me a better appreciation of how our surroundings or environment can affect our attitudes and emotions."

"Like a cold, rainy day makes you want to skip school," Tia said, skimming her hand over Erika's desk and smiling at the frog clock.

"Not you, of course," Erika said. "You've got the idea. Another example is how a drab room can make you feel tired."

Tia nodded. "My math room needs to be painted. It's dirty beige. I want to go to sleep every time I go to that class."

"Nothing to do with the subject," Erika teased.

Tia shook her head. "No, I'm serious. It's peeling and blah. Everybody skips classes in that room more than any other," she said.

"Then maybe *HomeStyle* could sponsor a classroom makeover," Gannon said from the open doorway. "I couldn't help overhearing you."

Tia looked Gannon over from head to toe, then glanced at Erika with raised eyebrows. "Who's he?"

"Tia Rogers, this is Mr. Gannon Elliott, executive editor of *Pulse* magazine," Erika said. "Mr. Elliott, Tia is teaching me how to be a mentor."

"She's doing pretty good for a new chick," Tia said, accepting Gannon's outstretched hand. "I thought the head dude for EPH was some old guy. You ain't that old."

Erika chuckled. "Patrick Elliott is the CEO of Elliott Publication Holdings. Patrick is Gannon's grandfather."

"Oh," Tia said. "Not to upset Miss Layven, but *Pulse* is way better than *HomeStyle*."

Gannon smiled. "Thank you. I'm partial to it. And Miss Layven will be moving permanently to the *Pulse* team as soon as we can arrange it."

Tia gaped at Erika. "That is just so cool."

"If you want to get a makeover for your math classroom, better start asking now," Gannon said.

Erika looked at him. "You're serious."

"Sure. Decorating, human interest and community service. I may even lift a brush in contribution."

Erika did a double take. "I didn't know you could paint."

He tossed her a dark look. "It's not that difficult."

"But do you have actual personal experience?" she asked in disbelief. After all, Gannon was a billionaire. Why would he need to *paint?*

Gannon nodded. "Yes. Teagan, Liam, Cullen and I painted the boathouse one weekend when we were teenagers. My grandfather thought it would build character."

"Did it?" Erika couldn't resist asking.

"It increased my desire to make good grades so I wouldn't have to paint for a living," he said.

A new story about Gannon's past. Delighted, Erika smiled, feeling as if she'd been given jewelry.

"Grades again," Tia said. "You sound like Miss Layven."

"Good to know we agree on a couple of things," he muttered. "How long are you two planning to be here?"

"We're actually leaving," Erika said. "Hot chocolate, then I'll put Tia in a cab. School night."

Tia wrinkled her nose.

"Mind if I join you?" Gannon asked. "I can offer the use of my car."

"Cool," Tia said. "Is it a limo?"

Gannon's lips twitched in humor. "Sorry, just a chauffeured Town Car."

"That's okay," Tia said. "It might look too pimpin' if we showed up in a limo in my neighborhood."

"You really don't need to do this," Erika said, thinking about the return ride in his hired car, alone with him. How was she going to stick to her two-foot rule in the backseat of his car?

"No problem. We can discuss the classroom makeover and then you and I can talk some *Pulse* possibilities on the return drive."

Erika grudgingly had to admit that Gannon was on his best behavior with Tia. He answered her questions, gently teased her and encouraged her about her studies. He picked up the tab for the hot chocolate and during the drive to Tia's apartment he asked her how she would like to see the room decorated.

"It needs to be a bright color so we'll stay awake," Tia said. "Yellow…"

"Research indicates that babies cry more in rooms painted yellow and people tend to become more emotional," Erika said.

Gannon threw her a questioning glance. "How do you know that about babies?"

Erika shrugged. "Just one of those things I picked

up through *HomeStyle*. Red is a stimulating color, but
some studies indicate an association with aggression."

Tia rolled her eyes. "We don't need no more aggression. There's fights every day."

"*Any* more aggression," Erika automatically corrected. "And there *are* fights every day."

"That's what I said," Tia said.

Gannon made an amused choking sound.

"Don't say no right away. But I'd like you to consider pink," Erika said.

"Pink?" Gannon echoed in a combination of disbelief and distaste.

"Put your macho attitude aside for a moment if you
can," Erika said.

Tia shook her head. "I can't do pink. The guys would
never stop making fun of me. And they would be impossible in the classroom."

"Studies indicate that students perform better in a
classroom painted pink. Not only do they perform better but they're happier."

Silence followed.

Gannon gave Erika a considering glance and rubbed
his finger over his mouth. Erika told herself to look
away from his mouth. Away.

He looked at Tia. "I think you should do some research on how color affects mood and write a very
short article. With Miss Layven's approval, *Home-
Style* can print your short article within the classroom redo feature. You choose the redo, within

reason, based on your research and you get a writing credit."

Tia dropped her jaw. "Me? Write an article for *HomeStyle*? Have *my* name in the magazine? I can't wait to tell my friends."

Erika couldn't help smiling at Tia's excitement.

"Omigod," Tia said. "I mean, it would be much more sweet to be in *Pulse* or *Snap* or *Charisma*," she said, listing EPH's most successful magazines. "But this is cool, too." She shook her head in disbelief. "My name in a national magazine."

"You'll need to do your research," Erika said.

"I will," Tia agreed.

"And Miss Layven will edit your article. You need to be prepared for rewrites," Gannon said.

"That's okay. I can do that," she said, nodding as the car pulled in front of her apartment building. She looked from Gannon to Erika, then back at Gannon. She reached out and grabbed his hand. "Thank you so much, Mr. Elliott! I won't disappoint you."

She turned to Erika and threw her arms around her. "Miss Layven, you're the best thing that ever happened to me."

Surprised at Tia's emotional display, Erika hesitated a half second before she returned the teen's embrace. Her heart twisted with an odd emotion. "I know you're going to do an awesome job, Tia."

"Yes, I will," Tia said and pulled back, pointing her index finger at Erika. "You can count on me."

Gannon opened the car door and slid out so Tia could climb out of the car. "Bye!" she said and darted for the front door of the apartment.

Erika and Gannon waited until she was safely inside, then Gannon got back into the car and gave Erika's address to the driver.

Her emotions swinging in several different directions at once, Erika didn't say anything for a long moment. A big part of her wished Gannon hadn't been so charming, so generous tonight. It would have been easier for her to not like him. His suggestion to allow Tia to write an article, however, felt like an arrow to her Achilles' heel. In an effort to keep from throwing herself at him, she put her purse on the bench seat between them. She needed a barrier. A steel wall would be best.

She swallowed over a knot of emotion in her throat. "That was brilliant and generous. Thank you. For Tia. For me. For *HomeStyle*…"

"You're welcome," he said. "Now you owe me."

Five

*Y*ou owe me.

Erika's heart stuttered and she felt her mouth go bone-dry. "Uh, owe you?"

"Yep," he said with a sexy grin playing around the edges of his mouth. "Payback's hell. I want you to play volleyball on Saturday afternoon."

The lascivious thought racing through Erika's mind came to a dead stop. "Volleyball? Excuse me?"

He shrugged. "I know you have athletic ability and you're tall. The family holds a friendly little game where employees from the magazines play each other. We need another woman on the *Pulse* team. We're only allowed one nonfamily stand-in and I have a hard time finding a female with the right height."

Erika didn't know whether to be amused, insulted or peeved. "Is this why you took Tia and me for hot chocolate and promised her that story? That was pretty low."

"Two minutes ago it was brilliant and generous."

"That was before I found out you wanted payment."

"It's not that bad a payment. Think about it. What's the worst that can happen? You sit on a bench for the afternoon."

"Why would I be sitting on a bench?"

"Well, you'd be an alternate, of course," he said.

"Excuse me? I played volleyball in college."

"That's why I chose you."

"To sit on the bench?"

"The guys get a little bloodthirsty," he explained. "It's all in fun, but I wouldn't want you to get hurt."

She shook her head. "So I'm supposed to be the token nonplaying female? If the rest of the female members of your family knew this, they would fry you," Erika said. "Can you imagine what Finola and Bridget would say?"

"Bridget's on Finola's team, so I can't ask her. It puts me in a bad spot. Besides it's *Snap* against *Pulse* this time." He sighed. "Do you remember Athena Wainright?"

Erika vaguely remembered the extremely tall, middle-aged copy editor for *Pulse.* "Yes, why?"

"She moved to Idaho. I need a backup player and I'm surrounded by pygmies."

She studied him, seeing the exasperation mar his handsome face. "I don't remember your being this competitive with your family."

His green gaze turned dark with an edge of sensuality. "When you and I were involved, I didn't want to waste time talking about volleyball games with my family."

Erika felt a quick rush of heat and resisted the urge to lower her window for a cold breeze. "One condition," she told him.

"What is it?"

"You let me play during the first fifteen minutes. If I don't pass muster, then you can put me on the bench."

He paused, then nodded. "Deal," he said.

"Any news on your attorney's return from his honeymoon?"

"Still out of town," he said. "I'll let you know when he gets back." The driver pulled in front of Erika's brownstone. "Let me walk you to your door."

"Absolutely not," she said, grabbing her purse and unlocking her door.

"You don't trust me?" he asked.

Erika didn't answer because the truth was she didn't know who she mistrusted more in a situation that put her in close quarters with Gannon—him or herself.

Gannon put Erika in for all three games. His uncle Daniel and cousin Cullen were clearly out for blood.

Erika spiked the ball just over the net, squeezing out another point for *Pulse*.

Gannon's brother Tag caught his breath. "Good thing you got Erika. It looks like Daniel and Cullen brought in a relative of the Jolly Green Giant," he said of Margo, the six-foot-four-inch woman playing on the opposite team. "What did they say her position at *Snap* is?"

"Temp," Gannon retorted, wiping the perspiration from his face. "If she worked there over a week, I'd be surprised."

"I repeat—good thing you got Erika since Charlie hurt his ankle."

"Yes, it is. My serve," he said, catching the ball as Cullen tossed it to him. The only downside of having Erika on his team was that his gaze and attention frequently dropped to the movement of her tight rear end. It had been tough to keep his eye on the ball when she offered such a tempting view. He knew what she looked like naked. What she felt like. The knowledge brought out primal instincts that didn't have anything to do with volleyball.

Cullen shook the edge of his T-shirt against his chest. "Seems to me Erika isn't officially working for *Pulse* yet, Gannon. I could have sworn I saw her headed for the fifteenth floor instead of the twentieth floor."

"You're just scared," Gannon said, tossing the ball above his head and hitting it hard and fast over the net.

His uncle Daniel smacked it back, directly in Erika's direction. Another woman would have ducked, but not Erika. She hit the ball with her head. Tag rushed forward and sent it across the net.

Cullen spiked the return, but Erika set it up again, this time with her fists. Gannon spiked it just inside the boundary.

Daniel groaned, then chuckled. "Gannon, you act like we're competing for the position of CEO."

"We're not?" Gannon said to his uncle and sent another hard serve over the net. Five minutes later Erika won the last point.

"All right!" Tag gave Gannon a high five and turned to Erika. "You saved our butts."

"That's an exaggeration," she said with a breathless smile. "But you're welcome. I'm glad I played one-on-one last week with the teenager I've been mentoring or I might have faded after the second game."

"Not you," Gannon said, lifting his hand to hers for a high five, then closing his hand around hers for just a moment. Erika's cheeks were pink and her face glowed from exertion. Her curly hair strained to be loosened from the elastic band that kept it from her face. The way she looked now reminded him of how she'd looked when he'd taken her to bed that first time. "How do you manage to look good even when you're sweaty?" he asked in a low voice.

The color of her cheeks deepened and she pulled her hand from his. "Nice try, but you owe me now," she told him quietly.

Gannon wondered what she meant and made a mental note to ask her later.

"Gotta run," Margo said. "Sorry about the loss, Mr. Elliott," she said to Daniel.

"Not your fault. I hate to admit it, but I think they wanted it more. Thanks for coming. Hey, Erika," Daniel called. "I'm sure we could find a place for a woman with your talents at *Snap*."

Gannon felt a quick kick of irritation. "Butt out," he said, stepping in front of Erika.

"Whoa," Cullen returned with a wide grin. "Territorial? You think she can get your father into the CEO office?"

"Who's eating *Pulse*'s dust right now?" Gannon asked, playfully egging on his cousin.

"This was volleyball, wasn't it?" Erika asked. "You are family, aren't you?"

"Yes to both," Daniel said. "But we like to win."

"At everything," Gannon added, extending his hand as his uncle ducked under the net.

"The important battles won't be finished until next year," Daniel reminded him.

"Eleven months and two and a half weeks," he corrected. "But who's counting?"

Daniel and Cullen chuckled. "Can't join you for a beer," Cullen said. "I have plans."

"Me, too," Tag said.

"That gives me an excuse to hit the hot tub and pretend my knees aren't killing me," Daniel said. "See you later. Nice meeting you, Erika."

Gannon grabbed a towel from the sidelines and scrubbed his face. "How about a shower and I take you to dinner as a thank-you for your participation?"

"Is that your way of saying I saved your butt?" Erika asked, resting her hands on her hips.

Gannon shook his head and snapped the towel at her, intentionally missing. "Never. But I'll still take you to dinner."

She held his gaze for a long moment, then sighed. "I don't think it's a good idea."

A ripple of surprise slid through him. "Why?"

She shrugged. "History repeating itself and all that," she said.

"I wasn't asking you to go to bed. Besides, you want to have my baby—"

She lifted her hand. "Wait a minute. I want to have *my* baby. I just want your genes."

His ego took a hit, but he recovered. "If you want my genes, then you must like something about me."

She sighed. "Unfortunately," she muttered and turned away. "I need to go."

He grabbed her arm. "Wait. You said I owed you."

"Right. One more reason you need to give me your genes. I'll see you Monday."

Watching her walk away, he felt the drag of irritation and something else in his gut. He frowned when he figured out the feeling. He still wanted Erika in his bed. She would be disgusted to know that she brought out in him the sexual urge to conquer and occupy.

She tempted the hell out of him, but he needed to keep a lid on his impulses. Since he hadn't been in day-to-day contact with her, he'd thought the chemistry between them had waned, but being around her reminded him of how hot it had been between them. Being around her left him with a nagging feeling of sexual deprivation.

He swore under his breath. Erika made a good point about history repeating itself. His grandfather had hammered it into his head that he needed to set an example for his generation of Elliotts. It wasn't as if he was a randy eighteen-year-old. He'd been able to shelve his attraction for Erika before. No reason he shouldn't be able to do it again. He just needed to dive into work as he always did.

Erika accepted a last-minute dinner invitation from Jessica and Paula. The three women met at a seafood restaurant. Paula mentioned Erika's position at EPH and the host seated them immediately and their cocktails were served in record time.

"That was low," Erika said, taking a sip of her martini and promising to limit herself to one tonight. "He probably thinks this will earn him a review in one of our magazines."

"You never know. You may mention this place to the right person and ta-da," Paula said, glancing at the menu. "Saturday night and none of us has a date. How sad is that?"

"Speak for yourself," Jessica said. "My boyfriend is working."

"Ah, the foot doctor," Paula said. "How is our boy Bill?"

Jessica smiled. "Podiatrist. Wonderful. But more

importantly, I have a prospective sperm donor for Erika."

Erika choked. "You what?"

"I found a TDH who's smart and has a sense of humor," she said in a singsong voice.

Paula smiled at Jessica's code word for a man who was tall, dark and handsome. "You can tell us all about him after we order," she said as the waiter approached. "I'm starving."

"Me, too. I think I burned a thousand calories playing volleyball today." Erika wondered if she should tell her friends she might have found her own tall, dark and handsome candidate.

Paula made a face. "Sounds sweaty. Why?"

"It was a company thing. Sort of," Erika said, thinking that turning down Gannon's invitation to dinner had been tougher than she'd liked. She'd put herself in an odd situation by asking the most attractive man in the world to donate sperm for her child yet swearing off sex or emotional involvement with him. "Sometimes I wish I were more like a man," she muttered.

"What?" Jessica asked.

"Nothing. I'll take the shrimp special," Erika said to the waiter and closed the menu. The other women placed their orders.

Jessica turned to Erika. "You wish you were more like a man?"

"Just able to detach myself emotionally," Erika explained.

"Like me," Paula said.

"Exactly." Erika smiled.

"Well, you may not need to detach yourself with the guy I've found for you. He's tall, dark, handsome, smart and he's got a sense of humor."

"How did you find him?"

"He's a friend of Bill's," Jessica said. "So we can double after you get to know him."

"Another foot doctor?" Paula said. "Bet he's got a fetish."

"That's not nice," Jessica said. "Bill doesn't have a foot fetish." She turned back to Erika. "This guy, Gerald, is very good-looking, and I've already told him about you."

Erika felt a shot of alarm. "What exactly did you tell him?"

"That you're gorgeous and smart and he should call you."

"You gave him my number? Did you tell him I want his sperm?"

"No, because I think you could want Ger more than his sperm."

Erika's first inclination was to politely decline. This would just complicate her plans with Gannon. He was going to father her child. He'd agreed. They just needed to get the contract signed.

She thought about how much he still affected her and took another sip of her martini. Her problem was that she still let Gannon overwhelm her. What if another man had the potential to make her forget him? Or at least help her get over him? What if Jessica's TDH could do the job? She shouldn't turn down the possibility without checking him out.

"Hey, if all else fails," Paula said, "you might get a decent pedicure out of the guy."

Erika skipped lunch and moved into her new *Pulse* office on Monday afternoon. She struggled with mixed feelings about leaving the *HomeStyle* offices, where comfort and cozy were key.

Pulse was more of a man's world, so if she took the books she'd read on climbing the corporate ladder seriously, she would need to hide her jar of M&M's in her desk drawer along with her hot chocolate mix with mini marshmallows.

She refused, however, to give up her frog clock or her small Tiffany lamp. She deliberately left her lamp turned on while she left to meet one of the couples she was interviewing for her baby article.

By the time she returned to the office, she was starving, but she wanted to type notes from the interview. Submerged in work, she had to force herself to answer the knock at her door.

"Sorry, I'm busy," she called. It didn't matter who it was. She needed to get down these last thoughts.

"Free gourmet food," Gannon called through the door.

Her stomach growled loudly. "Give me two minutes," she said and hurriedly typed some key words and phrases to help jog her memory when she returned to writing the article. She could keep the two-foot rule and eat at the same time. Besides her plans for later in the evening should help keep her from giving in to temptation.

She glanced at her clock, surprised at the time. Seven o'clock. She pulled on her boots and stood, stretching.

"Two minutes are up," Gannon said, opening the door and catching her midstretch. He carried two large boxes and a small box. His dark hair was slightly mussed, his tie discarded and the top of his shirt unbuttoned, giving her a glimpse of his muscular chest. His shirtsleeves were unfastened and pushed up his forearms. She didn't know which was more tempting, the man or the food. "Looks like you and I are the only ones left in the office."

"Really?" she asked, surprised. "What do you have and how did you get it?"

"The food editor received these this afternoon. She told me she's on Atkins and asked me to give them to someone else. It's packed in dry ice and perishable, so we either eat it or toss it."

"I hope it's already cooked," she said.

"I think it's a lot of fresh fruit," he said, opening one of the large cartons. "Help yourself."

"Nice of you to share. I didn't get to eat." She pulled out several containers. "Raw oysters, avocados, chocolate-covered bananas," she said, reading the labels. "What is this?" she asked, pulling out a split of champagne and two glasses.

"Aphrodisiac foods."

Erika pulled her hand away from the box as if it had burned her. She looked at Gannon suspiciously. "Why did the food editor give this to you?" *And why was he sharing it with her?*

"The food editor is Geraldine Kanode. She's sixty-three and was embarrassed as hell but didn't want to throw it away." His lips twitched. "She also said she didn't want to take this stuff home and give her husband any ideas. I can toss it…" He waved the container of chocolate-covered bananas.

Erika's stomach growled again. Hunger won over suspicion. "No, no, no. Wouldn't want it to go to waste." She motioned him over to her desk. "What are you still doing here?"

"An editor's work is never done," he said. "You know that."

She nodded and smiled, happy to put the desk between her and Gannon. "Can't disagree. I'm not big on raw oysters. They're all yours."

"Working on my sperm count?" He shot her a half grin that made her heart clench.

"That wasn't my first thought, but it's not a bad idea, is it?" She pulled out two plastic spoons and some napkins.

Gannon pulled a leather chair closer to her desk and

sat down. "Avocado with basil vinaigrette?" he said, of-fering the small tub to her.

"Sounds good," she said and took a bite of one of the halves. "Delicious. I wonder what this has to do with aphro—"

"Symbolizes the male testicles," he said and ate an oyster.

Erika swallowed a second bite along with a wave of self-consciousness. "Never thought of that," she said and looked at the avocado. She finished her half and shrugged. "Who would have known?"

"Champagne?" he asked, opening the split of bub-bly. At her nod he poured the liquid into each glass and read the attached note. "Says we're supposed to drop a vanilla bean in here."

"Why?"

"Something about a Mexican fertility goddess," he said and took a swallow. "Not bad, but it can't compete with Irish whiskey."

"Why doesn't that surprise me?" She inhaled the aroma of the vanilla and took a sip of the champagne. "Delicious. What's in the little box marked perishable?"

Gannon opened it and looked inside. "Fresh fig."

"Fresh?" Fresh figs were rare.

"Yep, and it's mine," he said, picking up the fruit and gently prying it open. "You know how a fig relates to the theme, don't you?" he asked, nibbling at the pink inner flesh of the fruit.

Feeling a rush of heat, she cleared her throat. Watching him savor the swollen, ripe layers, she couldn't help but visualize… "I can imagine."

"A fig resembles the female—"

"I see," she interrupted before he could finish.

"Genitals," he said and licked his lips.

The expression in his eyes was frankly sexual, making her burn from the inside out. She felt her blood rush to tender places and pool. Her nipples felt achy against her bra. She fought the urge to wiggle in her chair. Why was he taunting her? What was he trying to prove?

She should stop this right now and tell him to take his sex food away. The lure of one food was too great. The fruit of revenge. "I'll take a chocolate-covered banana."

"Phallic symbol," he said, and she felt his gaze linger on her as she took a large, indelicate bite.

"Very good chocolate and the banana is just right. Not too mushy," she said and took another bite. Encouraged by the expression of fascination in his green gaze, she drew her tongue along the length of the chocolate-covered banana.

Gannon's swift intake of breath was music to her ears. Closing her eyes, she took the banana in her mouth. "Mmm. This chocolate is delicious." She opened her eyes. "Wanna bite?"

He audibly swallowed and looked into the box. "I think I'll take the berries," he said. "Strawberry and raspberry." He met her gaze. "Nipple fruit." He lifted a raspberry to his lips and sucked it into his mouth.

A searing memory of his mouth tugging at her nipples while he pumped inside her burned through her mind, stealing her breath. She felt the restlessness between her legs grow. She bit her lip, thinking she was out of her league with Gannon. She always had been.

She needed to back down from the game of sexual chicken. After one more bite, she thought and took the last bite of chocolate-covered banana. She licked her finger and caught him watching her again.

A tempting shot of triumph sizzled through her. At least he was as turned on as she was. He held up two sticks of licorice.

She blinked in surprise. "Licorice. I always thought of it as a kid food," she said and took a bite.

"Chinese use the licorice root for medicine," he said, glancing at the label. "It's supposed to cause love and lust. Especially effective for women."

The bite stuck in her throat. Gannon didn't need all these foods. He was a powerful stimulant all by himself. She swallowed hard and smiled despite the arousal that raged through her like a hungry beast. "Well, I'll have to see if it works." She pointed at her watch. "I'm meeting a TDH for drinks in a half hour."

He frowned. "TDH?"

"Oh, sorry," she said, grabbing her coat and standing. She tossed the remains of their aphrodisiac feast into the box. "TDH is code for tall, dark and handsome."

He stood, staring at her. "You're meeting a man for drinks?"

She nodded. "I am."

His frown deepened. "I thought you wanted me to—" he narrowed his eyes "—give you my sperm."

"I do, but that doesn't mean I have to stop looking for Mr. Right. Thanks again for the snack," she said. "You're a lifesaver."

Six

Gannon looked over Erika's employment contract and glanced at his watch. After five. She would still be in her office. Deciding to deliver the agreement himself, he walked to her office and gave the door a quick rap before entering.

She glanced up from her desk, and he immediately felt a kick in his gut just from meeting her gaze. Closing the door behind him, he strolled toward her and gently tossed the contract onto her desk. "I told you we would have a quick turnaround on this."

She picked up the agreement and scanned it, then met his gaze again. "That *was* fast."

"We can discuss any questions you have about it over dinner," he said.

Her gaze fell away. "Oh, I think I'll look at it first and just ask my questions tomorrow. In the office."

"Afraid to have dinner with me?" he asked. Something about her made him want to get under her skin, make her react to him.

She looked up at him again. "Not afraid. I just want to be careful."

"If you're concerned about gossip, we can—"

She lifted her hand. "We did a lot of hiding last time around."

His chest squeezed at the sliver of hurt that came and went in her eyes. "Our feelings for each other were private. I was determined to keep it that way." He remembered feeling protective almost to the point of selfishness about his time with Erika.

"That didn't quite work out, though, did it," she said more than asked with a wry smile.

"Neither of us was ready for a commitment," he said.

"And that's no different now."

He couldn't disagree. With the competition for the head of EPH at stake, Gannon would be more focused on work than ever. "But you can't deny the chemistry between us."

"Can't deny it exists," she said. "But I learned an important lesson last time. Just because a man's hormones are involved doesn't mean his heart is involved."

"Ouch. You make me sound—" He paused. "Callous."

"No. You're just very practical. Even about your affairs."

"Being practical and up front protects things in the end. If I hadn't been honest with you from the beginning, you wouldn't have wanted to speak to me, let alone come back to *Pulse*."

"I'm not sure your theory is dead-on, particularly about women. But I adopted your practical approach about coming back to *Pulse*. I give you something you want in exchange for getting something I want."

His sperm. Gannon was starting to feel like a prize bull. He knew this wasn't the right time to start trying to persuade her that using his sperm for her baby was an insane idea. He'd given the idea repeated consideration, but he knew what he had to do—stall the sperm contract until Erika came to her senses.

None of this had comforted him last night after he'd done his best to arouse her only to hear she was meeting another man. "How was your TDH last night?"

She appeared to pull a deliberately neutral expression over her face. "He was nice. Very nice."

"Did the aphrodisiacs work?"

"That's not really any of your business," she said.

"It can be. I don't like lighting the fire of a woman to keep another man warm."

She stared at him in silence, then laughed aloud. "That's one of the most ridiculous things you've ever said."

"How so?" he asked, not sure if he felt more irritated with himself or with her.

"I hate to feed your ego, but most of the women in this office fantasize about you. You're too good-looking for the moral fortitude of pretty much the whole female race. Do you really think women don't get worked up over you, then unleash their frustration and passion on some lucky, unsuspecting male?"

He looked at her in disbelief, words eluding him.

She folded her hands together. "So what I'm saying is if you dislike the idea that you're heating a lot of pots when somebody else is getting the meal, you just need to get over it."

He raked his hand through his hair. "No one has ever said anything like that to me."

"It's just the truth."

"You can damn well be sure it hadn't occurred to me."

"Of course it hasn't. You're too busy being your handsome, sexy, workaholic self to notice."

"I'm trying to tell if you're complimenting or insulting me."

"Both and neither. I'm just being practical, like you. Telling you the truth."

Gannon looked into her eyes for a long moment. She'd grown stronger during their time apart. Smarter. More practical. He felt the burn of challenge chafe at him. It was the same feeling he'd given in to last year. Only it seemed even stronger now. Erika had always managed to turn his head and harden his groin as no other woman could. Her combination of mental toughness and hidden emotional softness drew him like a magnet.

Even though he knew getting involved with her could wreak havoc with his family's reputation and hers, he had a tough time depriving himself of going after her. Nothing and no one but his career grabbed his attention as she did. He'd broken the rules with her before and damn if he didn't want to again.

Gannon reined in the impulse to seduce her past her practicality until she was moaning with him inside her. He summoned a businesslike tone and said, "Let me know if you have any questions. I'd like to get the contract signed tomorrow."

"Okay, I'll look it over tonight."

"Good. And by the way, my father wants four representatives from *Pulse* at a cocktail party hosted by the United Nations ambassador from India. It's tomorrow night. You want in or not?"

He saw immediately that she did. In her eyes he saw a dozen lights signifying a dozen feature ideas.

"Yes," she said. "May I bring a guest?"

Gannon paused, feeling a quick, unwelcome spike of an unpleasant emotion he preferred not to examine. "Sure. As long as they can pass a security search. Give the name to my assistant."

The following morning New York City was hit by a nor'easter that brought a foot of snow. EPH allowed employees to leave early as reports of electrical outages and traffic accidents increased throughout the day.

Erika took advantage of the quiet and finished some work on *HomeStyle,* then turned her hand to editing one of the three articles for *Pulse* that had greeted her that morning on her desk.

An e-mail from Gannon's assistant informed her that the cocktail party was cancelled due to the weather, which was probably just as well since she was on the fence about whether she wanted to see Gerald, the TDH podiatrist, again.

When she'd met him for drinks, she'd found him tall, dark and handsome, funny and intelligent, but it seemed that every hour since she'd met him, for some reason unknown to her, her interest had waned.

Making a face, she turned her attention back to the article she was editing. At five o'clock she glanced out the window at the mess of weather and traffic and decided to fix herself a mug of hot chocolate instead of going home yet. She walked through the nearly deserted office to get some water for her coffeemaker, which she didn't use for coffee. On her way back she noticed the door to Gannon's office was ajar and the light was on.

Tempted for a second to say hi, she thought better of it and continued toward her office.

"You're not going to share?"

Gannon's deep voice traveled down the hall to tickle her ears just as she started to turn a corner. She stopped midstride and considered continuing on as if she hadn't heard. Her hesitation decided for her.

Gannon appeared just behind her and the sight of him made her stomach do a little dip. "I know that pot of water isn't for coffee. It's for hot chocolate. You steal the community coffee at work on the rare times when you want it."

"If it's community, I'm not stealing it. And I don't advertise my hot chocolate with marshmallows. I generally confine it to my office."

"You don't have to. We can smell it. There's a blizzard outside. We're the only two people left on the floor and you're not going to share your hot chocolate with me?"

Even though he was joking, she couldn't help feeling like a selfish little beast. "Okay, come on. I have a couple extra packets. What I don't understand is why you want my instant hot chocolate when you could get the real thing in the executive dining room."

"Proximity," he said, joining her as she walked toward her office. "Besides, the executive dining room is closed."

"You could tell your assistant to get it for you."

"Except she's not here. And although she would do what I asked, she'd think I'm a chauvinistic ass if I told her to get hot chocolate for me."

She couldn't help smiling. She poured the water into the coffeemaker and turned it on. "And you're not?"

He tossed her a dark look. "You've met my sister and my aunt Finola. Those two file their teeth on the bones of men who displease them."

Erika laughed. "Looks like you've successfully escaped their fury."

"It can be a tricky challenge. Which mug are you

going to give me? The one with the New York skyscraper scene?"

His ability to remember many of the little things he'd learned about her during their affair continued to surprise her. After he'd dumped her so easily, she'd decided she must not have been important to him at all. "Sorry. I think a cleaning person broke the skyscraper mug."

A look of trepidation crossed his face. "You're not giving me the PMS mug, are you?"

She laughed again. "No. I have a new one perfect for you to use." She pulled a mug from a box she hadn't unpacked yet. "I received this during a Chinese gift exchange at the *HomeStyle* Christmas party. I realize it's missing a zero, but I think it will do."

He glanced at the mug and gave a cryptic smile. It had a computer-altered image of a million-dollar bill wrapped around it. "I'll take it."

She dumped an envelope of hot chocolate mix into the mug and poured hot water, then stirred with one of the plastic straws she'd taken from the community coffee area. "You may *borrow* the mug," she said. "I'm not giving it to you."

"Thanks. You're growing more territorial in your advanced years," he said, taking the mug.

"Just embracing the boundaries that protect me," she said and fixed her own mug of hot chocolate.

"That sounds like a line from either a shrink or a self-improvement book."

"Paula's psychologist. It clicked for me."

"How about the TDH? Did he click with you?"

"So far," she said, surprised he'd asked and not wanting to discuss it further. She buried her face into her mug and took a sip of hot chocolate.

Silence followed.

"That's all? So far?" he prodded.

She nodded. "Uh-huh. What about you? How's your love life?"

He blinked at her question and looked away. "It's not a priority. I've got my hands full with this competition for the position of CEO of EPH."

"Is that your standard answer?" she couldn't resist asking.

He met her gaze and shook his head, then took a quick drink from his mug. "There was a time when you were intimidated by my position and name."

That was before you ripped out my heart and stomped it under the heel of your Italian loafer. "That was before you tried to guilt me into giving you hot chocolate from my private stash."

"I didn't just try," he said and took another sip from the mug. "I succeeded."

"So you did. Please excuse me while I finish editing this article."

He glanced at her desk. "Which one is it?"

"The one on the growing influence of women in sports," she said.

"I thought that might appeal to your feminist side."

"I suppose," she said. "We've still got a long way to go to catch up with the kinds of salaries men in sports make. But that's a matter of finding a commercial angle and creating a rabid fan base. There are plenty of barriers left to be broken." She paused. "I'd like to see some insets on some of the current barrier-breaking women and include a little personal information with each one."

He grinned and lifted his mug in salute. "It was a good article, but I knew you'd find a way to make it better."

"Thanks." His praise warmed her almost as much as the hot chocolate. Sinking into his green gaze, she caught herself. She might need more than a distance rule with Gannon. A time limit, too. "If you'll excuse me so I can get back to it…."

"You're hinting for me to go."

"Smart man," she said and moved to sit behind her desk.

"Thanks for the hot chocolate, Erika."

"You're welcome." She forced herself to look at her computer screen as he left the room. "I'll get the mug from you another time."

She focused her attention on the article for thirty minutes and then stretched as she glanced at her frog clock. She looked out the window, down to the street below. The traffic appeared lighter. She should be able to catch a train home without fighting the extra riders who usually took a bus or car. Wrapping her scarf around her neck, she pulled on her coat and hat. She grabbed her purse and cut off her lamp and light, then left her office.

She couldn't avoid passing Gannon's office on the way to the elevator. "Night," she called without stopping.

"If you'll wait a minute, I'll give you a ride home."

The offer stopped her in her tracks. Normally she would choose to avoid riding in a vehicle with Gannon because of her two-foot rule. But declining a chauffeur-driven ride home in a toasty-warm vehicle that would deposit her at her front door as opposed to walking two blocks in sleet from the train station would be insane.

"Thank you. I'll wait," she said.

Gannon appeared from his office in a long black wool coat with a cashmere scarf bearing his initials. "Just talked to my driver. He said there are outages all over the place. I'm glad my building has its own emergency generator."

"I don't usually have a problem with losing power. When I do, it only lasts a couple of hours. I can live with that, although I was looking forward to using my electric blanket tonight."

"TDH can't take care of that?" he asked, punching the elevator button.

"I'm sure he could if I invited him," she said, feeling prickly at his repeated references to Ger, even though Gannon didn't know who Ger was. "But the cocktail party was canceled, so he accepted a rain check. Why are you so interested?"

The elevator doors whooshed open and they stepped inside. "Just making conversation. Are you sensitive about discussing your TDH?"

"No," she said but felt as if she wasn't telling the truth. She pushed back. "How's Lydia?"

He did a double take. "Lydia?"

"Yeah," she said. "I think you dated her after you dumped me."

"I didn't dump you," he said.

"Yes, you did," she said. "I can repeat the dump conversation word for word for you if you like. 'Rumors about my involvement with you are getting back to me. I think we need to cool things down. This wouldn't be good for my reputation or yours.'"

They arrived on the ground level and the doors opened. "The car's here. We can finish this discussion later," he said and led the way.

Wind and sleet slapped Erika's face as she saw the driver appear to open the car door. "Good evening, Mr. Elliott. Ma'am."

"Sorry to drag you out in this mess," Gannon said as he waited for Erika to slide into the backseat.

She nearly moaned at the toasty temperature inside. A jazz CD played. Erika wouldn't mind spending the night in such comforting surroundings. Getting a cab would have been nearly impossible, and walking those blocks to her brownstone would have been a freezing pain in the booty.

He turned to Erika. "Did you ever think I ended our

relationship more for you than for me?" he asked in a low voice.

She looked at him in surprise. "No," she said in a quiet but blunt voice. "You told me from the beginning that we had to be discreet because your grandfather frowned heavily on Elliotts getting romantically involved with coworkers."

"Right," Gannon said. "Ever thought whose reputation would suffer most if our relationship had become public?"

She opened her mouth, then closed it. "No," she admitted.

"Who do you think would suffer more? Me? An Elliott? Or you?"

"A non-Elliott," she said. A non-Elliott without a tenth of Gannon's power, let alone his family's power.

"I don't want the press involved in my sex life."

"But what about Lydia?" she asked. "Her name and your name were all over the place after you dumped me."

"It's none of your business, but I was never intimately involved with Lydia. She didn't work for EPH and she loves making the society pages."

"She's quite beautiful. The two of you made a lovely couple," she said in a voice that couldn't hide her resentment.

"You still don't get it, do you?" he asked, shaking his head. "I went out with Lydia after you and I broke up to throw the attention away from you. I learned a long time ago that I didn't want the press commenting on my intimate relationships. On people I care about. So I keep the people I care about out of the limelight. I keep it private."

She looked at him for a long moment while his explanation sank in. Was he saying that he had *cared* about her? That their relationship had meant something to him?

"Since I graduated from college I've had a goal of getting engaged before the press could even guess at the woman I'll marry."

Erika shook her head. "I don't know, Gannon. With your family's high profile, that may be nearly impossible."

Gannon gave a half grin. "Maybe. But remember, nearly impossible is what Elliotts do best."

She couldn't argue with that. Her mind still humming with what he'd said about protecting the women he'd really cared about from the press, she stared out the window. As the driver turned onto her street, Erika noticed that the entire block was dark. No light emanated from the doorway of her brownstone. Her stomach sank.

"Looks like the power outage hit your place," Gannon said.

"Yes, it does," she said and shrugged. "It probably won't last long."

"Probably not," he agreed, and a full silence dangled between them, growing and swelling with each passing second.

"You could come over to my place," he offered.

She immediately rejected the idea for the sake of her sanity, her two-foot rule and her time limit, which she hadn't come up with yet. "That's nice of you but not necessary. I'm sure it won't last long. I've got a little battery-operated TV-radio that my father gave me for Christmas. He even gave me batteries, so I know it works. I have great quilts and snuggly socks."

"I know," he said, his voice holding an undercurrent of sensuality. "I remember."

Erika felt a punch of awareness in her stomach. It hit her so hard she instinctively covered her belly with her hand.

She ignored his response and reached for her door handle as the driver pulled the car to a stop. "Thank you for the ride. It was a treat to dodge mass transit *and* the snow."

"Just curious—why did you accept the offer of a ride when you wouldn't accept the offer to sit out your power outage in my apartment?"

"Well, there are two things you never turn down. A ride home during a snowstorm in a nice, warm vehicle as long as you know you're not riding with a serial killer."

"And the second?"

"A trip to South Florida in the winter."

"But you do turn down the offer of a warm apartment with power while your place is likely to be cold and dark. As long as the offer isn't from a serial killer."

"Yeah. Because in this case the offer is from the Big Bad Wolf." She smiled. "Thanks again. G'night, Gannon."

She stepped outside the car and struggled to maintain her balance and dignity as she trudged toward the door. When she arrived still standing, she turned to wave and received a snowball hit to her shoulder.

The icy splat surprised her. Gannon laughed and she looked up at him as he approached her. "What are you doing?"

"Sorry," he said without an ounce of sincerity. "I was aiming for your back, but you turned."

Peeved, she backed away as he came closer. "That's not even fighting fair. Aiming for my back?"

"Snowball fights are always dirty," he said. "I just wanted to get your attention. You're being stubborn and silly."

"Excuse me?"

"You are. I'm offering you the use of my warm apartment and you'd rather stay in your cold place. It's stubborn and silly." He lifted his hands. "I won't touch you."

His declaration pricked her ego. But it shouldn't, she quickly told herself.

"Unless you beg me to touch you," he added in a sexy, casual voice that should have disarmed her.

But she knew better. She knew how irresistible Gannon could be. She hadn't ever begged him to touch her because he'd always initiated their lovemaking until the breakup. After that, she'd been too wounded to consider approaching him.

"I'm not big on begging," she said.

"Too much pride," he said.

"No. I've never found begging necessary." She turned toward her door.

His hand on her shoulder stopped her, and her heart raced in her chest. "C'mon, Erika. It'll just be for a little while, and my genetically grown gentleman's genes would never allow me to let you freeze in the darkness while I'm warm with a glass of whiskey and watching the New York Knicks."

"Your guilt would spoil the enjoyment of the game," she said, turning back around to face him, unable to resist responding to him.

"Something like that," he said, his gaze holding hers the same way it used to when he'd looked at her as if she was the most fascinating woman in the world and he couldn't get enough of her.

She should run screaming into her cold, dark apartment. Now, she told her feet. Go now.

Her feet, however, didn't budge an inch.

Seven

Gannon could see the argument she was holding with herself flash in her eyes. His gut tightened. One of the things that had always fascinated him about Erika was the way her eyes told stories about what was going on inside her. He had the sense that if he paid attention, he could eventually read her like a book. She was a book he wanted to read again and again.

Breaking up with her had been necessary and he'd been mostly successful in putting her out of his mind, especially after she'd moved to *HomeStyle*. He hadn't second-guessed his decision. Breaking up had been the right thing to do for both of them. When his grandfather, however, had issued the challenge for CEO at New Year's, her image had shot to his mind, front and center.

Professionally Erika possessed a winning combination of drive and human insight. Personally she managed to both comfort and challenge him, something no other woman had done.

"If you don't come back to my place," he said, lifting his hand to brush snowflakes from her hair, "I'll start thinking you can't resist me."

Erika scowled. "You're so full of yourself. Despite the fact that you're loaded and entirely too good-looking, you are not all that and a bag of chips."

"What's not to love?" he asked, taunting a response out of her.

Her face turned serious. "At some point you have to love in order to be lovable."

He felt the punch of her statement in his gut.

"But maybe you just haven't found the right girl yet," she said and smiled. "I'll go to your apartment, but I need to grab a few things first."

"You're going in there in the dark?"

"It won't be the first time," she said and unlocked the door. "Probably won't be the last."

"Wait a minute," he said to Erika, then turned to the driver. "Can you bring me the flashlight you keep in the glove compartment?" he asked and Carl brought it to him. "Take the car around the block if you need to. We'll be a few minutes."

"We?" she asked, glancing back at Gannon in surprise. "You sure you can handle it?"

"I haven't been in your place in a while. I want to see what you've done with it."

"It's not bad," she said, automatically reaching for a light that didn't turn on. "I got some help from a decorator that contributed to *HomeStyle*. But you may not get the whole effect since it's so dark."

"That's okay. I really just wanted to smell it," he said and inhaled the combined scents of peaches, vanilla and sugar cookies.

He felt her gaze on him. "Smell it?"

"Your place always smelled good to me. Sometimes it smelled like cinnamon and apples. Sometimes it smelled like tropical fruit. It always made me want to come in and sit down and stay for a while."

"But not too long," she muttered under her breath. "Candles. You can experience these wonderful scents in your own home with candles."

Before he could interject, she went on as she led the way to the kitchen. He wondered if she was part cat with the way she could see in the dark. "Or since you're filthy rich, you can pay someone else to make your home smell wonderful." She rustled in a cabinet. "Could you shine the light up here, please?"

He illuminated the cabinet and watched as she pulled down instant hot chocolate and another box and a bag from one shelf and some kind of liquor from the upper shelf. "We came in for hot chocolate."

"And Godiva Liqueur," she added. "And a couple of apples and toiletries. If I remember correctly, you don't keep food in your apartment."

"I'm never there, so it goes bad. But I have a full bar."

"Bet you don't have Godiva Liqueur," she said and headed out of the room.

She was right. He didn't.

"Sissy liquor," she called from down the hall.

She'd taken the words from his mouth.

He heard something fall on her bathroom floor. "Oops. Flashlight, please."

He hurried down the hall and found her on the floor groping for her toothbrush. She glanced at him and smiled. "Don't leave home without it." She stood with an assortment of things cradled in one hand and with her other hand reached for his flashlight. "Need to borrow this for a minute. You just wait here."

"Why don't you let me go with you?"

"Because," she said and pulled the flashlight from his hand and left him in the dark.

"Does this mean you're getting a sexy negligee to surprise me?"

"No," she said, and a minute later the light from the flashlight bobbed toward him, signaling her return. She carried a tote bag along with her purse. "I'm ready now."

He wondered what she'd put in her tote. Lord, the woman made him curious about the most mundane things. He took the flashlight and led the way to her door. "If you were stranded on a desert island, what five items would you take?"

"Cell phone."

"Not unless you had satellite coverage."

"Like you," she said.

He turned abruptly and she walked into his chest. "Are you mocking my wealth?"

She looked up at him, and because of the darkness he could only see the suggestion of a glint in her eyes. "Yes."

Something inside him burst into flame and he hadn't even a little bit of a desire to snuff it out. Instead he slid his hand through the back of her hair and tilted her chin upward and lowered his mouth to hers.

Her soft inhalation cranked up the heat. He could taste her excitement on his lips. He rubbed his mouth over hers until she eased open her lips and he could slide his tongue inside. Her mouth hugged his tongue the same way her body would hug him intimately.

He thrust his tongue in and out of her mouth and felt himself grow hard with the sensual motion, with the heady suggestion of having more of her, of feeling her beneath him, wet, hot and ready....

He felt her drag her lips from his, turning her head to the side. "Oh wow," she whispered, her breath uneven. "I thought you said I would have to beg you to touch me."

Gannon forced his sex-muddled mind to clear. "You didn't? I could have sworn I heard you beg. But I haven't broken my promise even if you didn't say anything," he continued, feeling an odd tension build between them. It was about sex and something deeper, something he couldn't name.

She looked up at him, her eyes dark with arousal that ricocheted through him like a wild bullet. "How?"

He cleared his throat. "We're at your place, not mine.

I told you I wouldn't touch you at my apartment unless you begged."

She narrowed her gaze. "Sounds like a technicality. How can I trust you to keep yourself—" She broke off and glanced away. "How can I trust you to keep yourself to yourself at your apartment?"

"You can trust me," he said. "I give you my word." Even if I die from a hard-on that won't quit, he added silently.

An hour and a half later they'd eaten a frozen pizza and she was fixing s'mores in his microwave. A fire blazed in the fireplace and he was sinking into his favorite leather chair with a glass of whiskey. One minor adjustment would complete the picture.

If Erika would strip off her clothes, straddle his lap and kiss him into next week, the evening would be perfect.

Instead she was bundled in an extra sweatshirt, sipping her doctored hot chocolate and positioned too far away from him. It was only three feet, but Gannon knew it might as well be a mile.

"I'm glad you talked me into this," she said, leaning her back against the couch. She lifted her cell phone. "Since I asked my neighbor to give me a call when the power returned, I know it would still be cold and dark at home."

"Feeling grateful?" Gannon asked.

Erika met his gaze and caught his unspoken suggestion. She gave a tiny shake of her head. "Yes. I'll have to bake some brownies for you in a few days."

He swallowed a groan. He didn't want brownies. Why did this woman remind him that he hadn't had sex in a while? Why did she affect him so strongly? She was pretty but not drop-dead gorgeous. She clearly spent a minimal amount of time on her appearance. He was certain that was due to the fact that she had more important things to do.

He just wished she would *do* him into oblivion. Maybe that would get her out of his system. The problem with that theory was that he'd had an affair with her before. He should have gotten enough of her then, especially after the rumors started.

Something about Erika made him want to break all his rules. It was more than the need to get her sexually, although that need was damn strong. He liked just having her in his apartment with him. Her presence calmed and aroused him at the same time. He liked talking with her. He liked the way she didn't take crap from him, yet he could tell she admired him and was attracted to him. She clearly liked his genes, he thought, scowling as he recalled her desire for him to donate his sperm to her. For Pete's sake, this was a complicated situation, the kind he always avoided.

"You didn't ever tell me your five things you'd want on a desert island."

"Oh." She took a sip from her hot chocolate and

thought for a moment. "An iPod. With a battery that never dies."

He chuckled. "Okay. What music?"

"Everything," she said. "Alicia Keys, Seal, some beach tunes to cheer me up when I'm blue."

"For a girl from Indiana, you seem to have a thing for the beach."

"I do. I was landlocked entirely too long. I love the warmth, the sand, the water."

"The hurricanes," he interjected.

"Cynic," she said and gave a sniff. "You don't have to visit during hurricane season."

"Back to your music," he said.

"Some classical music played by a full orchestra, some standards and 'Marshmallow World' by Sammy Davis Jr."

"Sounds eclectic," he said, hiding a grin behind his glass of whiskey. "Two items left."

"Hot chocolate mix with marshmallows. I would be very sad without my hot chocolate and marshmallows. And the complete unabridged collection of Louisa May Alcott."

"No blow-dryer?" he asked.

She shrugged. "Why bother? The humidity would make my hair curly."

"No cosmetics?"

"Some soap would be really nice. Maybe I'd trade soap for the cell phone that doesn't work. What about you? Not that such a thing could ever happen to an Elliott because you, of course, would have a satellite cell phone. Plus a search party would be combing every inch of the planet for you."

"Are you mocking my wealth again?"

"No. Just your family position this time," she said with a sassy smile. "Five things."

"Sports radio with extra batteries."

"Can't do without your Knicks."

"Or Yankees, depending on the season. The complete works of Tolstoy. A bottle of great Irish whiskey. And a woman."

She blinked. "A woman? Who?"

He nodded. "A woman who satisfies my soul and body so much that I don't care if I ever leave the island."

"Tall order," she said, lifting her eyebrows skeptically.

He looked her over and remembered how she'd looked naked, how she'd felt in his arms, the sexy sounds she'd made when they'd made love. She was there. He was here. They were dressed. What a waste. He bit back an oath and took a long swallow of whiskey.

She pulled out his game of Scrabble and he beat her in the first round. She beat him in the second because he couldn't stop thinking about convincing her to play strip Scrabble. Just past midnight the Godiva Liqueur took effect and she began to yawn.

"Hot chocolate with a kick kicking in?" he asked, liking the way she looked with her eyes sleepy and her hair mussed.

"A little. Do you mind if I take your couch tonight?"

"I have a guest room."

She nodded and glanced at the fireplace. "But the fire is so cozy."

"It is," he agreed, wishing he hadn't made the stupid promise not to touch her unless she begged. Inbred cockiness had caused trouble for more than one Elliott.

"You can go to bed if you want," she said.

"No rush. I'll get a pillow and blanket for you." He ambled down the hall in his sock feet and pulled a pillow from the guest bed and a soft, warm blanket from the closet. He returned to find her with her legs folded against her, her arms wrapped around them as she stared into the fire.

"I always wondered why you didn't have a full-time servant. Or several," she mused aloud.

"Privacy," he said. "This is one of the few places I can be totally alone if I want to be. The cleaning lady takes care of everything when I'm not here."

"Phantom help," Erika said with a soft smile.

"Yeah, but she doesn't get a phantom check," he said drily. He watched her expression turn serious, pensive. "What's on your mind?"

"Just wondering."

"Wondering what?" he prodded, joining her on the sofa.

"You said that you keep the people who are important to you out of the press. I'm wondering how many women you've kept out of the press."

He studied her. "Not many."

"Not many is not a number."

"Three," he told her.

She glanced at him in surprise. "I would have expected more."

"You would have been wrong."

"Hmm," she said. "Are any of them still speaking to you?"

"Yes," he said, shooting her a hard look. "My breakups have always been civil. One of the women has gotten married. The other one lives in France."

"And the third?"

"Is sitting beside me right now," he said, meeting her gaze and feeling a snap of the electricity that sizzled between them.

"Neither of the other women threw a tantrum?"

"No."

"I could have," she confessed. "I was so hurt I wanted to scream and beat my hands against the wall. Throw dishes, expensive crystal with champagne at you, a pie in your face."

He looked at her in surprise. "You're joking. You're one of the most civilized, rational women I know."

"Yeah, well, I guess you could say you don't always bring out my civilized, rational side."

He stared at her, trying to visualize her throwing a temper tantrum, and he shook his head. "You're too mature for that."

Erika sighed. "Maybe. Maybe it's the Godiva Liqueur talking. But you know what they say—there's yin and yang, light and dark."

"If you're passionate in one way, you could be passionate in another," he added.

"Could be," she said and smiled slyly. "Bet I've scared you."

"Not quite," he said, feeling his temperature edge up a degree. He'd always gravitated toward relationships with women he knew he could ultimately control. Last year he'd been able to control his relationship with Erika. He wasn't sure it would be so easy now, and damn if that didn't make him want her more. He swallowed an oath. Where was this self-destructive streak coming from?

He cleared his throat. "I'll hit the sack and let you get some sleep."

"Thanks again," she said. "G'night."

He strolled down the hall, thinking about how much he'd like to strip off her clothes and sink inside her on his sofa. The visual would keep him awake for hours.

Erika awakened early and left a thank-you note along with a packet of hot chocolate for Gannon before she grabbed a cab downstairs. Her feelings for him jerked her from one extreme to the other. She wanted to be with him, craved his attention and knew she was insane to go down that road again. Hadn't she learned her lesson the first time? Playing with Gannon Elliott was like dancing barefoot on hot coals. There was no way she wouldn't get burned.

But oh, it felt so good before the burn singed her. She loved the way he looked at her, teased her and even played Scrabble with her. She knew he wanted her, and that knowledge made her nuts. Gannon was the most desirable man she'd ever met in her life. His desirability coupled with his obviously superior genetics was the reason she wanted him to father her child. Even if the fertilization took place in a tube instead of au naturel.

The problem was that Erika knew from intimate, personal experience that fertilizing au naturel would be so much more enjoyable.

Groaning, she entered her brownstone and told herself to get a grip. Luck finally smiled on her and the power came on within fifteen minutes of her return. She jumped in the shower and got ready for a full workday during which she would be focused on her work and not Gannon.

Her phone rang as she was putting on her mascara. She checked the caller ID before answering. Gerald. Answer it, she told herself. For the sake of your sanity, answer it. She snatched up the phone. "Hello?"

"Hey, Erika, how'd you survive the storm? I was worried about you when I heard about the power outages in your area."

How nice, she thought and felt a sliver of guilt at the same time since she'd ended up spending the whole night with Gannon at his great, warm apartment. "I made it okay. We got our power back. How about you?"

"Didn't ever lose it, thank goodness. I was wondering if I could call in my rain check tonight. I'd like to take you to dinner. It'll have to be a little late, though."

Erika held her breath, swallowing her instinct to refuse. Why did she want to refuse? Gerald was a perfectly eligible TDH. Plus he had great genes to contribute to her baby. "What time were you thinking?"

"Eight o'clock. I know it's late, but I'll try to take you somewhere worth the wait."

Nice again, she thought. "Okay, I'd like that."

"Good. I'll call you later today after I get reservations so you'll know where to meet me."

"Sounds good. Have a good day."

"You, too. I'm looking forward to tonight."

Erika frowned as she hung up. She needed to be looking forward to tonight, too. Maybe if she kept telling herself she was looking forward to seeing Gerald, she would start actually feeling that way. "I'm looking forward to seeing Gerald tonight," she chanted under her breath all the way to work.

She strode from the elevator at the office determined to focus on her work away from Gannon today. That was her best course of action.

No sooner had she taken off her coat and sat at her desk than her phone rang. Erika picked up the receiver.

"Mr. Elliott on line one," her new assistant said.

"Which Mr. Elliott?" Erika asked.

"Oh. Mr. Michael Elliott."

"Put him through please." Erika waited a half second. "Erika Layven. How can I help you, Mr. Elliott?"

"You can call me Michael. You may be calling me something else by the end of the day."

Erika heard exasperation in his voice. "What's the problem?"

"We have two feature articles that have to go to print, but they're disasters. I want you and Gannon to take care of them today."

Erika blinked. "Gannon?" she echoed, hearing a flushing sound as she saw her time and distance rules go straight down the toilet.

"Yeah. I hope you didn't have anything else planned today."

"Of course I had plans, but this sounds much more important. I can reschedule."

"Good. I've already told Gannon. You can work from his office."

"Yes, sir. 'Bye for now," she said and hung up, feeling a twinge of suspicion. Had Gannon set this up with his father to force her to be with him? She shook her head. She was being paranoid or maybe placing too much importance on herself. Gannon didn't have to resort to tricks to get a woman to be with him. Including her, she thought with a scowl. Grabbing her pen and a notepad, she headed for his office.

His assistant waved her inside.

Gannon looked up from his desk, which was uncharacteristically covered with papers and photos.

"How did this happen?" she asked.

"Current events. Breaking stories. Fill-in reporter,

new photographer." He shook his head in disgust. "The good news is the photographer took lots of shots, so we should be able to find something."

"Okay," she said, moving to his desk. "Tell me where you want me to start."

Eight

Erika and Gannon worked nonstop through lunch on the features, rewriting and editing. Erika made phone calls to obtain clarification. Gannon sent the photos they selected to their photo editor.

The time passed like lightning. If she thought about the way they worked together—as if she were one hand and he were the other—then it might have freaked her out. But they were too busy.

With her focus on the feature articles, she shouldn't have noticed him too much, but she did. She inhaled his aftershave and wanted to drown in it. He raked his fingers through his hair and she wanted to touch his hair. Once, his hand grazed hers and she felt a thrill race through her. She met his gaze and what she saw there stopped her heart.

As if both of them knew they couldn't let down their guard, they both looked away and forged on. By the end of the day, though, she couldn't help staring at his mouth when he talked.

At six-thirty, when they finished what had initially looked like mission impossible, she felt giddy.

Gannon sank into his chair and pulled his tie off. He'd loosened it hours ago. He met her gaze and chuckled. "Cheers to us."

She smiled in return. "Cheers to us. All we need is some champagne."

He lifted his hand. "I have some," he said and rose toward a minibar on the other side of his large office. Underneath the cherrywood bar he opened a small refrigerator and pulled out a chilled bottle of champagne. "Cristal."

She gaped at the bottle, then at him. "That's a little extravagant, isn't it?"

"Are you saying we don't deserve it?" he asked, unwrapping the foil. He grabbed a towel from beneath the counter and popped the cork.

"I guess it's too late to debate now." She stood. "Do you have glasses?"

He tilted his head behind him. "Lower left cabinet."

Erika walked to the cabinet and pulled out two crystal flutes. "These are beautiful. They look like Waterford."

"My mother gave them to me. Hinting," he said, moving toward her and pouring the sparkling wine into the glasses she held. "Have a seat," he said, pointing to the chairs on the other side of his desk.

Erika sank into her chair while Gannon sat next to her. "To conquering the mission impossible," she said, lifting her glass, enjoying his mussed look and the hint of a five-o'clock shadow on his jaw. She liked him when he looked a little rough around the edges. She also liked him when he was wearing a black suit. Then again, she really liked him with just a sheet or nothing at all.

He clicked his glass against hers. "To our friendship," he said.

She took a sip of the wine and then another. "Very good, of course."

"Very good."

"So what was your mother hinting about?"

"Me settling down and getting married."

"Ah. What did you tell her?"

"Same thing I always tell her. When the time and the woman are right."

She took another sip to cover the odd mix of feelings inside her. "I get some of the same thing from my mother."

"What do you tell her?"

"I change the subject and ask how her bridge game is," she said, and thought about the baby contract that Gannon hadn't produced. She told herself to be a little more patient.

"That's pretty good. I'll have to remember it for future reference." He topped off her glass. "Drink up. We should finish this."

"And end up with a champagne headache? I don't know. But maybe it's worth it if it's Cristal," she said, feeling a conspiratorial thrill as she let herself sink into his gaze. She took another few sips and felt a flush of heat. "Whew. With no lunch, this is going straight to my head."

"I can take care of that," he said in a voice that reminded her that he could take care of her in a lot of ways.

Feeling a twist of flat-out lust form in her belly, she closed her eyes and took another long sip. "Oh, what a day. A blur. Do you think your father will be happy with what we did?"

"Ecstatic," Gannon corrected. "In his way."

She smiled at his dry tone and opened her eyes. "He's not the kind to jump up and down very often, is he?"

"No, but he always makes it clear if he's pleased or not."

"And he's almost always pleased with you," she ventured.

"There have been a few times that I set him off, but I'm the oldest."

She understood because she was the oldest in her family. "The bar is higher."

Gannon nodded and lifted his hand to her cheek. "What about you?"

She should move away, she told herself. She was breaking both the time and distance rules, but she liked the way that one finger of his felt on her skin. The slow movement was mesmerizing. "I'm the oldest, too, but

I'm lucky. I don't work for my mother or father. I live in a different state. At the same time, you can take the girl out of Indiana, but you can't take Indiana out of the girl."

He smiled. "Soft heart under the black suit, hot chocolate. Do you miss your parents?"

She nodded. "Sometimes, but I think a little distance can be a good thing."

"Can't disagree."

"Yet you stay."

He shrugged. "I never considered anything else. I never really wanted anything else."

"Never? You never had a rebellious moment as a teenager or as a college kid?"

"Okay," he relented. "So there was a week or two when I seriously considered becoming a fly fisherman's guide in Montana."

She laughed. "I'm trying to picture you in rubber waders instead of a Brooks Brothers suit."

He moved his hand to her mouth and rubbed his thumb over her bottom lip. "Are you mocking me again? There was also that summer in high school when I was determined to play in a garage band."

Surprise raced through her. "Oh, I never knew. You never mentioned that before when we—" She broke off. "When we were involved. There's still a lot I don't know about you."

"You don't sound happy about that," he murmured, his gaze lingering on her mouth.

She wasn't, and the knowledge irritated her. "Not much I can do about it, is there?"

"You can do more than you think you can," he said and leaned back to toss back the rest of his champagne.

What an obscure comment, she thought, watching the muscles of his throat as he swallowed. She remembered kissing him there on his throat and hearing him groan in pleasure. The sounds he'd made when they'd made love had made her crazy to please him.

He tilted the bottle of champagne and filled his glass and topped off hers again. "Almost done." Meeting her gaze, he leaned closer. Then closer. So close her vision blurred.

"I'm going to kiss you."

"I didn't beg," she said in the only protest she could muster. She hadn't begged. Not aloud anyway.

"We're not in my apartment," he said and lowered his mouth to hers.

All the breath left her lungs. He moved his mouth over hers, caressing, exploring. His tongue slipped over her lips and she instinctively opened, letting him in.

He made a ghost of a groan that melted her thighs and turned her to liquid. He pulled back slightly. "Take a drink of champagne," he told her. "I want to taste it on your mouth."

Oooooh, wow. With a not-so-steady hand she lifted the flute and took a sip.

He slid his hand underneath her jaw and lowered his mouth again, slipping his tongue over her mouth and then over her tongue.

The kiss went on and on and she felt as if she'd been injected with a drug that made her move in slow motion. Nothing moved quickly except her heart. She felt the flute lifted from her hand.

The kiss turned deeper and Gannon pulled her from her chair onto his lap. A sliver of caution dented the thick aura of desire infusing her brain. "Is this a good idea?" she managed.

"We're just kissing," he said.

But her body wanted more, she thought. A lot more. He slid his hand around the nape of her neck and deepened the kiss, his tongue thrusting inside her mouth.

Almost of their own accord her hands went to his hair. His groan of pleasure rewarded her and she felt his hands on the sides of her breasts. Her nipples immediately peaked against her bra. One, two, three seconds passed and he touched her nipples.

The sensation sent a ricochet of tension down between her legs, where she felt wet and swollen.

"Do you want more?" he whispered.

The forbidden offer tantalized her unbearably. "How can I possibly think straight with the way you're touching me?"

"Is that good or bad?"

"Both," she muttered, biting her lip as he continued to rub his thumbs over her tender nipples.

"Tell me you want me to stop," he said, stopping the sensual movement.

So she was going to have to be a big girl after all. Responsible. She didn't want to think. She just wanted to feel him, every way, everywhere. She closed her eyes. "I can't say that I want you to stop," she admitted in a low voice.

He tugged her mouth back to his and took a long draw from her lips as if she were a drink he couldn't get enough of. At what felt like the speed of light he unbuttoned her blouse and unfastened her bra. With restless fingers she unfastened his shirt and pushed it down his arms, but he wore a T-shirt underneath.

Frustration bubbled from her throat. "Not fair," she said.

He quickly obliged her by removing his undershirt. She slid her fingers over his pecs and down his torso, thrilled by his quick intake of breath when her fingers dipped to his waistband.

He buried his face in her breasts, sliding one of her nipples into his mouth. The way he tugged on her nipple sent her temperature soaring and tightened the empty ache inside her. She shifted restlessly on his lap, sliding against his hard arousal.

He gave a groan that mixed frustration and pleasure. "You get me so—" He broke off and stood her between his legs, pulling down her stockings and the skirt she wore. She'd ditched her boots late afternoon in the middle of their intense work session.

His gaze dark with the same need she felt, he pulled

a condom from his pocket, unfastened his belt and shoved down his slacks and briefs. Sinking down onto the chair, he pulled her onto his lap.

He kissed her while his fingers searched and found her sweet spot. "Wet and good," he murmured in approval. His tongue stroked hers while his fingers caressed her intimately.

Erika got so hot she could barely breathe. Anticipation warred with anxiousness. "I want you inside me," she whispered to him. Then more to herself, "This is insane," she said, overwhelmed by the need to be with him, by the need to be as close to him as humanly possible.

Gannon lifted her hips over him and she slid down his shaft, taking him inside her. The way he filled her took her breath away.

He shuddered. "You have no idea how good…"

She lifted her hips and slid down him again, the friction stimulating all her most intimate nerve endings. "Oh, I think I have an idea."

And the rhythm began. He thrust upward when she rippled down over him. He drew her breasts to his mouth, sucking her nipple while he thrust inside her. The dual sensations made her crazy.

He slid his hand between them and stroked her sweet spot, and Erika felt an explosion of pleasure kicking through her blood like a current coming in fits and starts. He continued to move and she felt herself clench in a mind-blowing climax.

She heard him mutter something that was either an oath or a prayer. Or both. And he rocked his hips upward, thrusting, his body arched in release.

Squeezing her bottom, he swore under his breath. "Oh damn, that was amazing." He met her gaze with eyes dark with arousal and fulfillment. "You're incredible. Just—"

A knock sounded at the door. Shock raced through her. Someone might as well have thrown a bucket of water on Erika. "Oh no—"

He covered her lips with one finger and shook his head. Another knock sounded.

"Mr. Elliott? Cleaning service is here to take care of your office."

"Give me about fifteen minutes, thank you. I'm finishing a project."

Recriminations immediately filled Erika's head. What in the world was she doing? Had she learned nothing? She'd gotten involved with Gannon before and he'd hurt her so much she couldn't feel anything at all for another man.

This was even worse. They'd never gone this far in the office.

Bitter regret filling her throat, she struggled to climb off his lap, stumbling as she tried to stand.

Gannon stood and steadied her. "You okay?"

She could feel him studying her face and she refused to meet his gaze. "I could probably be better. Getting dressed wouldn't hurt."

He moved to lock the door. "It's okay. No one walked in on us."

"But they could have," she said, jerking on her clothes. "I'm in here bonking the boss and—"

"I'm not technically your boss," Gannon said. "I made sure of that when you returned to *Pulse*."

She sent him a withering glance. "That could have been anyone behind that door. And what if they hadn't knocked?"

"Everyone knocks on my door before entering."

"What about your father? What about one of your brothers or your sister? Or one of your thousands of cousins?" She tried to keep the hysteria from her voice.

He pulled up his pants and fastened them. She noticed it took him about one-tenth the time to pull himself together, while she was still dressing herself with hands that refused to steady themselves.

She struggled with the zipper on her boots and he brushed her hand away. "You need to calm down, Erika. Nothing happened. I would protect you. This thing between us…" he said and shrugged. "We just got carried away. We need to keep it private."

"I'm not sure we should keep it at all," she told him. "I already bought the T-shirt for this ride one time."

"But you want my baby," he said, meeting her gaze dead-on.

Her throat closed up and she looked away. "I want your genes. Otherwise you and I know it's not the right time or I'm not the right woman."

Silence followed, swelling between them, creating an unbearable tension inside Erika.

"Do we really know that?" he asked.

His question made her heart stop. It gave her a crazy kind of hope that she didn't want to buy into for her sanity and emotional safety. "We know it's not the right time. And if I were the right woman—the really right woman—then any time would be the right time." She successfully pulled up the zipper on her other boot.

"Erika," he said, putting his hand over hers.

She closed her eyes at the strong tug she felt, the wanting to be with him. "No, Gannon, for you this is just about the crazy chemistry between us and some amazing hot sex. And I'm hardwired differently." She glanced at the clock. Seven-fifteen. Her head clearing, she felt a nudge from her brain. What—

Remembering her late date with Gerald, she swore and began to gather the rest of her belongings. "Oh, great. Just great."

"What is it?"

"I have a dinner date in forty-five minutes."

Gannon went completely silent.

"You're not really going to meet him after we—"

She bit her lip and waved her hand. "I'll handle it. I'll take care of it. I'll, uh—" She swallowed over the terrible distraught lump in her throat. "I guess I'll see you Monday."

He reached for her and she stumbled backward. "No. Please don't touch me right now. I need to leave."

Nine

"**Y**es, Jessica, I had to cancel the dinner date with Gerald. I'm sorry, but I just couldn't make it. Something happened at work at the last minute." Something *stupid* happened at the last minute and she'd bashed herself the entire weekend for letting Gannon *happen* to her again. *In his office.*

Erika rolled her eyes at herself in disgust. The one good thing she could say about this Monday morning was that she hadn't crossed paths with the human object of her insanity.

"But you'll go out with him some other time, won't you?" Jessica asked. "I had to work to get this guy to do a blind date, Erika. You need to take advantage of this opportunity. He's a doctor."

Erika couldn't muster any enthusiasm about going out with Gerald and she feared that every time she looked at him, she'd be reminded of the reason she'd broken the date with him and subsequently reminded of what an idiot she'd been.

"I don't know, Jessica. I've just made a big change at work and it's going to be very demanding and—"

"Oh, Erika, don't pull the work excuse. Gerald is already thinking you're not interested. And really what's not to like about him? He's TDH with brains, a sense of humor—"

The light for her second line began to flash. "I know, Jessica, but—"

She heard a tap on her door, and her assistant poked her head inside. "Sorry to bother you, but a woman on the line said something about you being her niece's mentor and she sounded upset."

Erika felt her chest constrict with concern. "Jessica, I gotta go. I'll call you back when I can." She switched lines. "Erika Layven."

"Miss Layven, Tia's been hit by a truck," a woman said in a broken voice. "She won't be able to meet you."

Erika's heart stopped. "Omigod, what happened? Where are you?"

"It happened this morning on her way to school. I'm at the emergency room. I don't know what's going to happen. No one will tell me anything."

"Tell me where you are and I'll be there as soon as I can."

Gannon learned Erika wasn't in the office when he sent his assistant to deliver a feature article proposal to her. "How long will she be out?" he asked, wondering at the reason for her absence.

His assistant shrugged. "I'm not sure, but Rose said she thought she might not be back in until tomorrow."

He nodded, feeling a prickle of concern. Erika rarely missed work for any reason. After a meeting with a monthly columnist, he gave in to his curiosity and dropped by Erika's office.

"I'd like to get Erika's input on a feature proposal. Do you know when she'll be back in?" he asked Erika's assistant.

Rose shook her head. "No. When she left for the E.R., she told me to hold her messages and she'd check in at the end of the day if she could."

Alarm shot through him. "E.R.?"

"I'm a little sketchy on the relationships, but someone named Tia was apparently hit by a truck and was taken to a hospital."

Gannon recalled that Tia was the young teen Erika had been mentoring. He shook his head. "Do you know her condition?"

Rose shook her head sadly. "No, but how can it be anything but bad?"

Gannon frowned. "Did she mention which hospital?"

"Yes, I have it here somewhere," she said, rustling through some papers on her desk. "Here it is. St. Joseph's."

"Thanks," he said and tucked the information in his mind.

He went back to his office and sat down in his chair,

trying not to think of how frantic Erika must be. He could think of nothing else. Picking up his phone, he dialed her cell. No answer. His gut twisted. Not a good sign.

But not his problem, the pragmatic side of his brain reminded him. He clicked the mouse for his computer to check his schedule. He had a full plate of his own today.

Tia's aunt Brenda couldn't handle the sight of the blood from her niece's injuries, so Erika sat with Tia until she was taken into surgery. She alternately paced the waiting room and gave a hug of reassurance to Tia's aunt.

"I should have watched out for her better. I was in a hurry to get Jason to day care. I overslept, so we were all running late."

Erika put her arm around the young woman's shoulders. "You've got to stop blaming yourself. You couldn't have stopped that truck driver. You heard the officer. The guy was drunk," Erika said, still furious at the cause of the accident and shaken by Tia's close call.

"I just hope they can fix her. She's such a sweet girl. Smart. She deserves so much more."

"You do more than you know." Erika tried to reassure the woman at the same time she was worried.

"How is Tia?" a male voice asked from behind her.

Gannon's voice, she thought. It couldn't be. She needed to drink some water or eat something. She had to be imagining things.

"Erika," the voice persisted.

She glanced over her shoulder and was shocked to see Gannon in front of her. "Gannon?"

"Your assistant told me where you were. I thought I should check on you."

Still unable to believe her eyes, she glanced at her watch. "It's three o'clock. You left work early? You never leave work early." She shook her head, incredulous.

"This sounded serious. I thought I should come by."

Erika was too surprised to know what to think. The concern in his eyes touched her and took her completely off guard.

"Who's he?" Brenda asked.

"Oh, I'm sorry," Erika said, refocusing. "Brenda Rogers, Tia's aunt, this is my, uh— This is Gannon Elliott. I work with him."

Brenda wrinkled her brow as if his name was familiar. "Elliott. Where have I heard that before?"

Where haven't you? Erika thought. "The Elliotts are involved in several publishing ventures."

Gannon extended his hand. "I'm so sorry about your niece."

"I've been a wreck all morning, but Erika here has been a lifesaver."

"I'm sure she has," he said. "How is Tia?"

Erika responded. "Her leg is broken. It was a compound fracture. Other than that, she has a concussion and some cuts that required stitches. It's amazing that she survived it."

"It was a truck?"

She nodded. "The driver was drunk. At eight o'-clock this morning," she added, unable to keep her anger from her voice.

"But she's going to be okay?" he asked.

"It looks good. We're waiting to hear more from the doctor."

"I just want her to be okay," Brenda said, wringing her hands. "And I hope the insurance on my new job will cover most of the hospital bill." She took a deep breath. "I need a breath of fresh air if you don't mind. I've never liked hospitals. Please let me know if the doctor steps in," she said to Erika, then turned to Gannon. "Nice meeting you. I appreciate you stopping by."

Erika watched the woman leave the room. "I feel for her," she said. "She's trying to cover for her sister in jail and keep her own head above water."

Gannon moved closer to her and slid his hands into his black wool coat pockets. "What about the insurance?"

Erika winced. "The coverage may be iffy because Tia's aunt hasn't been working at this company long."

He paused barely a half beat. "Let me know if there are any gaps in coverage. It will be taken care of."

She stared at him in surprise. "Why? You barely know her."

"But you know her well and she's obviously important to you."

Her stomach dipped and swayed as if she were on a ride at an amusement park. Everything he said and did was indicating that she, Erika, was important to him. "I don't know what to say except thank you."

"Brenda Rogers?" a male voice said.

Erika whipped around to the doctor. "She went outside for just a second. I'll go get her."

Erika raced downstairs to find Tia's aunt just as she was walking inside. She escorted the anxious woman to the waiting room, where Gannon was talking with the doctor.

"Tia is in stable condition," the doctor told Erika and Brenda. "She may need some physical therapy, but after a week or two of rest with moderate daily movement, you'll be amazed at how quickly she recovers. Youth," he said and smiled. "She's groggy from the anesthesia, but I think she'd like a visit."

"Oh, thank God," Brenda said and grabbed Erika's hand. "Will you go with me to see her?"

"Of course." Erika glanced at Gannon.

"Give me a call later," he said.

She nodded, still trying to come to grips with why he had come to the emergency room. She never wanted to overestimate her importance to him. That had been her downfall before.

By the time Erika left the hospital it was midnight and she wasn't feeling anything like Cinderella. Taking a cab, she listened to her voice-mail messages on the way home. Her assistant had left several, and Jessica had called to gently bully Erika about Gerald.

She winced at that message and deleted it. Gannon had left two messages, one from much earlier in the day and one two hours ago instructing her to call him when she went home.

She replayed his messages two times and closed her eyes as she listened to his voice. She had always loved his voice, deep with just a hint of roughness around the edges.

She glanced at her watch again and shook her head. It was after midnight. No way she was going to call Gannon Elliott after midnight.

The following morning she dragged herself out of bed, called the hospital to check on Tia and ingested three cups of coffee. She would have mainlined it if it had been possible. She didn't fight her hair today, deciding to let it go curly as she applied what seemed like half a pot of concealer beneath her eyes.

For the sake of distraction, she rubbed on blush, lip gloss and mascara and wore a red sweater. She hoped it made her appear more alert when all she wanted was another half day of z's.

She rode the train to her office, took off her coat and prepared to sink into her chair.

A knock sounded at her door and Gannon walked into her office. Her heart gave a little bump at the sight of him.

"You didn't call," he said.

"It was after midnight."

He nodded. "You could have called anyway."

"Still awake?" she said in surprise. "I would have loved to have been asleep then. In fact, I think I may have dozed a little on the way to my apartment."

He cracked a half smile. "That sleepy?"

She nodded. "Oh, yeah. This afternoon I may pull out my yoga mat, put a Do Not Disturb sign on my door and take a nap."

"I thought yoga was for meditating."

"In this case meditating on the inside of my eyelids."

He chuckled. "How's Tia?"

"She was a little scared. She tried to put up a brave front for her aunt, and that just ripped out my heart, so I stayed until I talked with the night nurse and Tia conked out."

"You're a good person."

The simple affirmation from him stole all her pithy responses. He was treating her differently and she didn't know how to react. The way he acted could lead her to believe that something deeper than hot sex in his office was going on between them.

She glanced away to get her bearings. "This may sound strange, but Tia inspires me. She comes from this pretty terrible background with her mother being a re-peat drug offender, no father in sight and an aunt who's struggling to keep everything together. But I can tell Tia wants to do better. She's been working like crazy on the article for *HomeStyle*. She's a fighter and she's not afraid to go for it. What's not to admire about that?"

"And maybe you see a little bit of you in her?"

She opened her mouth, then closed it and smiled. "Now, that might be bordering on flattery. I've had quite a few more advantages than Tia has."

"But you've got the fight and the heart."

His gaze was doing strange things to her insides. She looked away again. "Thanks. And thank you also for the offer to cover any insurance problems. That will mean so much to Tia's aunt."

"No problem. What are your plans tonight?"

"Work, then hospital again."

"How long are they keeping her?"

"Another couple of days. I may try to go over to the house and give Brenda a break in the evenings."

He nodded. "Give me a call, and I mean that," he added in a stern voice. "I'll send over my car to take you home."

"That's not necessary," she said. "This isn't really your—" She shrugged. "Your thing."

"It's supposed to snow tonight. Are you going to turn down a ride?"

His gaze was dark with an edge of challenge. What was he trying to do to her? Confuse the hell out of her? Drive her crazy? He was succeeding.

But she absolutely refused to turn down a ride in a toasty car when the weather was horrid and she knew she would be tired.

"Thank you very much," she said.

"You're welcome," he said and left the room, leaving her to wonder.

The next two nights Gannon's car magically appeared to take her home. Erika told herself not to get used to it, but oh, the leather felt nice and the music soothed her. The second night when Carl, the driver, offered her a glass of wine, she accepted it. She talked with Gannon both nights, too.

Since Tia left the hospital on Thursday, he joined her as Erika visited the teen at home. Erika noticed him talking with Brenda while Erika played Scrabble with Tia. Hearing Brenda exclaim, Erika glanced at the two of them and saw Tia's aunt give him a hug.

She asked him about it on the drive home. "What was that about?"

"I just told her she didn't need to worry about the insurance and that I'd arranged for a nurse's aide to help with Tia for the next two weeks."

She shook her head. "When did you decide to get the aide?"

"Hey, I can be generous."

"Yeah, I know. You fund a dozen charities."

"More like nine," he said. "But I have ulterior motives in this situation."

Her heart skipped a beat. "What are those?"

"I'm concerned about your work performance. My dad needs you in top condition to help *Pulse* win my grandfather's challenge."

She blinked. "I haven't been slowing down on my job."

"What about the yoga-mat nap?"

"That was a joke," she said hotly.

He grinned. "I know."

She frowned. "What are you doing?"

"Will you admit you're exhausted doing double duty? Full day at the office. Long evening at the hospital."

She clamped her mouth shut.

"Should have known you wouldn't admit it. Okay, I want Tia taken care of so you can spend some time with me."

His bluntness stole the air from her lungs. She felt as if she were on a rocky ledge, grappling for something to hold on to. "I thought we weren't going to do this again." She glanced away. "We shouldn't have—" She broke off. "In your office, we really shouldn't have—"

His hand covered hers, stopping her rambling. "This is more than sex, Erika. I just want to be with you. Without interruptions. Without ducking and hiding."

She bit her lip. "How? I can't believe you want to date me publicly."

"No," he said. "I don't want to put either of us through the scrutiny." He closed his hand around hers. "Did I ever mention that I have a condo in South Beach?"

"South Beach as in Miami?"

He nodded. "I think we should go down for the weekend."

Her head was starting to spin. "Which weekend?"

"Tomorrow."

"Tomorrow?"

"We can use my private jet."

All she could do was stare at him. This was just too much for her to take in.

He lifted his fingers to her chin. "You said one of your rules was to never turn down a trip to South Florida in the winter."

Erika felt herself pulled in two opposing directions. The beach, warm sun and Gannon Elliott's undivided attention provided an irresistible lure. But she knew this could be one huge, honking mistake, especially if she fell for Gannon again.

The unsigned baby contract was becoming a bigger issue with each passing day. Every time she brought up the subject, he told her that his lawyer would handle it, but since it was such an unusual agreement, it would take time.

Sometimes Erika didn't know which she feared more: running out of time to be with Gannon or facing the prospect of an impersonal sperm donation from a stranger.

Ten

No lines, no intense security inspections, no skimpy snacks or yucky food and no waiting. As Erika looked out the window of Gannon's Cessna, she knew this was one aspect of wealth she could grow to love.

"Just curious," she said to him as he studied a report. "When was the last time you flew on a commercial airline?"

"When I went to Australia two years ago," he said. "No, wait. London, last year. It was a quick trip."

"Those are out of the country. They don't count," she said, knowing there were more perks and better customer service on international flights.

He wrinkled his brow thoughtfully for a moment. "Maybe when I was in college?"

Erika groaned. "You're so spoiled."

His gaze darkening, he shook his head slightly and slid his hand around the back of her neck. He drew her toward him. "Not spoiled enough."

She couldn't help smiling at his playfully dark tone. "Oh, really?"

"Yeah, being with you and not being with you makes me feel—" He broke off as if he were fighting saying the word.

"Cranky?" she offered.

He growled and the sound ruffled her nerve endings pleasurably. "Hungry all the time."

The revelation gave her a little thrill and she smiled. "For me?"

"Yeah, you," he said and lowered his mouth to hers.

Erika sank into the warm, seductive kiss and sighed. She lifted her hands to his shoulders and moved closer. The more miles they left between them and New York, the more she felt herself give in to their temporary escape. She knew all too well that the more she sank under his spell, the more she was going to hurt if and when Gannon lost interest…or changed his mind about her.

The reality poked at her like an annoying price tag left on her clothing. She deliberately brushed the sensation aside. His mouth, his attention, just being with Gannon felt too good.

She pulled back slightly. "Tell me about your condo. Is it near the beach?"

"Not near the beach. *On* a private beach. It's a nice getaway."

"Do you get away much?"

He shook his head. "I bought three of them a few years

ago as an investment. I turned two and kept the penthouse. A couple of my cousins have used it. I stayed in it once during a business trip to Miami. My assistant called to make sure it's stocked with food, wine and beer."

Erika felt a dart of concern. "Does she know who—"

He shook his head. "All she knows is that someone is using my condo in South Beach this weekend, but she doesn't know who. I left a message for my father that I would be back on Monday and that he can reach me on my cell. I made the flight arrangements myself."

"So I just need to make sure that if I get a sunburn, I don't get it on my face, right?"

"Yeah. But I don't want you to get a sunburn anywhere else either."

The way he looked at her told her he had wicked plans for her body. "You know, I've never been to South Beach."

"I plan to show you a good time. Good food, a visit to the bar at Delano's for one of their famous martinis and—"

"And?"

"And maybe I'll turn your head."

As if he hadn't already. As if she wasn't constantly struggling to get her head on straight when she was around him despite the fact that he'd hurt her horribly last year. Add in her crazy but somewhat brilliant idea that he provide sperm for the baby she wanted, and everything about this situation was sideways.

But she was headed for Florida in January with the sexiest, most fascinating man in the universe, and Monday would come soon enough.

Luck was with them. A change in weather brought hot temperatures, although the night turned cool. Gannon's condo oozed a combination of sophistication and comfort, and the view of the ocean nearly made Erika drool. His large balcony boasted chaise lounges ready for sunbathing or just vegging.

Gannon joined her on the balcony. "Get the lead out and change your clothes. It's time for dinner."

"Why should we leave?" she asked, gesturing at the view.

"Because I promised you a good time," he told her and tugged her back inside the condo.

Erika changed into a simple black dress and took along a sweater. Gannon wore a black sweater that emphasized his shoulders and his pecs. Another view that could make her drool, Erika thought.

He took her to dinner at a trendy restaurant that overlooked the activity on Collins Avenue and offered a view of the ocean. Afterward they went to Delano's bar, where they served generous martinis at ridiculous prices. "Now you're spoiling me," she accused. "How am I going to go back to New York in January after this?"

"Don't think about it. That's a rule. No talk about going back until Sunday afternoon."

"That could be dangerous," she muttered. "This whole thing could be dangerous."

"Why?"

She shook her head. "Too hard to explain. Since I have you here, though, I'd like to ask you some questions I didn't have the nerve to ask you when we were involved last year."

"Why couldn't you ask me last year?"

"I was too awed by you. Terrified of offending you."

"No more awe?" he asked with a lifted eyebrow.

"Quit looking for ego strokes. You get them all the time."

"Not from you," he said, dead serious.

As if he needed them from her. Her heart gave a bump. "You blew me away the first time I met you. You still make me…" She searched for words.

"Make you what?"

"Crazy, breathless." She swallowed over a lump in her throat. "Lots of feelings, but don't distract me. I want to know—what does a billionaire wish for?"

"Peace on earth," he said without missing a beat.

She laughed and grabbed his hand, leaning across the table. "Personally, professionally."

He sipped his martini. "The tough questions."

"Uh-huh," she said.

He was silent for a long moment. "I'm not dodging your question—"

"That's good," she interjected.

He tossed her another mocking, dark look. "But I

don't spend that much time thinking about what I want."

"Because you already have it?"

He narrowed his eyes thoughtfully. "I don't spend a lot of time musing. I spend more time doing."

"Well, if you were to muse, what would you want?"

"I haven't thought about it much. I just assume that someday I'll have a family. When my father retires, I'll be promoted into his position if I don't take another position at EPH before that happens."

"Would you like to be CEO of the whole shebang?"

"There's an appeal to having that kind of power," he confessed. "The idea of having that kind of influence over the media is seductive. Think of the impact you could have worldwide."

"Big responsibility, too," she said.

"That's why we check facts five times over on some articles. One wrong slip and four hundred people are killed in a country on the other side of the globe."

"That's one of the things I've always admired about you."

"What?"

"You're harder on yourself than you are on anyone else."

He toyed with her fingers. "Always knew you were a little too sharp."

"You'd rather be with someone not so quick?"

He lifted her fingers to his lips. "You're the one who's here, aren't you?"

"Yeah. So you've told me about your professional dreams. Still haven't said much about your personal dreams except a vague marriage and family...sometime."

"Oh, you're making me think." He groaned. "When I have time to think—and I stay busy enough to make sure that doesn't occur too often—I realize there's never a good time to try to develop a relationship the way I'd like."

Her heart twisted, but she took a breath to keep her voice light. "On the down low?"

He nodded. "But take time to do normal things. Be friends. I have too high a profile to have a normal relationship. I feel like I have to rob Peter to pay Paul."

She pulled her hand from his.

He met her gaze. "I obviously said something wrong."

"It's just that you feel so torn. I don't like being a part of that."

He shrugged. "So you screw up my head some. Yeah, it's true. But being with you makes me feel good. When I'm with you in the office, I have a tough time keeping my hands off you—and I'm not just talking about sex. I want to touch your hand. I want to share an inside joke. If I do that too much, other people will see there's something between us. That could cause problems for you and me. I sure as hell don't want you going back to *HomeStyle*."

"I won't go back to *HomeStyle* as long as you keep

your end of the bargain. Speaking of which, what's happening with the baby contract?" she asked.

He opened his mouth, then closed it. He finished his martini. "Good point. I'll make another call to my attorney first thing on Monday." He waved to a waiter. "Pineapple martini for the lady," he said to the server.

"I haven't finished my first one," she protested.

"Drink up."

"You're not trying to get me loaded, are you?" she asked, unable to keep from smiling.

"No, but I've gone along with your questions. Now you tell me. What does Miss Erika want professionally and personally, besides a baby?"

"I'm building my career to a place where I can have some flexibility."

"The make-yourself-necessary-and-the-company-will-do-anything-to-keep-you philosophy. I'd say you've succeeded at that," he said in a dry tone.

"Gosh, does that mean I should have asked for more money?" she joked.

"Keep going," he said. "What about the TDH?"

"A man. A husband. I would have preferred to do the husband before the baby, but I didn't anticipate any medical issues."

"The medical problem," he said. "Is it that bad?"

She bit her lip. "Bad enough to change my plans. I've even joined an organization for single mothers by choice. But I have to look on the bright side. My friends have already volunteered to be aunties," she confided.

"You told them?"

"Yeah, during a four-martini evening." She winced, remembering the hangover the next day.

"Four?" he echoed. "You've barely finished one."

"Yeah, but these are so big I could swim in them."

"So plying you with liquor is the secret to getting you to loosen your—" he deliberately paused "—tongue."

She laughed at his naughty humor. "Plying me with four martinis is a sure path to a hangover the next morning. That was a crazy night out with the girls."

"Did you tell them about your plan to get me under contract?"

"No," she said with a frown. "They don't even know that you and I were involved. Although they asked a lot of questions last year."

"Why?"

"Because I was sad."

He lifted his thumb to her lip. "No more of that."

Gannon took Erika to a sybaritic club and had no problem dodging photographers since several starlets were more than eager to pose for the camera. It may have been wiser to move their little party back to his condo, but he'd never taken Erika dancing. The two martinis she'd nursed seemed to have lowered her inhibitions, and he wanted to tease a few secrets out of her mouth before he got to her body.

Gannon knew that once he took her back to his

condo he would want to take her straight to bed—and not to sleep.

She laughed as she was pushed against him on the crowded dance floor. "There's nowhere to go," she protested.

"I think it's designed that way so you have to stay close to someone. Make sure it's me," he said, drawing her against him.

He dipped his head and drew in the subtle spicy scent of her perfume. "You smell great."

"So do you," she said. "Your aftershave makes me dizzy."

"It does?" he murmured, sliding his hands over her hips. She undulated against him, making him reconsider his plan to stay at the club a little longer.

She nodded and licked her lips, then pressed her mouth against his. An illicit thrill ran through him.

"I love the way you taste. Love the way you feel. Love the way you think. Most of the time," she added. "Love the way you talk."

"The way I talk?"

"Your voice is very sexy."

He swallowed a smile, wondering if two martinis had been a bit much for her.

She closed her eyes and looped her arms around the back of his neck. "But you're stingy with your heart."

He blinked. "What?"

"Or maybe it's just me. Just when I'm ready to write

you off as heartless, you do something like show up at the hospital the other day." She opened her eyes and met his gaze. "You shouldn't have done that. That kind of thing could make me fall in love with you."

"Ah," he said, thinking that he didn't mind the thought of her being in love with him. Maybe he'd had too many martinis, too.

"That's not a good thing."

"Why not?"

"I did it before and it was horrible when you stopped seeing me." She played with the back of his hair. "I probably shouldn't be here, but you did that nice thing by showing up at the hospital and taking my breath away and making me do crazy things."

"I kinda like being the man to take your breath away and make you do crazy things."

"There are consequences," she told him. "Can you handle the consequences?"

Her expression was so sexy and challenging, it made him so hard that he wondered if he would split the crotch of his slacks. "I think I can."

"Then why are we still in public and not alone in your condo?"

Not needing a second suggestion, he whisked her out of the club and to his condo in no time. As soon as they stepped into the elevator, he took her mouth in a long French kiss that made him sweat.

The way she drew his tongue into her mouth and shimmied against him sent his heart rate skyrocketing.

She slid her fingers into his hair, and the sensation of her touch on his scalp was oddly erotic.

Everything about her was erotic. The way she smelled, the way she moved, the way she tasted. He swallowed an oath and slid his hands up her thighs to cup her bottom, urging her against him to soothe the hard ache she caused.

"You make me—" She never finished the thought as she took his mouth again in an openmouthed kiss that robbed his breath.

He slipped his hands between her thighs, underneath her panties, and found her damp and swollen. It was the sexiest sensation, but he knew there was more.

"I make you what?" he managed.

She gasped as he stroked her.

"So hot," she whispered.

She did the same for him. The elevator dinged the arrival to the penthouse and he urged her through the door.

She tugged at his sweater. He pulled her zipper down and shoved her dress down over her hips along with her little black panties. The urge to be inside her was like a raging fire.

He pulled off his sweater and she unfastened his slacks. He ditched his shoes and slacks and pulled her against him. She wrapped her legs around his waist, her wetness taunting but not enfolding him.

In the back of his mind he remembered protection. For the first time in his life he wavered. She wanted a baby. In a way he'd never wanted before, he wanted to possess her, to mark her as his. An audacious, primitive thought.

He took a deep, not-so-steady breath and put her on the couch. "Back in a second," he whispered.

He grabbed his slacks and the condom inside the pocket and returned to her but made himself wait to look at her. Her hair spilled over the couch with abandon. The stiff peaks of her breasts invited him like cherries on cream. And her thighs were spread open, revealing her swollen femininity.

"You have no idea how sexy you are," he told her. "But I'm going to do my best to show you."

"Another thing I love about you is that you're an overachiever about everything you do."

She made him want to live up to being her overachiever lover. He lowered his mouth to her breasts and inhaled her groans, slid his lips down to her belly button and lower still to take her into his mouth. She arched against him and he decided the taste of her arousal had to be the most addictive thing he'd ever experienced.

"Inside," she whispered. "Inside."

He pulled on the condom and pushed her legs farther apart, plunging inside. She moaned. He groaned.

"Be careful," she told him as he sank into her moist, tight femininity and the deep turbulence of her eyes. "I don't want to love you too much again."

But he was a greedy man. He wanted her. Her body, her mind and her love. And he took everything she offered and gave her more than he'd planned.

Eleven

The trouble with a woman like Erika, Gannon realized after they returned from South Beach, was that being with her was habit-forming. He wasn't sure how she managed to be both comforting and stimulating, but she did it damn well.

Although he'd seen her that morning, his schedule had been too packed to get a chance to talk with her. Then he couldn't turn down his mother's impromptu invitation to a lunch that included his sister and brothers.

Despite his suggestion to make use of the executive dining room, his mother had preferred a café around the corner and indulged in small talk.

"Nice tan," his mother said, smiling as she lifted her brows in silent question.

"Yeah," his sister, Bridget, said. "It must be nice to be able to take time off for a trip to Florida in January."

"You could, too, if you didn't work for the female version of Attila the Hun," Tag said, joking about their hardworking aunt Finola.

"You'll be changing your tune when you report to her as the new CEO," Bridget retorted.

"Remember who your father is," Gannon said, feeling a sharp tug of competitiveness.

"It's just starting," Liam muttered. "We've got an entire year of this."

His mother lifted her hands and shook her head. "No arguments. This was supposed to be a nice lunch for a mother with her children."

"Sorry, Mom," Tag said.

"Back to Gannon's tan," Bridget said. "Take anyone with you?"

Gannon sipped his coffee. "No one I want to discuss."

His mother met his gaze. "Hmm. Must mean you like her if she hasn't shown up in the press."

Karen Elliott might be known for her easygoing nature, but she was shrewd when it came to reading what was going on with her husband and children. Gannon studied her for a moment. He was reluctant to admit to himself that he'd been distracted for most of the meal thinking about Erika, but now that he looked at his mother, he noticed she seemed a little on edge. Her hands were knotted too tightly and at the moment her brows were furrowed.

"What's up with you?"

She pushed her hair behind her ear in a nervous gesture. "Not much. The regular thing. Volunteer work, my reading club, visiting with Maeve." She glanced at her watch. "As a matter of fact, I need to leave for a meeting. But I just wanted to let all of you know that I'm going into the hospital for some tests."

Alarm shot through Gannon. "What?"

"Tests," Tag echoed. "What tests?"

"I don't want to make a big deal about it. It's not unusual to take all kinds of medical tests at my age." Karen was fifty-four.

"But this isn't routine, is it?" Liam asked.

His mother's face looked determinedly neutral. "I've told you as much as I need to."

"But, Mom," Bridget said, "you can't just drop this on us and not explain."

"You would prefer that I not tell you at all?" Karen returned.

Tag cleared his throat. "No. Not at all." He reached to cover his mother's hand. "But you're pretty important to us, so we want to know everything."

She patted his hand and gave a little smile. "Well, all of you are very important to me, too. Now I really should go. Gannon, if you don't mind, could you pay the bill?"

"No problem," he said and stood as Tag helped her with her coat. He leaned toward her and hugged her. "You know you can call me for anything."

"Including grandchildren?"

He groaned. "I should have known you'd find a way to slip that in."

"Don't make me wait forever. 'Bye, darlings," she said and kissed each of them before she left.

Silence fell over the four of them.

"This is weird," Bridget said. "I'm worried."

"She doesn't want us to worry," Liam said.

"What do you think it is?" Tag asked.

"I don't know," Gannon said.

"Has Dad said anything to you?" Tag asked.

"Not a word."

"I don't have a good feeling about this," Bridget said, and from the looks on his brothers' faces and the knot in his own gut, Gannon sensed she was speaking for all of them.

Erika plowed her way through the work that had piled up during her absence on Friday. The afternoon wore into early evening before she took a break and stretched. A light knock sounded on her door and Gannon walked in.

Her heart immediately lifted and she rose from her chair. "It's so good to see you," she said, smiling at the sight of him.

"Same here," he said, tugging her from behind her desk and into his arms. "Are you sure someone didn't try to pack two days into this one?"

"I'm with you on that, but the weekend was great," she said, relishing the feel of his arms around her. "It's like I turn my back and everyone races into my office and dumps their work on me before I can yell stop."

He chuckled. "Oh, this is crazy, but I've missed you."

Her heart tightened at his confession. "I guess we can be crazy together, because I've missed you, too."

He lowered his mouth to hers in a kiss that made her dizzy and warm. She pulled back slightly and looked at him. "That felt like two martinis on an empty stomach."

He gave only a half grin, making her take a second look. Something about him was different. Sure, the office brought the usual pressures, but he seemed more tense.

"What's wrong?"

He narrowed his eyes and glanced away. "Nothing. Regular headaches. Rough landing after my trip to paradise with my dream girl."

Her heart gave a little flip. "I appreciate the flattery."

"It's more than flattery," he told her, his gaze making her heart skitter.

"Thanks," she said, lifting her hand to his jaw. "Dream guy."

His jaw clenched slightly.

She frowned in concern. "Gannon, I don't want to pry, but something's wrong. You can tell me if you want, but you don't have to."

He closed his eyes, inhaling deeply, then exhaling. "My mother is going into the hospital for some tests. She won't tell us what's wrong. Neither will Dad. I grilled him this afternoon and couldn't get anything out of him."

The pain in his voice made her chest hurt. "Oh, Gannon, I'm so sorry. All of you must be sick with worry."

He shook his head. "My father may seem like the

rock of my family—and don't get me wrong, he's solid. But my mother…she's the glue. I mean, look at the personalities in my family. All of us kids have been a handful at one time or another, but she smoothes everything out and makes it work. I don't know what we'd do if something happened to—" He broke off, shaking his head again.

"You can't think that way until you find out the rest of what's going on."

"I prefer having all the information," he said in a rough voice.

"You like having control," she said.

He nodded.

"And you don't have it in this situation."

He sighed. "No. I don't. And I don't understand why she wouldn't confide in her own children."

"Don't you think she must have had her reasons?" she asked.

"She's usually the most reasonable person in the world."

"Then you're going to have to give her some room to do what she feels she needs to do."

"None of us likes being shut out."

"I'm sure you don't. You think she'll tell you more after she gets the test results?"

"Yeah, I just wish I knew…"

"So you could fix it," she added. "What can I do to help you?"

He met her gaze. "You're doing it."

The way he looked at her made her feel light-headed. The way he looked at her made her feel necessary. Was that possible with a man like Gannon?

After that, they spent every night together. It was as if the puzzle pieces between them had clicked together and neither wanted to question it. It just felt right.

Gannon joined her when she visited Tia and he waved coffee under her nose in the mornings to help her wake up. They made love every night and she fell asleep in his arms.

The fact that he still hadn't produced a contract from his personal lawyer bothered her. She'd brought it up several times once he'd insisted it was in its final draft. She had to believe he would come around. Maybe this time she would get the man *and* the baby. Maybe she would get it all.

The prospect made her so breathless she couldn't overthink it.

Gannon joined his family for dinner one of the weekend nights but showed up at her apartment afterward. Erika knew she was falling more deeply in love with him with each passing moment and she couldn't find any motivation to stop herself.

Monday started out the same way. She and Gannon worked their jobs and he surprised her with a rose that evening. Erika carried the secret pleasure of the rose and his attention all through the next day.

Late Tuesday afternoon he entered her office with a

somber expression on his face. He closed the door behind him and adjusted his tie.

Erika felt a spike of alarm. "What's wrong? Is it
your mother?"

She rushed toward him, but he held up his hand to
stop her. "No. Not my mother."

"Then what is it?"

Shoving his hands in his pockets, he sighed. "The rumors have started again. A copy editor mentioned to an
intern that she'd seen us together. It must have been
when we took that walk the other night."

She fought a wave of apprehension. "You're not
dumping me again," she said.

He shook his head. "No. Not dumping. We just probably need to cool things down for a while."

She didn't find his response at all reassuring. "What
do you mean by cool down? And how long is a while?"

"Cool down means we probably shouldn't see each
other outside of work for a while."

A knot of ugly tension formed in her throat. "And a
while is?"

He shrugged. "I don't know, Erika. Maybe we
should put this off until the CEO challenge is over."

She gasped. "But that's a whole year."

His jaw tightened in displeasure. "Yeah, I know. But
it might be best."

"For whom?" she demanded.

"For everyone," he said, his impatience bleeding
into his voice. "This isn't what I want."

"Well, you sure made the decision fast. I think I was in your bed this morning."

"C'mon, Erika. This is a tough time. My focus has to stay on *Pulse* and getting my father into the CEO position. I have feelings for you, but this isn't the right time."

Feeling like the worst kind of fool, she fought a mix of fury and tears. She felt totally betrayed. He hadn't made promises, she reminded herself, but it didn't matter. She'd allowed herself to believe. She'd let down her guard.

Gannon might watch out for *Pulse,* his father and her job, but he wasn't going to watch out for her heart.

Her throat was so tight she could barely speak. "I don't know what to say. I didn't expect this from you. Again."

"It's not the same thing," he said.

"Yes, it is." She shook her head to clear it. She had to take care of herself. "I can't stay with *Pulse.*"

"What?"

She shook her head again. "I can't stay with *Pulse.*"

"You're not going to use that as a trump card to force me to go public with our relationship, are you?"

He may as well have slapped her. "This isn't about you," she said. "This is about my emotional well-being. Not that you would understand that. I don't want to have to see you every day and—"

"We can make arrangements so we don't have to interact as much," he said.

She shook her head. "No. I don't want to be on the same floor. I'm not going to do that to myself. I'm going back to *HomeStyle* immediately."

"You can't," he said.

"I can. You never signed a contract for me and my contract stipulated that I could return to *HomeStyle* at any time."

He stared at her in disbelief.

An ugly suspicion boiled inside her. "You never even intended to give me your sperm, did you?"

Gannon gave an exasperated sigh. "It was an insane idea. I hoped I could make you see—"

"My insanity," she interjected, fury rising inside her. "Yes, I can and I will return to *HomeStyle,*" she repeated, clinging to the resolve growing inside her. "I'm getting off your seesaw, Gannon. And I'm not getting back on."

Gannon stayed up until nearly dawn, prowling his empty, lonely two-story apartment. He could still smell the scent of Erika, hear the echo of her laughter. He didn't want to sit on the sofa because she wasn't there smiling up at him.

As he watched the sun rise over the cold city from his window, he searched his mind for ways to keep her in his life. Sure, he wanted her at *Pulse,* but he wanted her after work even more.

In fact, the want was feeling a lot closer to need. More than sexual, though heaven knew he couldn't get enough of her in bed either.

There had to be a way to negotiate this situation. There was always a way.

Riding the wave of her anger and refusing to give in to her hurt, Erika went to work early and moved her belongings back to her *HomeStyle* office. Her successor hadn't gotten completely settled in, so Erika just stacked her boxes against the wall next to the door.

She left a note for Michael on his assistant's desk simply telling him that she preferred to return to *Home-Style* because the position suited her better. She arranged a transfer to a highly coveted position for her temporary replacement. No need for the woman to get the shaft just because things hadn't worked out for Erika at *Pulse*.

She kept busy putting her office in order and reacquainting herself with the business of producing *HomeStyle*.

Midmorning an e-mail from Gannon popped up. Even the sight of his name made her heart jump. Disgusted with her reaction, she vacillated over whether to delete it without reading it, but some sick part of her couldn't resist.

He was surprised she'd moved so fast. They should talk about things. A year wasn't so long.

Maybe not for him, she thought and deleted the message.

She told herself she was doing fine—not great but okay—until she walked out of her office and nearly plowed into him. Seeing him shocked the air out of her lungs.

"Hi," he said.

"Hi," she managed.

"We need to talk."

Talking with Gannon got her into trouble. Looking at Gannon got her into trouble.

"I'm busy," she said and was amazed that her feet followed her mental direction to step away from the fire that had burned her twice.

I'm busy became her mantra. She practiced it at odd moments when he invaded her mind. She said it to him when he tried to invade her office. She even began to repeat it in her sleep for the next two nights.

On Wednesday she received an unexpected invitation. Tea on Thursday with Maeve Elliott, the wife of Patrick Elliott, current CEO of Elliott Publication Holdings. Cameras and recorders permitted.

She was so excited she could barely stand it. For months she'd requested an interview with Maeve at the family townhome, but Maeve's assistant had always put her off.

She couldn't believe her luck. What a coup. She immediately began to plan for the meeting, jotting down notes and arranging for a sensitive, polite and talented photographer. She told herself the fact that Maeve was Gannon's grandmother wasn't part of her intense curiosity about the woman. Her interest was purely professional.

Which sounded like bull and she hadn't even said it aloud. The following morning she changed her clothes three times and took an extra outfit to work in case she spilled something on herself.

A half hour before her appointment with Maeve, she and the photographer took a cab to Ninetieth and Amsterdam Avenue. Gannon had told her the place was huge by Manhattan standards, with three stories of living space and an unheard-of half-submerged garage. Erika also knew that Maeve and Patrick's orphaned twin granddaughters lived at the townhome during the week since both of them worked at EPH.

As the cab driver slowed in front of the address, she took in the Manhattan home of Gannon's grandparents. The black wrought-iron gate covered in ivy discouraged uninvited guests. The gray stone building with white trim and a red front door sat back from the street about ten feet.

The photographer, Tom, gave a low whistle. "Nice place."

"It's beautiful. We won't take outside shots in order to protect their privacy."

He nodded in agreement. "I've got my flash ready for inside."

"I'll ask her permission before you shoot," she said, feeling a mixture of excitement and nerves. "Are you ready?"

He nodded and got out of the car, then turned to assist her.

"Thanks," she said. "Great manners. That's part of the reason I chose you."

He smiled. "My mother will be delighted to hear it."

They rang the doorbell and a woman answered the door. "Mrs. Elliott will have tea in the library," she said and led Erika and Tom to the room left of the foyer. The grand entrance boasted a ceiling that went up to the roof and showcased a stained-glass skylight.

Erika spied a grand piano farther down the entryway. She heard the quiet click of Tom's camera as she entered the formal library. The lovely room emanated a warm ambience while filled with antiques.

A silver tray was already set with tea, tiny sandwiches and pastries. Three place settings of delicate rose-covered bone china were placed on the cocktail table.

"I wonder who—"

"Hello, Erika," a familiar voice said from the foyer.

Gannon. She looked at him in surprise. "What are you doing here?" she whispered.

He laughed. "I'm having tea with my grandmother."

Realization sank inside her. "You set this up," she said, unable to keep an accusing tone from her voice.

"Yes, I did. And you're glad I did. Right?"

She opened her mouth and worked it, wanting to stalk out of the town house. But that would have been unbearably rude, and she couldn't give up the opportunity to meet Maeve even with Gannon there.

He turned behind him and extended his hand. "Grandmother Maeve, this is Erika Layven, the managing editor of our new magazine *HomeStyle*."

A small-boned, thin woman with mostly white hair pulled into an elegant updo entered the room. She wore a well-tailored dress and a locket around her neck, but what captured Erika's attention was the spark in her eyes and her kind smile.

"Erika, it's lovely to meet you. Gannon has told me you're a clever, industrious woman with a good heart. He mentioned your involvement in the mentoring program." Maeve extended her hand in welcome as she spoke in her lilting tone.

Erika fought an odd urge to curtsy and shook Maeve's hand instead. "Thank you for inviting me today. I'm honored."

"Please sit so we can enjoy our tea," she said, waving her hand toward the chair across from the settee. "You, too, Gannon. It's been a long time since you took afternoon tea."

Gannon smiled gently at his grandmother. "Can't deny that. I'm usually drinking coffee around this time to get a second wind."

"Tea's better for you," she said and turned to Tom. "Would you like to take a few pictures now?"

"Thank you very much, ma'am," he said and began to snap away.

"May we take a couple with Gannon, too, please?" Erika asked.

Maeve beamed. "I'm always happy to have my picture taken with my handsome grandson."

Gannon threw Erika a questioning glance. "You'll let me see this if you decide to print it."

"Of course," she said, feeling her stomach knot with a sense of loss as she watched him treat his grandmother with such deference. Erika longed to be part of Gannon's whole life, his work, his home and his family. But it would never happen.

Tom took a few more shots and Maeve lifted her hand. "That's enough. I'll ask Annie to bring another setting and you can join us, too."

Tom glanced at Erika with a look of desperation. He was obviously terrified of taking tea with Mrs. Elliott.

"I know Tom would love to stay, but he has another assignment today," Erika said.

"Exactly," he said. "I hope you'll excuse me."

"That's fine," Maeve said. "Don't let us keep you. Be careful with the wind. It's a bit nasty today."

"Thank you, ma'am," he said and smiled, then left for the door.

"What a polite man," Maeve said. "You don't see that often enough these days. Let's have Annie serve the tea and we can chat."

Erika was scrupulously polite during the visit, biting back the urge to scowl at Gannon for ruining the time with his intrusion. She didn't want to be distracted by the way he stretched out his long legs or the way he laughed at his grandmother's tales. She didn't want to notice the deference with which he treated her. She didn't want to think of him as capable of sweet attentiveness. She much preferred the cold-monster image she'd built in her mind as a form of protection.

"Tell Erika how you and Grandfather met," Gannon suggested.

"I was a seamstress in Ireland and he had come for a visit. I was nineteen years old and Patrick was tall with black hair and eyes as blue as the sea. And relentless. When he makes up his mind, there's no changing it," she said, shaking her head. "Back then I had long red hair and a few men wanting my hand, but Patrick just pushed them out of his way. Swept me off my feet and took me away from Ireland, and that was that."

"It sounds like you didn't stand a chance," Erika said.

"Oh I didn't. Patrick, he was already too handsome for his own good. A bit like this one here," she said, pointing to Gannon. "But it was his personality, his will. He had the energy of a summer storm." Maeve smiled. "He still does," she said, her smile fading slightly as she touched the locket hanging around her neck. "We've had our losses, but we have a lot of joy." She glanced at Gannon and squeezed his hand. "It's good to see you. You should take tea more often."

"I should," he said and kissed her cheek. "Thank you for having us."

"I'm always happy to see my grandchildren. And you're right about Erika. Smart and lovely. I can see the good heart," she said.

"Thank you, Mrs. Elliott. This was such an honor and a pleasure."

"I can give you a ride," Gannon said. "My car's waiting."

Erika opened her mouth to protest but didn't want to appear ungrateful in front of Maeve. She bit her tongue. "Thank you."

Maeve led them to the door. As soon as Erika stepped outside, she shot toward the street, feeling a misty moisture in the air that she hoped wasn't a preface to a rainstorm.

"Hey! Wait up," Gannon said, his long stride catching up with hers in no time. "What are you doing?" he asked when she lifted her hand to hail a cab.

"I'm getting a cab."

"I said I'd give you a ride."

"I don't want one from you," she told him, although the misty moisture turned to drizzle.

"Don't be ridiculous. It's almost rush hour. It'll take forever to get a cab and you'll end up paying a fortune."

"I can charge the company," she said, throwing him a dark look. Several taxis passed her by, and getting a taxi in the rain was nearly impossible.

He stood and waited while she waved her hand for several minutes. Frustration ground her down.

"Okay," she grumbled, her tiredness winning. "Thank you. I was going back to the office, but I think I'll just head home."

Gannon opened the door for her and she got in, moving as far to the opposite side of the seat as she could and placing her purse on the seat beside her as a puny barrier.

"I thought you would enjoy meeting Maeve."

She crossed her arms over her chest and stared straight ahead. "I did. Thank you for arranging the visit. I didn't know you were going to be there."

"Would you have turned her down if you'd known I was going to be there?"

"It would have crossed my mind," she muttered.

"But you still would have gone," he said. "Because you've been dying to meet her."

"The meeting gave *HomeStyle* a terrific feature. What's not to like?"

"What did you think of her personally?"

She wished he would stop trying to engage her, but at least he wasn't talking about their relationship. Or lack of it. Erika felt as if a hard rock was lodged in her throat. Every time she breathed it hurt.

"Maeve was lovely and warm. I bet she was always an openly affectionate grandmother."

He nodded. "She was."

"So what happened to you?" She bit her tongue too late. The flip comment flew out of her mouth before she could snatch it back.

Gannon pinned her with his gaze. "Is that a request or a challenge?"

His stormy expression made her a little nervous. "Neither. Forget I said it."

"No. I want you to explain."

"Well, we just don't always get what we want, and it may be hard for you to accept, but that includes you, too."

"Are you saying I'm not affectionate enough for you?"

The interior of the car seemed to close in on her. She became aware of his aftershave and his long legs just inches from hers. She saw one of his hands on his leg and remembered how that hand had felt on her bare skin, how he'd held her and touched her intimately.

She inhaled slowly. "I didn't say you weren't affectionate."

He paused a half beat. "Openly affectionate."

Silence hung between them and her hurt bloomed like a man-eating flower. To be openly affectionate you had to be willing for everyone to know how you felt. Gannon wasn't. After this second go-round, Erika couldn't pretend his insistence for a secret relationship didn't signal a huge lack of commitment.

"Have you missed me?"

"Like a toothache," she said, refusing to let him get at her one more iota.

He gave a rough chuckle. "I miss you," he told her. "I don't want to do without you."

Her heart twisted. "That was your call, not mine."

He took her hand. "All I said was that we needed to cool things down for a while."

Her resentment rose inside her like a bubbling volcano. "Have you successfully cooled off? Has it been that easy for you?"

"No," he said, his eyes changing colors like a turbulent sea. "I'm still burning up for you and I bet you're still burning for me."

He lowered his head and took her mouth in a carnal, possessive kiss that rippled with emotion. She could feel the want and felt an echoing response inside her. With that caress, he ripped aside the fragile construction of her protection against him, and she felt the aching need tear through her like a hurricane out of control.

He pulled back slightly and whispered against her lips. "You still want to be with me. I can taste it."

She pushed against him, upset with herself for giving in so quickly. "Just because I want you doesn't mean I'll be with you. Trust me. I'm used to wanting you and not having you."

Twelve

The crowd roared as the Knicks scored again, putting the home team ahead by six points. Gannon automatically stood, but he couldn't muster much enthusiasm.

Gannon had never lost at anything that was truly important to him, but he was starting to feel as if the wind was turning against him. He had a bad feeling in his gut about his mother's medical tests. His father had seemed distracted the past few days and he still refused to discuss the subject with Gannon.

And there was Erika.

Rather, there wasn't Erika. Every time he thought of her, his chest squeezed so tight he felt as if he were caught in a vise grip.

After he'd given her a ride home following the tea at his grandmother's, he'd called her, but she hadn't picked up her phone or returned his call.

She'd meant it when she'd said no more. She might still have feelings for him, but she'd given up on him.

The reality alarmed him. Unaccustomed to that emotion, he struggled with a sense of emptiness that went deeper than his bones.

He had thought he could reason with her, negotiate, but she was slamming the door in his face every way it could be done.

Damn, he hadn't realized he'd gotten this involved with her. He'd thought he'd been in better control of his emotions than this. He always had before.

Even now, as he sat in prime seats in Madison Square Garden watching the Knicks with his uncle and a few cousins, he felt completely disconnected.

The half-time buzzer sounded and his uncle Daniel nudged him. "You look like you need a beer or two," he said. "We're going to the VIP lounge. Come on."

He opened his mouth to make an excuse, but Daniel interrupted. "No. We're not letting you stay here looking like that."

Gannon reluctantly got to his feet and joined his cousins and uncle for the mob-filled trek to the VIP room. His cousins scattered while Daniel and Gannon nursed beers at a table near the bar.

"You going to tell me what's wrong?" his uncle asked.

Gannon shook his head.

"Then push aside your sadness for the moment and celebrate with me. I've finally found a way to get my estranged leech of a wife to agree to a divorce."

Surprised, Gannon automatically lifted his beer in salute. Everyone in the family knew that Sharon,

Daniel's second wife, had clung to him and everything she could get from being an Elliott despite the fact that Daniel had wanted a divorce for years. "That's great news. How'd you do it?"

"Paid her off. She finally realized there was no way I would reconcile. Word of advice—don't let your father choose your wife. Choose your own. You have to live with her. Your father doesn't."

Daniel's words struck him like a two-by-four. Even though Gannon's father wouldn't dream of choosing wives for his sons, Gannon couldn't help feeling that he was putting off being with the woman who made him feel happier than he'd ever been because of his grandfather's aversion to scandal and the recent CEO challenge.

Daniel paused midgulp, studying Gannon. "You look like you just took a right hook to the jaw."

"Close," Gannon said, a dozen emotions churning inside him.

Daniel narrowed his eyes. "I'm not the most intuitive guy on the block, but this is looking like a woman problem."

Not bothering to deny it, Gannon nodded.

"I haven't seen you take much of a fall for any woman," Daniel said, then gave a rough chuckle. "I guess it's your turn."

"It sure is bad timing," Gannon said, shaking his head.

"It's almost always bad timing. Bad timing is easier to deal with than the wrong woman, though. Trust me."

Gannon took another long swallow. "What are you saying?"

"Despite the fact that I'm facing my second divorce—or maybe because of it—my advice is simple. If you find a woman who makes you whole, do whatever it takes to get her and hold on tight."

At five after ten on Tuesday morning a dozen beautiful red roses blooming with fragrance arrived at Erika's office. There was no card attached.

Erika felt a sinking suspicion Gannon had sent the flowers. The absence of a card was consistent with his goal to stay under public radar.

The notion filled her mouth with a bitter taste and she considered tossing the arrangement out the window. But the roses were so pretty and smelled so lovely.

She could pretend anyone had sent them.

A second bouquet of roses arrived at ten-thirty. Again no card.

A third bouquet arrived at eleven. No card. A fourth at eleven-thirty. A fifth at noon.

Erika began to feel self-conscious. Her office smelled like a florist's shop, and coworkers knocked on her door to see the arrangements placed on every available surface.

Another dozen roses arrived at twelve-thirty. Furious that Gannon had made a spectacle of her, Erika dialed his extension. When his assistant picked up, she demanded to speak to him.

"I'm sorry. He's on another line right now. I'll give him the message that you called."

A knock sounded on the door and Erika ground her teeth and hung up the phone. Her assistant, Cammie, peeked inside, her face lit with excitement. "More roses!" she said and brought in yet another bouquet.

Erika swore under her breath. "I want these taken to the hospital."

Her assistant gaped at her. "What? But you can't. They're for you. And they're beautiful."

"And I have too many," Erika said. The flowers made her nervous. Red roses signified love, the long-lasting kind, and being surrounded by all these American Beauties underlined the fact that Gannon didn't love her the way she loved him. "Call the closest hospital and ask if there are four people who could use some roses to cheer them up."

Her assistant looked crushed. She sighed. "Okay. If you really want me to."

"I really want you to," Erika said firmly and closed the door after her assistant left.

Seconds later another knock sounded at her door. Her temper ratcheted up another notch. Another interruption. Probably another coworker wanting a look at her office full of roses. She jerked open the door. "This is not the company sideshow provided for your viewing entertain—" She broke off when she saw Gannon with a man she didn't recognize by his side, along with his assistant and hers.

They were all staring at her.

She cleared her throat, embarrassed and more rattled than she could recall. If it had just been Gannon, she would have verbally scalded his gorgeous self. But there were others. She was forced to save her blasting of him for later. "Is there something I can help you with?"

"Yes, there is," he said, his gaze deadly confident.

Erika's nervousness intensified. That expression of his had always foreshadowed trouble for her. Big trouble. "I'm busy this afternoon, but—"

"This will just take a few minutes," he said and led his troops into her space. "Nice roses."

"Beautiful," she said. "But a little overdone considering there was no card. Anonymity requires less courage, don't you think?"

His lips twitched slightly. "I agree. That's why I brought along my personal attorney, Harold Nussbaum, and my assistant, Lena, and yours. I wanted witnesses."

Confusion raced through her and she swallowed an oath. Had he changed his mind about the insemination? And was he going to let the whole office in on it? She glanced past him to the open door.

"Should we close the door?" she asked.

He shook his head. "The more, the merrier." He moved closer to Erika, his gaze purposeful.

Her heart rate picked up.

"I'm here to tell you in front of witnesses that I love you."

Her assistant, Cammie, gave an audible gasp.

Erika's heart shot into her throat. She stared at him in shock.

"You make me laugh. You make me think. You make me feel more than I ever thought I could. I want to be with you all the time. I want the chance to love you forever. I think you're better at this loving thing than I am, but if you're patient with me, I know I can learn."

A well of emotion expanded in her chest, making it impossible for her to breathe. Was she hearing things? Was this really happening?

He got down on one knee and she felt light-headed. She had to be dreaming.

He extended his hand toward her, waiting for her to reciprocate with her own hand, but all she could do was stare.

"Give him your hand," her assistant whispered.

Erika tentatively slid her now ice-cold fingers onto his warm palm. His hand enclosed hers and she met his gaze, swallowing over the lump of emotion in her throat.

"I love you. I want us to be together always. Will you marry me?"

She met his gaze and could have sworn all the clocks in the world stopped. But she was still afraid. Was she having a monster delusion? "Could you please repeat the question?"

She heard his assistant give a nervous giggle.

"I said, will you marry me?"

"Are you sure you want this?" she asked, ignoring everyone but Gannon.

"More sure than I've ever been about anything."

"Why? Why are you so sure?"

"Because I've found the woman of my dreams—you. And I don't want to waste one more minute of my life without you."

His words filled her like a warm breeze. His hand holding hers and the commitment in his gaze told her she wasn't having a delusion. He was real and so was his love for her.

Her eyes burned with a sudden infusion of moisture. "I feel like I've been waiting for you forever."

"Thanks for letting me catch up," he said. "Will you?"

She nodded. "Yes, yes, yes."

His assistant and hers made sniffling sounds as he rose to his feet and took her in his arms.

"This was lots better than any card you could have sent with the roses," she said. "But you didn't have to bring witnesses."

"I didn't?" He held her tight against him, making her feel cherished.

"No, but I'm glad you did. If I'm afraid I dreamed it, I have someone to call."

"You won't need to call anyone," he said and pulled a black velvet jeweler's box from his pocket. He flipped it open to reveal a huge diamond ring, then he lifted her hand to put it on her finger.

"That stone is ridiculously large," she murmured.

"I wanted you to have a tangible reminder of this day."

She was so full of joy and amazement and love. "I want you to be my tangible reminder."

"Oh, sweetheart, you can count on it," he said and took her mouth in a kiss. A crowd of coworkers craned to see inside, but Erika didn't care if anyone else saw what she and Gannon had going on. The most important person in the world had just told her that he loved her. Nobody could top that.

A crazy question nudged at her. "Which magazine will I work for? *Pulse* or *HomeStyle*?"

"Whichever one you want. As long as you remember that you and I will be working on making a baby every night," he whispered.

Erika felt every cell in her body smile. "Something tells me you won't let me forget."

* * * * *

TAKING CARE OF
BUSINESS

by
Brenda Jackson

BRENDA JACKSON

is a die-"heart" romantic who married her child-hood sweetheart and still proudly wears the "going steady" ring he gave her when she was fifteen. Because she's always believed in the power of love, Brenda's stories always have happy endings. In her real-life love story, Brenda and her husband of thirty-three years live in Jacksonville, Florida, and have two sons.

A *USA TODAY* bestselling author, Brenda divides her time between family, writing and working in management at a major insurance company.

You may write to Brenda at PO Box 28267, Jacksonville, Florida, 32226, USA, by e-mail at WriterBJackson@aol.com or visit her website at www.brendajackson.net.

A special thank you to the interracial couples that I interviewed who provided the feedback I asked for. It was deeply appreciated and proves that true love is colour-blind.

Live happily with the woman you love through the fleeting days of life, for the wife God gives you is your best reward down here for all your earthly toil.
Ecclesiastes 9:9

One

"**M**s. Williams, Mr. Teagan Elliott is here to see you."

Renee Williams took a deep breath, slipped off her reading glasses and pushed aside the medical report on Karen Elliott, bracing herself to deal with the woman's son, who from what Renee had heard was causing problems.

Since learning of his mother's breast cancer, and trying to assist Karen in dealing with all the paperwork for her upcoming surgery, Teagan Elliott was going about it the wrong way by putting unnecessary pressure on the hospital staff just because his last name was Elliott.

She pressed down the respond button on her phone and said, "Please send him in, Vicki."

Renee silently prayed that her confrontation with him would go well. She didn't want to remember the last time she had taken a stand against a man who thought his last name was the key to open any and all doors.

Her job as a social worker at Manhattan University Hospital meant helping everyone and making sure they were treated fairly, regardless of their economic, educational and cultural backgrounds.

A knock on the door brought Renee's thoughts back to the business at hand. "Come in."

She stood and placed a smile on her face when the man she knew to be Teagan Elliott, of Elliott Publication Holdings, one of the largest magazine conglomerates in the world, walked into her office dressed as if he had just posed for a photo shoot in *GQ* magazine. Renee had to concede he was a handsome man with all the sure-sign characteristics, which included expressive eyes, a symmetrical face, a straight nose and a chiseled jawline.

Moving from around her desk, she met him halfway and offered him her hand in a firm handshake. He automatically took it. "Mr. Elliott?"

"Yes, and you're Ms. Williams, I presume."

His northern accent was polished, refined and spoke of old money and lots of it. "Yes, I am. Would you like to have a seat so we can discuss the matter concerning your mother?"

He frowned. "No, I don't want to sit to discuss anything. I want you to tell me just what will be done for her."

Renee lifted a brow as she stared into the icy blue eyes that were holding hers. So he wanted to be difficult, did he? Well, he would soon discover that when it came to handling difficult people, she could be a force to reckon with. She crossed her arms over her chest. "Suit yourself if you prefer standing, but I've had a rather long and taxing day and I don't intend to stand."

With that, she resumed her seat. The glare he gave her was priceless, and if it weren't for the seriousness of the situation at hand, she would have quirked her lips into a smile. Evidently, not too many people sat down and left him standing.

"Now, about your mother," Renee said after taking a sip of her coffee, which had turned cold. "I see that her surgery is scheduled for—"

"I think I need to apologize."

Renee glanced up, put down her mug and gave him a look. The eyes staring back at her were no longer icy but were now a beautiful shade of clear blue. "Do you?"

"Yes." A smile touched his lips. They were lips that Renee thought were beautifully shaped.

"Normally I'm a likeable guy, but knowing what my mother is going through right now is a little hard to deal with. It wasn't my intent to come across as an arrogant ass. I just want to make sure she's getting the best of everything," he said, coming to take the seat across from Renee.

A part of Renee wondered if there was ever a time an Elliott hadn't gotten the best of everything. "That's what I'm here for, Mr. Elliott. My job is to make sure that not only your mother, but anyone faced with emotional concerns that can impede their recovery is given help to deal with those issues."

He nodded and his smile widened. "Have you met my mother?"

Renee returned his smile. For some reason she was drawn to it. "Yes, I had a chance to talk to her a few days ago. I found her to be a very beautiful person, both inside and out."

He chuckled. "She is that."

Renee could tell Teagan loved his mother very much. In talking with Karen Elliott, Renee had discovered the woman had three sons and a daughter. Teagan, at twenty-nine, was the third child, youngest of the sons, and a news editor at one of the family magazines, *Pulse*. Renee had also discovered during her talk with Karen that of all her children, she and Teagan had the closest relationship.

"So tell me, what are we up against, Ms. Williams?"

Teagan's question broke into Renee's thoughts. "Now that the doctor has given your mother the diagnosis and a decision has been made for surgery, what Karen needs from her family more than anything is support. I understand some of you don't comprehend her reasons for having a double mastectomy when a tumor was found in only one breast. She wants to have both removed as a precaution. Doing so is her choice and should be accepted as such.

"Karen also will need all of your love and support when the surgery is over and during her period of recuperation before she starts her chemotherapy treatments. Again, although there is no sign the cancer has spread to the lymph nodes, she has decided to undergo chemo as a precaution. The outlook at this point is still guarded, but I truly believe everything will work out in your mother's favor since the lump was found early."

Renee leaned back in her chair. Now that it was pretty obvious that Teagan Elliott was just trying to help his mother, although he had approached it in the wrong way, her heart went out to him. It was admirable for a son to care so much for his mother the way he did.

"Do you have any idea when the surgery will take place?" he asked.

"Right now, it's scheduled for next Tuesday."

Teagan sighed as he stood. "I really appreciate you taking the time to explain what the family needs to do. And again I apologize for my earlier attitude."

Renee smiled as she also got to her feet. "You are forgiven. I completely understand how an unexpected medical condition can cause havoc to even the mildest-mannered individual."

He laughed. "I said I'm normally a likeable guy. I never said anything about being mild-mannered."

Renee grinned. Nobody had said anything about him being a handsome hunk, either, but the proof was standing before her. With his six-foot athletic build, jet-black hair and blue eyes, she couldn't help wondering if anyone had ever told him that he bore a marked resemblance to what she perceived would be a younger-looking Pierce Brosnan. He was definitely worth taking a second look at. But she knew a look was all she'd ever take. Men with the kind of money the Elliotts had didn't bother dating people out of their social class. Besides, he was white and she was black.

"Here's my business card, Mr. Elliott. As your mother's social worker, I'm here whenever you need me. Just give me a call."

Teagan accepted the card and placed it in the pocket of his jacket. "I appreciate that. I'll get the family together tonight and we'll talk about what you and I have discussed. Right now my mother's health, as well as her peace of mind, is the most important thing. Thanks for everything."

Renee watched as he turned and walked out of her office.

Teagan, better known to family and friends as Tag, stepped into the elevator, glad he was alone. He released a deep sigh that came all the way from his gut. What the hell had happened to him while in Renee Williams's office? The woman was definitely a beauty, and radiated an almost palpable feminine presence that nearly knocked him to his knees. Nothing like that had ever happened to him before while sharing space with a woman.

When she'd spoken, the silkiness of her voice was enough to stroke everything male inside of him. It had been like a physical caress on his senses. And when their hands had touched in that handshake, it had taken everything he had to control the urge to pull her closer to him. He figured she was about five feet five inches without the pumps, and the outfit she'd been wearing, a tangerine-colored business suit, had definitely defined her curvy figure.

Then there was the coloring of her skin, a creamy color that reminded him of rich caramel. Combined with long, black hair that flowed around her shoulders, and dark brown eyes that had stared at him, she reflected, in addition to striking good looks, compassion, intelligence and spunk.

He actually had to chuckle when he thought of what she had told him when he had initially refused to sit down. Yes, she had spunk, all right, and he would give anything to have the opportunity to get to know her better. But he knew that would be impossible. A romantic involvement with anyone was the last thing he had time for. Since his father had decided, and rightly so, that spending time with Tag's mother was more important than what was going on at the office, Tag was more involved with the magazine than ever. And then there was that blasted challenge his grandfather, Patrick Elliott, had issued that had sparked a rivalry between EPH's top four magazines.

Each of the four magazines was run by one of Patrick's children. There was *Pulse,* the one run by Tag's father, Michael, which was a world-class news magazine; *Snap,* a celebrity magazine run by Tag's uncle Daniel; *Buzz,* which focused on showbiz gossip and was headed by Tag's uncle Shane; and *Charisma,* a fashion magazine run by Tag's aunt Finola.

Last month, Patrick had decreed he was ready to retire and whoever made his or her magazine the biggest success by the end of the year would be given the position of CEO of the entire Elliott Publication Holdings.

When the elevator came to a stop on the bottom floor, Tag couldn't help but look forward to the day his and Renee Williams' paths would cross again.

"So, there you have it, the gist of what the social worker said today," Tag said to his siblings at dinner that evening. The four of them had met at a restaurant in Manhattan, not far from the building that housed the Elliott publications. Gannon, at thirty-three, was second in command to his father at *Pulse*; Liam, at thirty-one, was currently working in the corporate financial department and Bridget, who was twenty-eight, was the photo editor for *Charisma.*

"And you're sure this social worker knows what she's talking about?" Bridget asked, taking a sip of her wine. There was a worried expression on her face. "The decisions Mom has made lately are so unlike her. It's as if she's going to the extreme."

Tag nodded, knowing where his sister was coming from, especially their mother's decision to have a double mastectomy. But all he had to do was recall his meeting earlier that day with Renee Williams to know the woman did know what she was talking about. She seemed very competent and professional…as well as beautiful. The latter seemed to stick out in his mind and he couldn't let go of it. Even now, he couldn't help but remember the smiles he had coaxed out of her after apologizing for his behavior.

"Yes, she knows what she's talking about," he finally said, responding to Bridget's question. "But as I was reminded today, it was Mom's decision to make and what she needs from all of us is our love and support."

Tag felt that he and his siblings always had a rather close relationship, and a crisis such as this was making them that much closer. After thanking the waitress who handed them menus, he turned to his older brother Gannon. Gannon had recently become engaged and Tag, like everyone else, was happy for him. Erika was just what Gannon needed, not to mention, as an editor, an asset to *Pulse*.

"How is Dad holding out?" Tag asked Gannon.

Gannon, who had been studying the menu, glanced up at his youngest brother. "He's doing all right. Today he cancelled an important meeting with a representative from St. John's Distributors to fly with Mom to Syracuse to check on one of her charities there."

"It's hard to believe he's actually putting all work aside," Liam said, shaking his head. All of them knew what a workaholic Michael Elliott was, but even so, they also knew what a strong marriage their parents had.

"That just goes to show how much Mom means to him," Bridget said smiling, touched by the way their father was devoting his time to his wife during her medical crisis.

Bridget glanced over at Tag. "This social worker you met with today. What can you tell us about her?"

Tag leaned back in her chair and smiled. "Her name is Renee Williams. She's African-American, probably about your age. She's very professional and definitely seems to know her business. There is also a calming quality about her that can make anyone feel comforted and reassured."

Liam nodded. "She sounds like just the person Mom needs. This illness has made her spirits decline, and that bothers me more than anything."

That was bothering Tag as well, but he believed Renee could help his mother get through this particular emotional stage. "Ms. Williams is also very beautiful."

The moment the statement left Tag's lips he knew it was a mistake, because it immediately captured the attention of his siblings.

Gannon raised a dark brow at Tag. "Oh, you happened to notice that, did you?"

Bridget and Liam chuckled. Everyone knew how it was with Tag when it came to his interest in women. His mind was spent more on business than romantic pursuits.

Tag knew where his siblings were coming from and smiled. "Yes, I noticed." The last thing he needed was to be thinking about a woman, especially one as good-looking as Renee Williams, but he couldn't help himself. There was just something about her that had touched him on a level that no woman had done before.

"Mmm, the salmon looks good tonight."

Tag glanced over at his sister who was studying her menu. However, his brothers were still staring at him with curious gazes. Uncomfortable with being the center of their attention, he frowned. "Hell, it was just an observation. Don't try and make anything of it."

Gannon laughed. "If you say so, kiddo."

Two

"Ms. Williams? This is a pleasant surprise."

Renee glanced up from the novel she was reading to gaze into the friendly blue eyes of Teagan Elliott. "Mr. Elliott, how are you?" she said, smiling and adjusting her reading glasses on her nose. "And how is your mother doing?"

She watched his lips thin and a worried look appear in his eyes. "She's not her usual vibrant self and isn't saying a lot about her upcoming surgery to any of us. I talked to Dad and he says it's the same with him."

Renee nodded. "How she's handling things is understandable. Just give her time to come to grips with everything. She has a lot to deal with right now."

Tag shook his head. "I know you're right, but I'm still concerned about her."

"That's understandable. All of you will get through this and so will your mother."

Tag couldn't help but return her smile. Just as he'd told his siblings, Renee Williams had such a calming nature about her. From the first time he had met her a few days ago, he had quickly concluded that she was the perfect advocate for her patients. He knew his mother liked her and spoke highly of her often.

"So, what brings you to Greenwich Village? Do you live close by?" he asked. He had been walking down the street checking out paintings by various artists when he'd happened to spot her in the window seat of the café. At first he hadn't been certain it was she, but then, from the way his body had responded, he'd known for sure. Whether he liked it or not, he was definitely attracted to this woman, and seeing her today wasn't helping matters.

In her office there had been this professional demeanor surrounding her, but here on a Saturday morning, sitting at a window-seat table at a small café and wearing a wool skirt and a blue sweater, she made him even more aware of just how beautiful she was. Even her ponytail didn't detract from that beauty. The temperature was in the upper fifties, one of those inexplicable, rare heat waves that warmed New York in February.

"No, I live in Morningside Heights. I was supposed to meet someone here this morning, but they called at the last minute to cancel. I decided to come here, anyway."

"Oh, I see." Tag couldn't help wondering if the person she'd planned on meeting was a man, then wanted to kick himself for even caring. He quickly decided the blame wasn't all his. He was someone who appreciated beauty and Renee Williams was one of those women whose sultry good looks rang out loud and clear. "Well, I'll let you get back to your reading. I didn't mean to interrupt you."

She tilted her head to the side, her eyes holding his captive. And when she took her tongue to moisten her lips, he found his gaze glued to her mouth. "You didn't interrupt me. In fact, I'm glad I ran into you," she said, giving him a throaty chuckle that did something to his insides.

He gave her a crooked smile. "In that case, do you mind if I join you?"

He could tell she was surprised by his question, but without missing a beat, she said, "No, I don't mind."

As soon as he pulled out a chair, a waiter came to take his order. "Can I get you anything, Mr. Elliott?"

"The usual, Maurice." The man nodded and quickly walked off. Tag looked across the table to find Renee watching him with open curiosity. "Is there anything wrong, Ms. Williams?"

She shook her head, grinning. "No, but I take it that you're a regular here."

His mouth curved into a smile. "Yes, I have a condo in Tribeca and come here often, usually every Saturday morning. I love art and there's nothing like seeing an artist at work." He watched her smile again and wondered if she had any idea how seductive it looked.

"I like art, too. I even dabble in it every now and then."

"Really?"

She laughed. "Yes, really, and when I say *dabble* I mean *dabble*. I've never taken any art classes or anything. I think I just have a knack for it. I believe it was something I inherited from my mother. She was an art major and taught the class at a high school in Ohio."

"Ohio? Is that where you're from?"

"Yes. I even went to college there. Ohio State."

Tag leaned back in his chair. "What brought you to New York?"

Renee sighed deeply. She didn't want to think about Dionne Moore, the man who had broken her heart. After graduating from college she had taken a job at a hospital in Atlanta where she had met Dionne, a cardiologist. She'd thought their relationship was special, solid, until she'd found out that Dionne was having an affair with a nurse behind her back.

What was sad was that while she hadn't known about the other woman, several of the other doctors—friends of Dionne—had known and had been taking bets as to when she would find out. Once she did, it had caused quite a scandal that had had everyone talking for days.

Embarrassed, she had promised to never allow herself to be the hot topic over anyone's breakfast, lunch or dinner table. To repair her heart and put distance between her and Dionne, she had jumped at the chance to relocate to New York when Debbie Massey, her best friend from college, had told her about an opening at Manhattan University Hospital. That had been almost two years ago, and since then she had pretty much kept to herself and had refrained from dating altogether.

"It was a job offer I couldn't refuse and don't regret taking," she finally said. "I love New York."

"So do I."

At that moment they were interrupted when the waiter returned with a tall bottle of beer for Tag. Tag tipped the bottle to his lips, then setting it down on the table looked over at Renee. "So, Ms. Williams, how do you—"

"It would make me feel better if you called me Renee."

"Okay," he said slowly. "And I'd like it if you called me Tag, which is what everyone calls me."

"All right, then, Tag it is."

He glanced at her glass. It was almost empty. "Would you like another drink?"

"No, thank you. The fruit punch here is delicious, but too rich. I'm going to have to do a lot of walking to burn off the calories."

"I'm sorry your date didn't show up."

Renee laughed. "Don't be. It's not the first time Debbie has gotten called away at the last minute. When duty calls, you have to go. She's a friend of mine who works at *Time* magazine."

"Ouch, they're *Pulse*'s strongest competitor."

Renee chuckled. "Yes, that's what I hear."

"But we're definitely better."

Renee reared her head back and laughed. "And of course, I would expect you to make that claim."

Tag took another long pull of his beer. The sound of Renee's laughter was breathy and intimate and he immediately felt a jolt of desire in the pit of his stomach.

He couldn't remember the last time he had allowed himself to unwind, certainly not since his grandfather had challenged the family, sparking everyone's competitive nature. But for once his mind was on something else besides work. It was on a woman. This particular woman. If she could have this sort of effect on him just by being in his presence, he didn't want to think what would happen if he were to touch her. Kiss her. Or better yet, make love to her.

The image slammed into him, sizzling his brain cells and making slow heat flow through every part of his body.

"I guess it's time for me to get up and start browsing the shops."

He glanced over at her, not ready to part ways. "Would you mind if I browse with you? There are a couple of places that are giving private showings today that you might be interested in."

Renee met his gaze. What he hadn't said was that the only way she could attend those showings was with him. The Elliott name carried a lot of weight. She sighed and chewed the inside of her cheek. She had heard about those private art showings and knew that now was her chance to go to one. So why was she hesitating? Browsing the shops and attending a private show or two with Tag wouldn't be so bad as long as she kept things in perspective. She was his mother's social worker and he was being kind. End of story.

She drained the last of her drink before saying, "Are you sure you don't mind me attending those showings with you?"

He placed his beer bottle down. "Yes, I'm sure. I'd like to spend some time with you, anyway."

She licked her lips. "Why?"

He tried not concentrating on her mouth. Instead, he gazed directly into her eyes. "Because I've been working a lot of hours lately and this is the first opportunity I've had to grab time for myself. And because I really enjoy your company."

Her smile was slow but he knew it was also sincere. "Thanks, I'm enjoying your company as well, Tag."

"Then," he said calmly, "that pretty much settles it."

There was a moment of silence, and Renee quickly wondered if anything between them was settled, or just about to get pretty stirred up.

"Oh my goodness, this is simply beautiful."

Tag glanced at the painting Renee was referring to and had to agree. The piece, titled *Colors,* depicted an African-American child standing beneath a rainbow. The artist had been able to vibrantly capture all the colors, including the child's skin tone, as well as the blue-green ocean that served as a backdrop. The happiness that shone on the toddler's face was priceless, and the way the painting was encased in a black wooden frame made all the vivacious colors stand out. "Yes, it is, isn't it."

He picked up the tag attached to the painting and glanced at it. "It's a Malone and the price isn't bad, considering he's making a name for himself now. I was able to purchase several of his paintings at a private art show when he first got started."

Renee could envision the paintings adorning the walls of Tag's condo. Alton Malone, who was of mixed

Caucasian and African-American heritage, had a wide range, but she personally liked his contemporary ethnic paintings the best.

It was obvious Tag liked fine art. But then, so did she. The only difference was that money to buy it came more easily to him than to her.

At the moment, the difference in their incomes wasn't the only thing on her mind. So was the difference in their skin colors. Although New York was one of the most diverse cities on earth, some people's opinions about interracial dating just didn't change. More than once, as they strolled along the sidewalk together, darting in and out of various shops, Renee had felt people's curious eyes on her. Whether accepting or disapproving, she wasn't sure. But the stares had been obvious, as were a few frowns. There was no way Tag hadn't noticed. However, he didn't seem bothered that people were erroneously assuming they were a couple.

"It's four o'clock already," he said. "What about grabbing something to eat before I take you home?"

Renee glanced over at Tag. Earlier, he had asked how she had gotten to Greenwich Village and she had told him that she had ridden the subway. He had offered to drive her home, saying his car wasn't parked too far away. She had graciously declined the offer. Hanging out with him on a lazy Saturday was one thing, but she didn't intend for him to go out of his way to take her home.

"Tag, thanks for the offer, but I'm used to taking the subway wherever I need to go."

"I'm sure you are, but I don't have anything else to

do. Besides, it will be late evening by the time we finish eating."

Renee shook her head as a smile touched her lips. "I wonder when it will dawn on you that I didn't agree to eat with you."

He grinned. "Sure you did. That was our deal, remember?"

Renee lifted a brow as they continued to stroll along the sidewalk. "What deal?"

"Don't you remember?"

She eyed him suspiciously. "No, I do not."

"Then you must be having a senior moment."

"No, I don't think so," Renee said, enjoying this camaraderie with him. "I'm twenty-eight and way too young to have senior moments."

"Not so," he said, teasing Renee. "I'm twenty-nine, but I used to have—"

"Hey, Tag! Wait up!"

Tag and Renee stopped walking when the person called out to him. They turned to see a man—who appeared to be about Tag's age, dressed in a jogging suit and running shoes—trot over to them.

"Hey, man, where have you been keeping yourself?" the man asked Tag when he finally reached them and the two men shook hands. "It's been ages since I've seen you at the club."

"Work has been keeping me busy," Tag said. He then glanced at Renee. "Renee, I want you to meet a friend of mine from college, Thomas Bonner. Thomas, this is Renee Williams."

Renee accepted the man's hand. "It's nice meeting

you, Thomas." She could immediately feel the unfriend-
liness in the handshake and watched as he plastered a
phony smile on his face.

"Uh, yes, nice meeting you, too." Then, as if she was
of little importance, he dismissed her and glanced up at
Tag through disapproving eyes. "Evidently, you're not
too busy to carve out some colorful playtime."

Renee immediately picked up the censorship in his
expression. Evidently, Thomas Bonner thought that she
wasn't the type or the color of woman that Tag should
be seen with. But his insinuation that she was nothing
more than an object of Tag's amusement really got next
to her. Breathing deep, she held back her anger, deciding this man wasn't worth it. However, Tag evidently
disagreed. He placed his hand on the small of her back
and eased her closer to him.

She could hear the iciness in his voice when he said,
"You should know I'm too serious a guy to ever indulge
in playtime. Besides, when a man meets someone this
beautiful he doesn't waste his time by acting a fool. If he's
smart, he uses it wisely to impress her. And what I'm doing, Thomas, is trying to impress. Wish me luck."

Renee could tell Tag's comments left the man at a
loss for words. "Uh, well, I'd better continue my run.
Give my best to your family," Thomas finally stumbled
out before jogging off without looking back. Renee
could just imagine the rumors that would be flying
around in Tag's social circle tomorrow. Maybe he could
handle a scandal, but she could not. She had been there,
done that. And she didn't want to ever live through it
again.

She glanced up at Tag. "Why did you give him the impression that we're romantically involved?"

The corners of his lips turned up and she hated admitting how much she liked the way his smile seemed to touch his eyes. "Does it bother you that I did?"

She shrugged. "I could handle his comment. He's not the first prejudiced person I've met in my lifetime and he won't be the last. Over the years, I've experienced my fair share of bigotry," she said softly.

"Well, that's one thing I won't tolerate."

She believed him.

They began walking, and neither said anything for a few moments, then Renee decided to break the silence. She glanced over at him. "You never did say why you did it."

Tag sighed. There was no way he was going to tell her that for a moment he hadn't been able to help himself. He had refused to let Thomas think that his intentions toward her—if there had been any—were anything less than honorable. To insinuate that she wasn't someone he could possibly take seriously had hit his last nerve because it was so far from the truth. And that, he quickly concluded, was the crux of his problem. Renee was someone he could take seriously if he was free to engage in a serious relationship. But he wasn't. The situation with his mother was bad enough. Add to that what was happening at Elliott Publication Holdings and it was enough to make a nondrinker order a bottle of gin and guzzle the entire thing.

Knowing that she was waiting for an answer, he decided to give her one. "Thomas was going to think whatever he wanted without any help from me. You're a beautiful woman and I don't consider myself a bad-looking guy, so quite naturally people will assume we're a couple."

"And that doesn't bother you?"

"No, but it evidently bothers you. I learned early in life, Renee, not to care what other people think."

Renee ceased walking and placed a hand firmly on Tag's arm. "And that's probably just one of the many differences in our upbringings. I was raised to care what others think."

Tag nodded. "In this case, with us, now, today, why should it matter?"

She raised her eyes heavenward. Did she have to spell it out for him? It wouldn't matter if it were today or tomorrow. The circumstances would still be the same. "Because I'm black and you're white, Tag."

He smiled, and his eyes sparkled as if he'd just been told something scandalous, simply incredulous. "You're joking," he said in mock surprise. He took her hand, held it up to his, denoting the obvious contrast of their skin coloring. "Really? I hadn't noticed."

She couldn't help but chuckle. And she couldn't help but decide at that moment that she liked him. "Get real."

"I am. And what's real is that I like you and I enjoy your company. This is the most relaxed I've been in a long time, especially since finding out about my mother's cancer and taking on added responsibilities at work. And I'm not about to let a bunch of prejudiced fools decide whom I should or should not date. As for my caring what others think, I've had to deal with people's misconceptions all my life. They think just because my name is Elliott that I've had it easy."

She hated admitting that she'd assumed the same thing. "And you haven't?"

"Far from it. There's no such word as easy with a grandfather like Patrick Elliott."

Renee glanced over at Tag. "Tell me about him."

They had reached the café where Tag had mentioned earlier would be a good place to eat. They sat down right away, the crowd from earlier that day having thinned out.

"Patrick Elliott is one tough old man. He was raised by Irish immigrants who instilled in him a strong work ethic. He worked to put himself through school and because of his keen mind and street smarts, he went to work at a magazine company and eventually founded his own empire."

He paused when the waitress delivered their waters and gave them menus. Renee, who'd evidently been thirsty, took a deep gulp and licked the excess from around her lips. At that moment, a surge of desire hit Tag. It was so overwhelming, he had to briefly look away.

"And?"

He blinked at her single word. "And what?"

She smiled. "You were telling me about your grandfather, but I don't think you were finished."

He chuckled, thinking of how he'd gotten sidetracked. "Oh, yes, where was I?" he said, leaning back in his chair after taking a sip of his own water. "While in Ireland visiting family, he met and fell in love with a young seamstress named Maeve O'Grady. They eventually married and raised many children together. My grandparents have a very loving relationship. However, it's my belief that my grandfather's fear of poverty is what has made him devoted to his business."

Tag paused for a moment, reflecting on what his next words would be. "Although my grandfather dotes a lot on my grandmother, he hasn't always spent a lot of time with his children and grandchildren and isn't very demonstrative, although we all know he loves us. Over the years we've accepted that his true love is his empire, Elliott Publication Holdings, or EPH for short. All of his children are working for the company and he runs a strict ship. He also insists that all family members, including his grandchildren, must earn their way to the top by working their butts off within various levels of the business. No exceptions."

Renee took another sip of water before asking, "How old were you when you began working at the company?"

He smiled, remembering those days. "I was sixteen and started out in the mail room without any special treatment because my last name was Elliott. I later got a degree in journalism from Columbia University."

At that moment, the waitress returned to take their order. They ordered hamburgers, milkshakes and fries. After the woman left, Tag turned to Renee and said, "I don't remember the last time I ate junk food. I'm usually too busy."

Renee looked surprised. "You're kidding. Most people eat junk food because they don't have time for the real thing. So what do you eat?"

"Too much nourishing food. The guy who lives next door to me is a chef and he keeps my refrigerator loaded."

"Jeez, life must be good," Renee said as a smile touched her lips. "Especially since you could call me the microwave queen. I don't have time to cook. I'm so busy, I barely have time to change my clothes after work before tackling some project or another. It's easier for me to just pop a meal in the microwave."

Tag swallowed. Heaven help him, but he could picture her rushing through her house after a long, taxing day at work and taking her clothes off. He wondered how many or how few underthings she wore. He then wanted to kick himself for even letting that speculation rule his thoughts. It wasn't like he was ever going to get involved with her, and needed to know.

"I meant what I said earlier, Tag. You don't have to take me home."

Tag glanced over at her. So they were back to that again, but he was determined to dig in his heels. There was no way he would put her on a subway when it wouldn't be any trouble giving her a ride. "You did say you've met my mother, right?" he asked, looking deep into Renee's eyes.

The blue gaze almost held her spellbound. "Yes. Why?"

"There is one trait she has that you may not have picked up on yet, and of all her children I'm the one who inherited it the most."

Interested, Renee couldn't help but ask, "And what trait is that?"

"Stubbornness."

"Ah," she said, nodding. "And what if I told you that I can probably be just as stubborn as you?"

He studied her a moment before a smile touched his lips. "The only thing I can say is that a standoff between the two of us ought to be very interesting."

Three

"Okay, I concede, Teagan Elliott. You won this round."

She might have to concede on that issue, Tag reasoned, but he personally had to concede that she looked good sitting in his car. "Now come on, Renee. Did you really think the gentleman in me would have you roaming all over New York in the dark?"

She gazed at him in obvious frustration when he brought his vehicle, a Lexus SUV, to a stop at the traffic light. "I don't see why not, since I do it all the time. And riding the subway isn't roaming. It's getting from point A to point B."

Tag couldn't help but shake his head and silently admitted that he had totally enjoyed the time he had spent with her today. It had been clean, honest, wholesome fun. Although he would be the first to admit that developing a relationship with her would be high on any man's agenda, it wasn't on his. Not that he wasn't interested, because he definitely was. He just didn't have the time. *Pulse* was the only thing he was romancing these days. *Pulse,* and his family.

"I live in the next block."

Her voice reined his thoughts back in. "Nice neighborhood. I used to jog a lot in the park while attending Columbia."

She smiled over at him. "I jog there a lot now. I'm a member of the Morningside Park Coalition. We work with the city to preserve and improve the park."

When he came to a stop in front of her apartment building, she said, "You don't have to walk me to the door."

A part of Tag couldn't help wondering if the reason was that she didn't want to be seen with him. For some reason the thought bothered him. He leaned toward her and touched her cheek. "Sorry, there's no way I can deliver you home halfway. My task wouldn't be completed until I walked you to the door and made sure you got into your place okay."

"Thanks. I didn't wanted to put you out." She smiled and he immediately felt her warmth. Relief ran through him that she wasn't uncomfortable being seen with him. Still, he sensed her nervousness. Was she worried that he would try to kiss her goodbye? What if he did? Would she reciprocate? There was only one way to find out.

Renee watched as Tag came around the front of his vehicle to open the door for her. She couldn't help but think about how much difference there was between him and Dionne. Other than the obvious skin coloring, there was the way they regarded women. Because Dionne had been raised by a single mother who'd evidently been a superwoman, he had expected a woman to be able to do just about anything for herself, including opening her own car door and seeing herself into the house. The only time he'd walked her to the door was when he had expected to spend the night.

"Thanks," she said when Tag opened the door and offered his hand to help her out of the vehicle. Her heart fluttered at the feel of their hands touching, and she couldn't help wondering if the reaction was one-sided. Evidently it wasn't since he continued to hold her hand while walking her up the steps to her apartment.

He continued to hold her hand while walking her up the steps to her apartment.

He stepped aside while she unlocked the door. She wondered if he was waiting for her to invite him in. All day they had enjoyed being together without any type of flirtation, or promises of getting to know each other better. So why was her heart beating a thousand beats a minute, and why was she feeling heated from the way he was looking at her?

She cleared her throat. "Thanks again, Tag. I really enjoyed today."

"So did I. And bundle up good tonight. I understand the temperature will begin dropping around midnight."

"Okay." She thought of her huge bed where she would be sleeping alone, and for the first time in two years the thought actually bothered her. It also made her realize that Dionne had been the last man she'd been serious about. Once she moved to New York she had spent more time developing her career than seeking out any worthwhile relationships with the opposite sex. She had kept telling herself she was only twenty-eight and there was no rush. Now she suddenly felt... rushed.

"Will you have dinner with me tomorrow night?"

She blinked, then gazed into Tag's piercing blue eyes. She swallowed the thickness in her throat. "Dinner?"

"Yes, dinner. Tomorrow night."

Renee sighed. Okay, he had asked the million-dollar question, so how would she respond? She had to be honest with herself. If he had been an African-American male she would probably not have hesitated, but there were issues she needed to consider with him being white. The difference in their race was a major factor, but then so was the difference in their social backgrounds. His family owned a magazine publishing company whose headquarters took up an entire Manhattan block, for crying out loud. He lived in Tribeca of all places. An area known for its high-rise condos, quiet streets, good schools and wealthy lifestyles. It was a haven for the well-to-do. For people like the Elliotts.

"Renee?"

She glanced over at him. "Yes?"

"Can we step into your apartment to finish this conversation? I think we're drawing unwanted attention."

Renee glanced around, noting his statement was true. A couple of people in her apartment building were openly staring at them. She returned her gaze to his. "Yes, let's go inside."

She opened the door, and the moment they stepped over the threshold, heat filled her insides in a way it hadn't ever before. "Can I get you something to drink?"

He leaned back against her closed door, placing his hands in the pockets of his jeans. "No, I'm fine, but what you can do is give me an answer to my question about dinner tomorrow night."

Renee nervously licked her lips.

"Don't do that."

"Do what?"

"Lick your lips like that. You've done it several times today and each time I've wanted to replace your tongue with my own. Even now I'm standing here fighting the urge not to."

His words fanned an already heated spot deep within her. Her heart suddenly began beating faster. Out of habit she automatically licked her lips again and when she realized what she'd done, she quickly said, "Oops. I didn't mean to do that."

His eyes stayed glued to her face. "Too late. It's been done."

He slowly moved away from the door, removing the distance separating them. When he came to a stop in front of her he studied her with an intensity that she felt all the way to her toes.

"This is crazy," he said in a deep, husky voice, "but I'm dying to kiss you."

Yes, it *was* crazy, she silently agreed. Because she was dying for him to kiss her. Earlier, she had listed in her mind all the reasons they couldn't become involved, but at that very moment, the only thing she could concentrate on was the way he was looking at her, the heat that seemed to take over her body and the desire that was flowing through her veins. No man had ever made her feel this way before.

He was watching her as carefully as she was watching him. They both knew their next move would be one they wouldn't forget in a long time—if ever. Tag studied her lips, saw them quiver nervously and knew the exact moment she would lick them with her tongue.

He was ready.

His tongue captured hers outside of her mouth, tangled with it as he thoroughly explored all of her, taking this intimate pleasure to a level he had never taken it before. Kissing was a special way to communicate without words, and what they weren't saying was turning him on even more, stirring emotions he had denied himself for so long. Affection, passion and even lust ruled his thoughts, his mind and his body.

He thought her lips were beautifully shaped and her response to him had been spontaneous. He liked her taste, he was drowning in her fragrance and he was taking the kiss to a level he hadn't known was possible.

Renee was literally panting for breath, but the thought of their mouths disconnecting was something she didn't want to think about. She had never been kissed like this before. Tag was taking the art of French kissing to a whole other level. He wasn't just keeping her tongue busy, he was intimately mating with it, leaving her breathless, weak in the knees, moaning out loud. He seemed to be lapping up each and every sound she made.

A part of her brain wanted to shut down everything

she was feeling. It tried reminding her that what they were doing wasn't good. He was white, he was rich, his mother was her patient…and so on and so forth. But at that very moment, the only thing that was getting through to her was the tingling she felt all the way to her toes as well as the pool of heat that had settled right smack between her legs. And there was also the hardness of him that she felt against her thighs, and the sensitive feel of her nipples pressed against his solid chest.

Slowly, he pulled away, drawing in a deep breath. The sound filtered through her like a soft caress. The blue eyes staring at her held such intensity it made her pulse race even faster.

"That," he said softly, "was my first."

She held his gaze, had been drawn into it, was locked into it. "Your first what?" she somehow managed to ask in a tone that sounded like a whisper.

"My first real kiss." His brow furrowed as if he was somewhat troubled at the thought. "I've never given so much of myself to a woman before."

His words touched her in a way she had never been touched before. They were just as deep and profound as his kiss had been. He reached out and lifted her chin with the tip of his finger. "You are simply beautiful." He then shook his head as if amazed. "No, I take that back. You are beautiful. There is nothing simple about it."

He leaned forward and kissed her lips again. "Now to repeat my earlier question, will you have dinner with me tomorrow night?"

Renee released a long, drawn breath. Her mind, thanks to Tag, was jumbled in mass confusion, but the one thing that rang clear was the fact that they shouldn't see each other again this way for a number of reasons on which she didn't want to dwell at the moment. "I don't think having dinner with you is a good idea."

He lifted a dark brow, angled his head and asked, "Why not?"

She sighed deeply. He was making this difficult. What was obvious to her evidently wasn't to him. That kiss had revealed too much. Too many more of those and she would be falling hard and heavy for him, not caring about the differences between them.

Knowing he was waiting on an answer, she decided to take the easy way out. "Your mother is my patient so we shouldn't be getting involved."

Tag opened his mouth to say having dinner with him was not getting involved, but that wouldn't be completely honest. If he were to take her to dinner, he would want to kiss her good-night, and another kiss like the one they'd shared just might have him begging for a taste of something else. When they had kissed, and he had stroked her tongue with his own, her lips had been so soft, her tongue welcoming and her flavor so sweet....

"For how long?" he asked, leaning back against the closed door.

Renee blinked. "How long what?"

"How long will my mother be your patient?"

Renee nervously shoved her hands into the pockets of her skirt. "Officially, until after her surgery and she is released from the hospital. But I'll still be there for her if she needs me once she begins her chemotherapy."

He nodded. "And this rule about not getting involved with your patient's family is yours or the hospital's?"

Renee swallowed. The blue gaze that had her within the intensity of its scope seemed to burn fire wherever it touched. Right now it was on her lips and her mouth was feeling the heat. She nervously licked her lips and saw the moment his stomach clenched and remembered his reaction whenever she did that. "It's mine, but I think it's for the best."

"Do you?" The smile that suddenly appeared at his lips was challenging, sexy and brazen. "Then I guess I'm just going to have to prove it's not for the best, won't I?"

He reached out, gently pulled her close, gave her a hug and then whispered close to her ear, "Stay warm tonight and think about me." And with that he turned and left.

"So how's your weekend going, Tag?"

Tag glanced up from pouring wine into two glasses and met his brother's gaze. Liam had dropped by for a visit but Tag could tell how he'd spent his Saturday was the last thing on his brother's mind; however, he answered anyway. "It was rather nice. I decided to take some time away from work and attended a couple of art shows in the Village."

Liam rubbed his hand down his face. Tired. Frustrated. Agitated. All three. "It's good to know someone can put work on hold for a while to enjoy himself."

"So can you," Tag said, leaning back against the counter. Liam, financial operating officer at EPH, was known as a financial wizard. "Taking time off to rest and relax won't put the company in the red, Liam. Besides, you deserve it."

Liam sighed deeply. "Speaking of putting the company in the red," he said, after taking a sip of his wine, "I'm worried about Granddad's challenge. Personally, I don't see it helping the company. In fact, I see it hurting us in the long run. What on earth could he have been thinking to pit us against each other like this? Yesterday I was walking down the hall and as soon as I turned the corner whatever conversation Aunt Finola and Scarlet were having practically died on their lips when they saw me. It was as if they considered me a spy or something."

Tag nodded at what Liam was saying. He'd encountered a similar situation last week when he'd walked in on a conversation between his uncle Daniel and his cousin Summer. It was weird how everyone had begun acting all secretive because of his grandfather's challenge.

"Granddad is a smart man," Tag said. "Although I don't understand why he would do such a thing, I have to believe he'd never do anything that would eventually hurt the company. You know how he feels about it. It's his baby."

Liam, grudgingly, had to agree. "So, are you ready for Tuesday?" he asked, taking another sip of wine.

Tag shook his head. Tuesday was the day their mother was scheduled for surgery. "No, but the sooner Mom gets it over with, the sooner she can get better."

Liam closed his eyes for a moment in sheer exhaustion. "Yes, you're right." He then checked his watch and stood. "I think I'm going to stop by the office and finish up a couple of things before going home."

After Liam left, with nothing else to do, Tag showered and got ready for bed. The moment he crawled under the covers he thought about Renee. He hadn't meant to kiss her but he had and that had been the beginning of his problem.

He hadn't expected to develop a taste for her, but he'd done that as well. He had wanted to keep on kissing her, tasting her, mating their mouths. To keep indulging. Her lips had felt warm beneath his. Warm and heated with a surrender she hadn't wanted to make but he had coaxed out of her anyway, each and every time he had lowered his mouth to hers.

And earlier today, while with her in Greenwich Village, they had talked about a number of things. She had shared with him that her parents were both deceased. When she was ten years old her father had died of a work-related injury, and her mother had died of colon cancer when Renee was in her last year of high school. She had remembered how kind the social workers and hospital staff had been to her and her mother, and eventually followed in their footsteps, obtaining a degree in social work, with a specialty in health services.

During the time they had spent together today, he had watched her and had been touched at how the smallest thing could make her smile. He'd watched how she interacted with people in general; always respectful, courteous, polite and considerate. Even when she hadn't needed to be…like with Thomas Bonner.

The man had seen something in Renee that Tag hadn't. Color. To Tag, Renee was a beautiful woman. He didn't see her as a woman of a particular skin tone but as a desirable woman he wanted. But he had a feeling it hadn't been the same with her. He had seen the same frowns, stares and censored expressions that she had today. However, while he'd merely chalked them up to ignorance, he could tell they had bothered Renee. All day with her he'd assumed they were developing a friendship. But after kissing her, tasting her, he wanted more. He wanted something he hadn't thought about sharing in a long time with a woman. He wanted a relationship.

Damn.

How could he decide something like that after spending one day with her? Sharing one kiss? He wasn't sure just how deep he wanted the relationship to go but he did know that he wanted one. He wanted to take her out to dinner, the movies, and the theater…just to name a few places. He wanted to show up at her apartment some afternoons and discuss how his day had gone and hear how hers had gone as well. He wanted to invite her over to his place and cook for her…or have Lewis, his friendly chef next door, do the cooking. And he would love taking her to Une Nuit, his cousin Bryan's restaurant, and introducing her to his entire family.

He shook his head and sighed deeply. He'd never thought about introducing any woman to his family before, but he wanted to do it with Renee. He wanted to share all things with her.

He ran his hand down his face, frustrated, because she didn't want any of that. He knew he had to give her time, space and not rush her. Not only would they be engaging in an affair, but it would be an interracial one.

At least that was probably how she would see it. He saw it as simply a man and woman who were attracted to each other deciding to take it to the next level.

But that had to wait. Right now, he had to be content to see her on Tuesday at the hospital. Somehow, though, that wasn't good enough.

Four

"Your wife's surgery was a success, Mr. Elliott."

Tag could see profound relief on his father's face as well as on the faces of his siblings gathered in the waiting room. "And you think that you got it all?" Michael Elliott asked.

Dr. Chaney nodded. "Yes, although her condition will still be guarded for a while, I believe we got all the cancer. She will remain here for a few days, and then I'll release her to you for convalescent care."

"How soon can we see her?" Gannon asked with his fiancée by his side.

"Not for a while yet, possibly an hour or so. She was put under heavy sedation and is still in the recovery room. I suggest all of you go grab a bite to eat. When you come back, she should be awake."

After the doctor left, Michael met his offspring's intense gazes. "Your mother is going to be fine now. When she's released I'm taking her to The Tides to recuperate."

Tag nodded. The Tides was the Elliott family's five-acre estate on Long Island. His grandfather had purchased the estate forty years ago when he became successful and had moved his young family out to the island because the area had reminded Tag's grandmother of her Irish homeland. It sat on a bluff like a fortress and overlooked the Atlantic Ocean. Tag agreed it would be the perfect place for his mother to rest, relax and heal.

"I like your mother's social worker," Michael Elliott said. "It was nice of her to drop by and check on us earlier."

Tag's head snapped up. "Renee was here?" He noticed the way his father looked at him, probably surprised with his use of the woman's first name, indicating some personal familiarity.

"Yes, she dropped by an hour or so ago, when you, Gannon and Liam had left to go downstairs for coffee."

Tag nodded, absorbing that statement silently. He wished he had been there when she'd shown up. He checked his watch, making a quick decision. "Since Dr. Chaney said it will be at least another hour before any of us can see Mom, I think I'm going to walk around a bit." He glanced over at his brothers and their expressions clearly said, *Walk around? Yeah, right.*

Ignoring them, Tag excused himself and headed for the nearest elevator.

* * *

"Is it true that you're Karen Elliott's social worker?"

Renee glanced up from her sandwich and met Diane Carter's curious gaze. Diane was a trauma nurse and one of the hospital's worse gossips. She was quick to get upset if someone got into her business yet she made it a point to get into everyone else's. Usually Renee avoided the woman at all cost but every once in a while she would join Diane for lunch when no one else would.

Renee had to concede that with Diane's blond hair and blue eyes she was a natural-born beauty. But rumor had it that besides having a problem with loose lips, she also had a tendency to be too clingy, which turned off a lot of the men in whom she'd shown interest.

"Yes, I'm Karen Elliott's social worker," Renee finally said after taking a sip of her lemonade.

"Boy, aren't you the lucky one," Diane said with a smirk. "Have you met her sons?"

Renee thought about Tag. "I've met only one. Teagan Elliott."

"And what do you think of him?"

The last thing Renee would do was tell Diane what she really thought of Tag. "He's okay."

Diane leaned back and looked at her like she definitely had a few screws loose. "Just okay? I've seen photographs of him in the society section of the newspaper a few times and he's so handsome he makes your eyes ache."

No sooner had Diane's words left her lips, Renee's hand froze on the glass of lemonade she was about to bring to her lips when Tag walked into the hospital's café. He glanced around as if he was looking for some-one, then his eyes lit onto her.

The connection of their gazes did funny things to Re-nee's insides. It didn't take much to remember the kiss they had shared three days ago; a kiss that still heated her all over whenever she thought about it.

"Renee, are you all right?"

She quickly looked at Diane. No, she wasn't all right, but Diane would be the last person she would tell why. "Yes, I'm fine." And with as much effort as she could muster, she took a sip of her lemonade then bit into her sandwich, trying not to notice that Tag was standing across the room staring at her.

Tag sucked in a deep breath the moment his gaze slammed into Renee's. He wanted her. How could he not? Why had he thought for one moment that he'd con-vinced himself he could not get involved with her or anyone because he didn't have the time? Who was he kidding? He definitely wanted to get involved when the object of his attraction was Renee.

He drew in a deep breath of air as he began making his way across the room. He had gone to her office and was told by her secretary that she was at lunch and chances were he would find her in the cafeteria. He had hoped she would be alone but it seemed she was dining with someone. But that didn't stop him from wanting to see her, talk to her.

Renee hadn't realized that Tag had crossed the room until he was standing right next to her table. She glanced up and felt the sensuous undercurrents automatically ra-

diating between them and wondered if Diane noticed
them too.

Immediately putting her professional facade in place
Renee leaned back in her chair, cleared her throat and
in her best businesslike voice, said, "Mr. Elliott, how are
you? And how is your mother?"

Tag sensed her nervousness, saw the guarded look in
her eyes and watched how she caught her bottom lip between her teeth. He gave her companion no more than
a cursory glance, but quickly registered how she eyed
him with keen interest. He knew what Renee was silently asking him.

"My mother is fine, Ms. Williams," he said in his own
businesslike voice. "Her doctor indicates the surgery was
a success. However, that's what I want to talk to you about
and I hate to intrude on your lunchtime, but I was wondering if I could speak with you privately for a moment."

Renee felt Diane's eyes on them, taking it all in, and
was glad Tag had picked up on her silent warning. The
last thing she needed was for the nurse to start rumors
floating around the hospital. "Yes, I was finished here
anyway. We can go back to my office."

Feeling a gentle kick to her leg under the table, Renee realized Diane was eager for her to make introductions. "Mr. Elliott, I would like for you to meet Diane
Carter. She's one of our trauma nurses."

Diane was beaming when she presented Tag her
hand. "Mr. Elliott, it's so nice meeting you."

"The same here, Ms. Carter. I hate to take her away
from you, but there is this pressing matter I need to discuss with her."

Diane waved off his apology. "Hey, there's no reason to apologize. Trust me, I understand."

Renee doubted that Diane really did when she herself didn't.

Warmth spread through Renee's veins the moment she and Tag stepped into the elevator together. Alone. Neither of them said anything and as they rode up to the sixth floor, she tried to remind herself of all the reasons they could not become involved.

"I'm sorry I missed you earlier when you came to see how my family was holding up."

"It's part of my job to check on the family of my patients during surgery, to see if there's anything I can do for them."

Tag leaned against the paneled wall. "That's good to know, since there is definitely something you can do for me."

"And what can I do for you, Mr. Elliott?"

"For starters, since we're alone now, you can stop pretending Saturday night never happened. That we never kissed. Touched. Lost our heads and minds to passion."

He heard the air when it suddenly rushed from her lungs. He saw the shiver that passed through her body, but before he could make another comment, the elevator came to a stop.

When the door slid open, Tag stood back to let Renee step out. Neither said anything as they crossed the lobby to her office, walking side by side. Her secretary looked up and smiled before returning her attention to her computer. Renee appreciated the fifty-something woman who had been her secretary for the nearly two years Renee had worked there. Vicki was efficient, trustworthy and someone who respected Renee's need for privacy.

Renee opened the door and stepped into her office. Tag followed and closed the door behind them. He watched as she quickly crossed the room, and couldn't help but admire how she looked in her chocolate-brown business suit. The skirt hit her just above her knees, and his first thought was that she definitely had a great pair of legs.

"I'm glad you mother's surgery was successful."

Tag's gaze moved from her legs to her face. She was standing in the middle of her office, eyeing him nervously. "So am I."

She cleared her throat again. "In the cafeteria you said you needed to talk to me about her."

He shrugged, deciding to be completely honest with her. "It was something I said to get you alone."

He watched her eyes narrow. Okay, so she wasn't happy hearing the truth, but seeing her standing here, alone in the room with him, made him realize the lie had been worth it. He smiled.

Renee wished she could somehow banish the sight of Tag standing there dressed in a tailored suit, like he was the epitome of every woman's fancy. But then she had to quickly concede that he could have been dressed in a T-shirt and a pair of tattered jeans and he still would have looked good.

And then there was the way his mouth could curve

into a smile. The way it just did. She swallowed. "Mr. Elliott, I'm going to have to treat this strictly as a business meeting."

"If you'd like."

Renee was becoming frustrated and Tag wasn't helping matters. "I have a job to do."

He leaned back against the door and chuckled. "You don't have to remind me since your job is what brought us together."

"We aren't together."

"It depends on your definition of the word," he said easily.

Deciding enough words had been said, he moved forward, closing the distance between them, and came to a stop in front of her. "I need to get back. My mother should be coming around and I want to be there when she does." He paused briefly and then added, "But I wanted to see you, just to assure myself that Saturday had been real and not a pleasant figment of my imagination."

Renee crossed her arms over her chest and lifted her chin. "So what if it was real? That was then and now is now. I should not have let things get out of hand like that."

"You sure about that?" Tag asked. He wanted to kiss that lie right off her mouth. There was no way she could convince him that she regretted what they'd shared Saturday.

"Yes, I'm sure."

"And you don't want me to kiss you again?"

"Absolutely not! I wish you'd never kissed me in the first place!" Renee glared at him and noticed his eyes seemed more intense than ever. She sucked in a deep breath when he leaned down and brought his mouth close to hers, mere inches away.

"Now tell me again that you wish we'd never kissed," he whispered hotly against her lips.

Renee opened her mouth to say the words and had planned to come up with a comeback that would set him back a notch. But she couldn't make the words come out and quickly closed her mouth. She gazed at the face so close to hers and knew frustration, want, desire as she felt herself being pulled in, falling helplessly into the depths of his bottomless sea-blue eyes.

"Tell me," he whispered against her lips.

She inhaled deeply as a throbbing sensation took over her body that seemed to start in the nipples of her breasts and was slowly moving down past her waist to land right in the middle between her thighs.

This was not supposed to be happening to her. She'd never been drawn to a man this way. And she had always stayed within what she'd considered her comfort zone while dating. Although she'd accumulated a number of white male friends over the years, she'd never given thought to developing a serious relationship with any of them. But there was something about Tag that defied logic. Her logic anyway. He seemed to find her as sexually appealing as she found him.

And she wanted to kiss him again.

Knowing that she would regret her decision, she tilted her chin which brought their mouths closer. But he didn't move. Instead he stood there, cool as you please, his gaze holding hers while sending delectable shivers down her body. The shivers, combined with the racing of her heart, were having one hell of an effect on her. But still he stood there, immobile, letting her know that if she wanted the kiss she was going to have to be the one to take it. With a moan she hadn't known she was about to make, against her better judgment she leaned closer and captured his mouth with hers.

She grabbed his shoulders and welcomed his tongue when it entered her mouth, mating it with hers, stroking it and sending tremors of pleasure through her body.

Then the tempo of the kiss changed when he took it over. It went from soft and gentle to hot and possessive. And she responded automatically, feeling her abdominal muscles clench. Intense heat pooled between her legs and the scent of all male teased her nostrils.

The ringing of the phone intruded and Renee pulled back, breaking off the kiss. Inhaling deeply, she reached across her desk and pushed the respond button on her phone. "Yes, Vicki?" she managed to say while heat continued flowing around in her stomach. She glanced over at Tag. The eyes staring at her were smoldering with desire and he was standing there waiting, as if he hadn't finished with her yet.

"Your one-o'clock appointment is here, Ms. Williams."

Renee moistened her lips nervously. Kissing Tag had made her forget everything, including the fact that this was her office and she was standing in the middle of it, kissing him. What if someone had walked in on them? She could imagine the scandal that would have started.

"Thanks, Vicki. Give me a few minutes to wind things up with Mr. Elliott."

Renee then turned her attention back to Tag. He was still standing in the same spot, staring at her. Okay, so she had been the one to initiate the kiss this time. Call them even. It didn't change the fact that they couldn't become involved and she needed to make him understand that. She had more to lose than he did. "A relationship between us won't work, Tag," she said slowly, distinctively stating each word.

"You don't think so?"

"No."

"Because my mother is your patient?"

"Among other reasons that are just as important," she said, deciding to spell it all out for him since he was acting like he didn't have a clue. Surely he could see the obstacles they faced as a couple as well as she could.

He crossed his arms over his chest. "And what are these other reasons?"

"I don't believe in casual affairs, which includes involving myself in relationships that I know upfront won't be going anywhere. You're white and I'm black. You're a wealthy businessman and I'm a social worker whose income won't come close to yours in a million years."

He continued to stare at her. "And your point?"

Renee narrowed her gaze. *Her point?* How could he ask her that when it was so clear? But if he wanted her to break it down even more, then she would. "My point is that I've never dated outside my race. I prefer staying in my comfort zone, and I'm not a woman who ever dreamed of marrying rich."

He laughed, but she could tell he wasn't amused but was rather pissed-off. "Are you saying you're basing your decision on my skin color and my finances?"

Hearing him say it made her feel no better than Thomas Bonner. Immediately, she put her defenses up. "Why would you want to become involved with me, Tag? Come on, let's get real here. Am I a woman your family would expect you to bring to dinner?"

His eyes darkened in anger and he quickly closed the distance between them. "First of all," he said in a low, angry tone, "I don't recall asking you to have a relationship with my family, just with me. Second, my family has never, nor will it ever, dictate how I live my life and with whom. Of course I would be lying if I said I wasn't raised with a certain set of values, but one of the things my grandparents and parents instilled in me more than anything was to judge a person on his character and not his outside appearance. And it's obvious that you're not doing that. If you're judging me by the way I look and by the size of my bank account, then we have nothing left to say."

He turned and walked out the door.

This was one of those days Renee was glad she didn't have any more appointments scheduled after her one o'clock. She needed to leave work as soon as she could to clear her mind of any lingering doubts she had regarding Tag. The words he'd spoken, the accusation, were still hanging there in her mind, refusing to move on. Why had he made things so complicated? Why didn't he understand her decision had been to spare them undue heartache and pain and unnecessary gossip?

Oh, she was sure there were a lot of interracial couples out there falling in love and making things work despite the odds. But it was those odds that bothered her more than anything. He wasn't living on another planet. He knew the rules that society dictated and the problems you could encounter if you decided to go against them.

She remembered all too well Cheryl Hollis and how she had sneaked behind her parents' backs and dated a white guy while they were in high school. Cheryl had gotten pregnant and both set of parents had been up in arms. The guy's parents had money and threatened to cut him off if he so much as claimed the child as his. So he had done exactly as his parents had dictated, leaving Cheryl alone, pregnant and brokenhearted.

Granted, Tag wasn't a high school senior dependent upon his parents' income, but he was still an Elliott. His family's influence and wealth ranked right up there with the Kennedys and Bushes. Heck, his grandmother could probably call Oprah directly and invite her to dinner. Renee ran a frustrating hand down her face. She refused to let Tag lay a guilt trip on her. She wasn't prejudiced, just cautious.

But still, as she shut down her computer for the day, she couldn't erase from her mind that Tag Elliott had done something no other man had been capable of doing since Dionne. He had reminded her she was a woman—a woman with emotions, wants, physical needs and desires. She just wasn't used to a man making her lose control. Even now her palms were sweating just from her thinking about the kiss they had shared earlier here in this office.

She drew in a frustrated breath. No matter what, she had to believe that she had done the right thing letting Tag know where she stood and how she felt. But if that was the case, why was doing the right thing making her feel so bad?

Five

"I don't understand what you're saying, Dad. What do you mean Mom doesn't want to see us?" Tag asked, completely baffled.

Michael Elliott met the confused looks of his four offspring. He'd known this conversation would be difficult but somehow he needed to get them to understand how things were with their mother.

"As you know your mother is being released from the hospital today and I'm taking her to The Tides to recuperate. She has requested that when we get there she be left alone for a while. She doesn't want to see anyone. Not even the four of you."

"What?" Tag, Liam, Gannon and Bridget exclaimed simultaneously in shocked voices.

"Are you sure that's what she said, Dad?" Gannon

asked, shaking his head, finding his mother's request hard to believe, totally unacceptable.

Michael nodded sadly. "Yes, and I hope all of you can understand how Karen is feeling right now. She's been through a lot, both emotionally and physically. She needs this time alone."

"What she needs is time with her family," Bridget said, her eyes huge, dark and hurt. "We need to do something if she feels that way. Can't we call her social worker since it's obvious Mom's going through a deep state of depression?"

"I agree with Bridget," Liam said. "There has to be something we can do to lift her spirits."

"I agree as well," Tag chimed in. "I'll visit with Renee Williams to see what can be done." Just saying Renee's name caused pain to ripple through him. It had been almost a week since that day he had angrily walked out of her office. He knew she had visited with his mother a couple of times in the hospital but she'd done so when he hadn't been around to run into her.

"How soon can you meet with Ms. Williams?" Gannon asked, regarding Tag thoughtfully.

"I'll go and see her today."

It was one of those days when Renee had needed to stay at the office after closing hours to get a few things done. She glanced over at the clock as she shut down her computer. It was close to seven o'clock. Normally, she would have left hours ago. Vicki, bless her heart, had hung around to assist Renee in finishing a report.

"I'm out of here," Vicki said smiling, sticking her blond head in the doorway.

Renee returned the older woman's smile. "Thanks for your help. I'm glad we've gotten everything finished for tomorrow's meeting."

"Me, too. I'll see you in the morning. Don't stay too late."

Renee grinned. "Don't worry. I won't be too far behind you."

Minutes later Renee had put everything she needed into her briefcase and glanced up when she heard the knock at the door. Thinking it was the maintenance crew to clean the office, she didn't look up when she said, "Come on in, I'm just about finished and—"

She lifted her head and the rest of the words died on her lips when she saw that the person standing in her doorway was Tag. Suddenly, heat flowed through her body and blood rushed through her veins. He didn't say anything. Neither did she. The silence between them stretched, weaving around them like a silken thread.

Renee breathed in a deep, shuddering breath. She hadn't seen him since that day they'd had words and couldn't help wondering why he was here. They had said everything that could be said and would never see eye to eye on things, so why bother?

Sighing deeply, she closed her briefcase with a click. Instinctively, she squared her shoulders, putting her protection gear in place since it appeared his entire expression was an unreadable mask. But even with that he was a very handsome man. She would always give him that.

"Tag, what are you doing here?"

He stepped into the room and closed the door. "I saw your secretary downstairs and she said you were still here. I need to talk to you."

Renee shook her head. "I don't think there's anything else we need to say."

"I don't want to talk to you about us, Renee. I want to talk to you about my mother." At her raised brow he added, "And that's no lie this time."

It was then that Renee noticed a couple of things about him. His rigid shoulders, the lack of spark in his eyes, the strain of controlled emotions in his features. She quickly crossed the room to him. "What is it, Tag? Has something happened to Karen?"

"No," he said calmly, attempting a faint smile. "Nothing has happened to Mom."

"Then what's wrong?"

He cleared his throat, finding it still hard to believe and even harder to get the words out. "She told Dad that she doesn't want to see any of us while she's recuperating at my grandparents' home."

Renee slowly nodded, understanding. The last time she had met with his mother she could tell that Karen had begun slipping into a state of depression. It had been the same day the doctor had unwrapped her chest to show Karen how to go about caring for her stitches after leaving the hospital, although Renee knew that Michael Elliott had hired a private nurse for his wife.

"None of you should take your mother's request personally, Tag."

Tag's eyebrows snapped together in anger. "What do

you mean we shouldn't take it personally? She's our mother and—"

"She's also a woman with a lot to deal with at the moment. Having both breasts removed isn't something any female would take lightly. For a while, when her chest was bandaged, she was going through denial. But now since she's gotten a chance to see the surgeon's handiwork, reality has set in and she's combating it the only way she knows how, which is with anger, fear and withdrawal. I was with her the day she became angry. Dr. Chaney and I were prepared for it. We were also prepared for the days when she went through stark fear, thinking that perhaps the doctor didn't get all the cancer and it would return to other parts of her body and that she would be eventually lose those parts as well."

Renee sighed deeply, knowing she had to get Tag to accept his mother's present state of mind. Accept it as well as understand it. "Now she's going through withdrawal. She doesn't want to deal with anything or anyone, even those whom she loves. If she could, she would block your father out as well but he won't let her do so, although trust me she has tried."

Tag closed his eyes, not wanting to believe what he was hearing. His mother had always been the strong one in the family. Like his grandmother, she was the one who could always hold things together in a crisis. Now she was going through her own personal crisis and he was finding it hard to conjure up even a little bit of the strength his mother always seemed to have had.

He leaned back against the closed door, suddenly

feeling exhausted. "So what are we supposed to do? Let her continue to wallow in self-pity and do nothing?"

Renee shook her head. "No. To start with, you should all honor her request and give her the space she needs right now, while working together behind the scenes and doing something that can and will lift her spirits."

"Like what?"

Renee shrugged. "Anything that will make her appreciate the fact that she's alive. I understand she enjoys working with her charities. You can arrange for her to continue to do so even while she's convalescing. Remember, she'll be going through both physical and emotional healing. The most important thing is helping her to get beyond her ordeal and concentrate on something else."

Renee studied Tag's expression and knew he had absorbed her words. His next question, however, surprised her. "Will you help, Renee?"

She shook her head. The last thing she needed was complications, and Tag was nothing if not that. "No, I don't think that's—"

"Please."

Renee nervously gnawed the insides of her mouth. Could she handle doing what he was asking? She let out a small breath. Yes, she could handle it if it meant helping Karen. Over the past few weeks she and Tag's mother had developed a relationship that had gone beyond social worker and patient. She admired Karen for all the good things she did for others, especially all her charitable work.

"Will you do it, Renee?"

She glanced into Tag's face and saw the heartfelt

plea in his eyes. And then she knew what her answer would be. "Yes, Tag, I'll help out with your mother any way I can."

Both relief and appreciation shone on his face. "Thank you, Renee. Are you willing to meet with my sister and brothers and explain everything to them as well? Tomorrow night we're having dinner together at Une Nuit, a restaurant owned by my cousin Bryan. Is there any way you can join us there?"

Anyone living in New York had heard of Une Nuit, the restaurant whose patrons oftentimes included a number of celebrities. Now that she had agreed to help him lift Karen's spirits, Renee knew she had to move forward. At least she and Tag wouldn't be dining at the restaurant alone. She wasn't sure how many times she could be alone with him without wanting to comfort him and assure him that everything with his mother would be all right. But she knew to comfort him meant she would also want to kiss him, take his pain away, touch him....

A sexual awareness she only encountered when she was around Tag tried taking over her mind, but she fought it. "Yes, I'll be glad to meet with you and your siblings tomorrow night."

Tag nodded. "I'll pick you up around seven."

"You don't have to do—"

"Yes, I do. I don't want you taking the subway to meet with us. Okay?"

She sighed, knowing his stubbornness was coming out and to argue with him would be pointless. "Fine."

He smiled. "Good. And do you need a ride home now?"

"No, I'm meeting Debbie at a restaurant not far from

here. She's leaving in the morning for an assignment in London so we decided to make it a girls' night out. I'll be fine."

"Are you certain?"

"Yes." She'd never met a man who was so concerned for her well-being. Tag was so thoughtful, caring and attentive.

"Then the least I can do is walk you there."

She knew telling him that wasn't necessary would only be a waste of her time. Clutching her briefcase, she walked out with him, stopping to turn out the lights. Moments later they stepped into the elevator and as the car descended she couldn't help hoping that busybody Diane Carter had left for the day. The last thing Renee needed was to run into her in the lobby. No doubt she'd get the wrong idea about her and Tag.

When the elevator came to a stop and the doors slid open, Tag stood back to let her step out. "You really don't have to walk me to the restaurant, Tag. It's only a few blocks from here," she said, stepping into the hospital lobby. "I'm sure you have more important things to do."

"No," he said, slanting her a sideways glance. "There's nothing more important."

Darkness enfolded them as they stepped outside and began walking. The sidewalks were congested and more than once he gently pulled her closer to him to avoid her getting trampled by someone hurrying past.

When they reached her destination, she turned to him. "Thanks."

"And thank you, Renee, for everything. I'll see you tomorrow night at seven."

"All right."

She quickly entered the restaurant and when she glanced over her shoulder through the window he was still standing there, looking at her.

Tag leaned forward on the conference table with his palms down as he stared at the man and woman sitting at it. "I want anything and everything you can find on Senator Vince Denton, especially his activities over the past year. No one walks away from politics after thirty years without a good reason, especially someone that close to the present administration."

"He gave us his reason. He's been in politics long enough and wants to return to his farm in South Carolina and live the rest of his days in peace and harmony. Sounds like a damn good plan to me," Peter Weston, *Pulse*'s special edition editor, said, carelessly throwing out a paper clip. Peter was responsible for *Pulse*'s campaigns, opinion polls and surveys.

Tag met the man's nonchalant expression. "I don't care how good it sounds, I'm not buying it and I suggest you don't either." He sighed. It was time Tag and his father had a serious talk about Peter's lack of interest in his job. Peter had worked for *Pulse* for over fifteen years, starting out as an investigative reporter—one of the magazine's best—and working his way up through the ranks. Lately, it had been noticed by a number of co-workers that he lacked the hunger, instinct and drive he used to have. Peter had been placed on paid administrative leave on two occasions when his work habits had begun declining and it appeared things were beginning to go downhill again.

Rumor had it that Peter was involved in an affair with a Radio City Rockette and was sacrificing everything, including a good marriage, to be at the woman's beck and call. It was Tag's opinion that what Peter did on his free time was one thing. What he did on *Pulse*'s time was another.

Peter's interest in *Pulse* had started waning a few years ago when Gannon had gotten a position that Peter evidently thought should have been his. He was of the mind that Gannon's name and not his hard work had gotten him where he was, which was not true.

"I thought his resignation was rather strange, too," Marlene Kingston said, scanning the notes she'd taken from an earlier meeting. At twenty-seven, she had been working for *Pulse* since college and always had a good eye for the news. Currently she edited the analysis pages and wrote editorials. "I find it odd that he would resign right before next week's vote on that big oil bill," she added.

Tag liked the woman's sharpness. However, he could tell by the glare Peter had given her that he did not. "That's a good point, Marlene, and one we should look into. Just make sure whatever you have to report is accurate and from a reliable source." He sighed deeply then added, "Pull out all stops and let's dig to see what we can find. Make plans for us to meet in a few days, same time, same place, with some answers."

Half an hour later Tag was poking his head in the room where the smell of ink teased his nostrils. Making his way past old issues of *Charisma*, canisters of ink and reams of paper, not to mention numerous pictures of Elizabeth Taylor plastered on the wall, he made it to the workstation of Edgar Rosewood and sat down in the chair next to it.

The man sitting at the desk looked up at him beneath bushy eyebrows. Edgar, who would be celebrating his seventieth birthday in a few months, had been hired by Patrick within a month of EPH opening its doors, and to this day refused to call it quits by retiring. That was fine with Tag since Edgar had been Tag's father's mentor as well as mentor to Gannon, Liam and himself when they'd come through the ranks. Tag always had and always would consider the man someone special and an asset to *Pulse*. To this day, one thing Edgar retained was a sharp eye for headlines that were so well buried that even a hunting dog couldn't find them.

"What's bothering you, kid?" Edgar asked, his tone rough, his frown deep. "Personal or business?"

Another thing Tag liked about the old man was that he knew how to cut to the chase. Not wanting to delve into his personal problems, not even with Edgar, Tag said, "Business. I think there's more to Senator Denton's resignation than meets the eye."

Edgar swung around from his computer. "So do I."

Tag lifted a paperweight off the pages of last month's magazine. He felt good knowing Edgar was also on to something. "I just hope we can find out what it is before *Time* does."

"We will, as long as you let Marlene Kingston do the digging. She has a nose like a bloodhound. If Denton's not clean, she'll find out just what's dirty. Personally, I like her."

Tag couldn't help but smile. "Why? Because she re-
minds you of a young Elizabeth Taylor?"

The old man smiled. "Yeah, that's one of the reasons.
The other is that she's a good newswoman. The best
thing you can do is get her from under Peter and have
her work with Wayne Barnes. Peter has been taking
credit for Marlene's hard work long enough. The only
interest he seems to have these days is a pair of breasts
pouring out of a Rockette costume. He's doing nothing
but stifling Marlene's growth."

Tag had to agree, which was something else he
needed to talk to Gannon about.

Edgar looked at him, studied him. "You sure there's
nothing else bothering you?"

Tag shrugged. "Of course this thing with Mom is
constantly on my mind."

"That's understandable but I think you might have
another problem."

"What?"

Edgar gave him a pointed look. "The absence of a
good woman in your life."

Tag smiled. Edgar had given him and Liam that
same speech after Gannon had announced his engagement to Erika last month. "Still trying to marry me
off, are you?"

"There's nothing wrong with settling down. I've been
with my Martha for over fifty years and have been involved in a secret love affair with Elizabeth for forty of
those fifty."

Tag chuckled and raised his eyes to the ceiling. "In
your dreams." He stood and checked his watch. A part

of him couldn't wait to see Renee later. He had been thinking about her all day. Gannon, Liam and Bridget were anxious to meet with her tonight as well, to hear what she had to say.

"Time for me to get back to work," Tag said, walking toward the door. He paused in the doorway and stared at the huge poster of Elizabeth Taylor on the wall next to it. "What do you think about when you look at her?" Tag asked Edgar over his shoulder.

He could hear the old man chuckle softly. "Passion and desire."

Tag turned around. "And what do you think about when you look at Martha?"

Edgar stretched out his legs, leaned back in his chair and locked his fingers behind his head. "Same thing, but added to those two is love. And that's the key, kid. Find a woman who can ignite you with passion and desire and who can also fill your heart with love."

Tag grunted. He doubted there was a woman in existence who could fill his heart with love, but when it came to passion and desire there was one face that readily came to mind.

Renee's.

"Thanks for picking me up," Renee said as she eased into the leather seat of Tag's SUV.

"You don't have to thank me, Renee." He closed the door and came around the other side and slid into the driver's seat.

He glanced over at her. "You look nice. But then you always do."

His compliment made her smile. "Thank you."

"You're welcome." He pulled out into traffic.

She was silent, her gaze skimming the buildings and people as they drove by. Although she had never eaten at Une Nuit, she had heard of a lot of nice things about the restaurant. According to what Tag had told her earlier, his cousin Bryan had gotten out of the family business a few years ago to try his hand in the restaurant business. The change in careers had proved successful. Tag had also mentioned that Bryan traveled quite a bit and when he did, the restaurant was managed by a capable Frenchman by the name of Stash Martin.

"My sister and brothers are looking forward to meeting you tonight. They appreciate all you did for our mother while she was in the hospital."

To say what she'd done was merely her job would sound rather cold, Renee thought, especially when she considered the time she'd spent with Karen more valuable than that. She glanced over at Tag. "I'm looking forward to meeting them as well and look forward to doing what I can to help lift your mother's spirits."

When the vehicle came to a stop at a traffic light, she said gently, "Tell me about them." She inhaled sharply when he turned and met her gaze. The depths of his blue eyes shone darkly under a flashing street sign. He did something to her each and every time he looked at her, whether she wanted the reaction or not.

"Gannon, who is thirty-three, is my oldest brother and the second in command to my father at *Pulse*. He always loved his carefree bachelor lifestyle but last month he became engaged to a woman he'd had an affair with over a year ago by the name of Erika Layven. You'll also get to meet her tonight."

Tag hit the brakes when a yellow cab carelessly darted out in front of his Lexus. "Liam," he continued, "is thirty-one and is EPH's financial operating officer." He chuckled. "We tease him about being my grandfather's favorite grandchild because he's the one who keeps tabs on the money, and trust me, he does a damn good job of it. He's sharp when it comes to numbers.

"Last but not least, there's Bridget, who is your age. She's a photo editor for *Charisma* and according to what she tells me, she's still trying to find herself."

He glanced over at Renee. "And there you have it." And with that timely ending, the car came to a stop in front of Une Nuit.

Six

If Renee had felt strange and uncomfortable when she'd first walked into Une Nuit with Tag, then those feelings were definitely behind her now. His siblings had a way of making her feel relaxed, and she could easily tell that the four of them shared a rather close relationship.

The inside of the restaurant looked sensational and the place was filled to capacity, with a number of celebrities in the house. She and Tag bypassed the long line of patrons waiting to be seated and were escorted to the "Elliott Table" where Gannon, Liam and Bridget was waiting for them. Gannon's fiancée, Erika, joined the group a few minutes later.

Tag was quick to explain that with so many family members frequenting the restaurant, Bryan had designated a rear table as the "Elliott Table."

Renee had blinked twice when she'd met the restaurateur. With his jet black hair and blue eyes, she could easily tell that he and Tag were related. And he was so laid-back and friendly.

"Are you sure you don't prefer wine, Renee?" Gannon asked, smiling.

Renee liked Tag's brothers and his sister, as well as Erika. She thought there wasn't a pretentious bone in Erika's body, and like the others, she went out of her way to make her feel comfortable. "No thank you," Renee said. "I better stick with this coffee since there's work tomorrow."

"Yes, there is that. And we want to thank you for your willingness to help with Mom," Gannon said, acting as spokesman for the group. The others nodded in full agreement.

Renee's smile spread to each corner of her lips. "None of you has to thank me. Your mother is a wonderful person and I'm happy to do anything that I can to help her." She had explained earlier exactly what Karen needed. All of them had listened attentively and had thrown out several good ideas and suggestions, but it was Gannon and Erika's suggestion that everyone decided was the best.

In light of Karen's breast cancer, the couple had decided to fly to Vegas and marry at the end of the month instead of having a traditional wedding. However, if planning a wedding would give Karen something to do and lift her spirits, they would certainly change their plans. It was decided that Erika would contact Karen and ask her assistance in planning a small wedding.

The family had already made plans to gather at Patrick and Maeve's Hampton estate at the end of the month to celebrate the older couple's anniversary, and Gannon and Erika thought it would be special to exchange their vows on the same exact date Gannon's grandparents had fifty-seven years ago. Since everyone knew how much Karen loved planning special events, they hoped assisting Erika with her wedding would lift Karen's spirits.

While Renee sipped her coffee she couldn't help but notice when Gannon leaned over to Erika and whispered something into her ear. Whatever he said brought a smile to Erika's face, and she tilted her head for him to kiss her on the lips. Renee was touched by the romantic gesture, just one of several that had passed between the couple that night. She'd been surprised by how open they had been in admitting their love for each other and their desire to get married and start a family right away.

"Ready to leave?"

Renee nearly jumped when Tag leaned over and whispered into her ear. She lifted her gaze but she didn't dare move her head. Doing so would have their lips practically touching. Yet, they were so close there was no way their breath wouldn't mingle when she did speak. "Yes, I'm ready."

She regretted having to say good-night to everyone and was surprised when Bridget slipped her business card into her hand and told her to call her one day soon so the two of them could do lunch. Erika did the same thing.

"I enjoyed myself tonight," Renee said to Tag when they were in the SUV and on their way back to her place. "You have special siblings, and after meeting your parents I can see why. They did a great job in raising all of you."

Tag glanced over at her and smiled. "Thanks." Although she had given him a compliment, he couldn't forget it had just been a few days since she had stood in her office and practically said she could not have a relationship with him because of their different races and his family's wealth.

"What's this joke about the family feud?"

Renee's question interrupted Tag's thoughts. He glanced over at her. "It's no joke, it's the truth. My grandfather is retiring at the end of the year and has decreed that whoever makes their magazine the biggest success by the end of the year will be given the position of CEO of EPH."

Renee glanced at him with widened eyes. "You're kidding, right?"

Tag chuckled. "No, I wish I was but I'm dead serious. And what's so crazy is that although the four magazines are run by a different offspring, the staff is mixed. For example, Bridget doesn't work with me, Gannon and my father at *Pulse*. She works with Aunt Finola at *Charisma*. So in essence, in trying to put *Charisma* on top, she won't be rallying to our father's side in his bid for the CEO position."

"Uh-oh, that can be a pretty sticky position to be placed in," Renee said, wondering why Tag's grandfather would do such a thing in pitting his family against each other that way.

"It already is and personally, I don't like it. The feud

between the different magazines is making things tense at the office."

Renee turned her head and recognized the deli on the corner. They were within a block of her place. She shifted in her seat, suddenly feeling nervous. When Tag had picked her up earlier she had been dressed and ready to go and had walked out of the apartment before he'd had a chance to knock. She couldn't help wondering, considering their argument in her office over a week ago, if he would just drop her off at the curb and keep going. She had to be realistic enough to know that the only reason he had shown up at her office last night was to ask for her help with his mother.

When his car turned the corner and came to a stop in front of her apartment building, she began unbuckling her seat belt. In a way, she was sorry the ride had ended. "Thanks again for tonight."

"I should be thanking you, and I do," he said huskily, seconds before opening his door and quickly walking in front of the car to open the car door for her. He offered her his hand.

She took it and immediately felt flushed from the top of her head all the way to her toes. All it took was a look in his eyes to know he'd felt it, too. Tingles of awareness were electrifying the space between them. A yearning sensation was spreading all through her limbs and she suddenly longed for the feel of his lips on hers. She blinked, forcing those thoughts away, and knew she had to take control of what was happening to her. Put a stop to it immediately.

They didn't say anything as he walked her to her

apartment, and when they reached her door he stood silently by while she took the key from her purse and unlocked it. She turned to him. "Thanks for walking me to the door, Tag."

"You don't have to thank me, Renee."

If she had been focused more on her surroundings than on Tag, Renee would not have noticed the deep timbre of his voice or the intensity that filled his blue eyes. But she did notice those things although she wished she hadn't, because in doing so she felt more heat spread through her.

She remembered their conversation that day in her office. She knew every single word she had told him, could probably recite it in her sleep. But now, at this very moment, none of it mattered. She was dealing with an emotion she'd never dealt with before and she knew, whether she wanted it to happen or not, she had fallen in love with Tag.

Forbidden love.

She sucked in a deep breath at the realization and wondered how she could have let such a thing happen. The big question was not how he had gotten through her defenses so quickly, but how he had managed to get through them at all. They were completely wrong for each other, on different ends of a spectrum, worlds apart. They could never share a happy life together without stares and frowns. There was no reason to think about a future with him, but there was something they could share tonight that would be theirs and theirs alone.

"Good-night, Renee." Tag leaned down and kissed her cheek before turning to leave. He took a few steps, stopped, and then, as if he was compelled to look at her just one more time, he turned back around.

The moment their gazes reconnected she knew she was doomed. She loved him and she wanted him. It was as simple as that. At least for tonight it would be simple. "Would you like to come in for a drink or something?" she asked softly, unable to hold her silence any longer.

With a smile that would have endeared him to her for life if he hadn't already been so, he recovered the distance separating them and whispered, "Are you sure you want to be alone with me tonight, Renee?"

Emotions clogged her throat. She knew what he was asking.

He had tried walking away but couldn't. Like her, he had reached the end of his rope. Desire had thickened their minds, taken control of their thoughts, and, God forbid, pushed them over the edge. Once they stepped into her apartment there would be no turning back and they both knew it.

"Yes, I'm sure," she said, her mind completely made up. They would have this night together. With that decision made, an unexpected rush of relief and pleasure washed over her, forcing any and all opposition from her mind. He was man. She was woman. And at this moment, he was the man she loved and wanted.

"If you're sure," he said, slowly opening the door.

"And I am," she said as an assured smile touched the corners of her lips.

"In that case, I think we should take this inside."

He held the door open to let her go in first and then he followed, closing and locking the door behind him.

* * *

There was definitely something sexual and elemental about being alone with the woman you desperately wanted, Tag thought as he leaned against the closed door.

He watched as Renee went to stand in the middle of the room. She was nervous. He could tell. But then he was aroused and he knew that she could tell that as well. There was no way his body could keep something like that a secret. He suddenly felt like holding her in his embrace, needing to feel the heat of her body against his.

He held his hand out to her. "Come here, Renee," he said in a voice that wanted to retain control but was slowly losing it.

She placed her purse on a table and crossed the room to stand in front of him. His hands automatically slid around her waist. "I want to hold you for a little while," he said, bringing her body closer to the fit of him. Renee's head automatically rested upon his chest.

Tag knew there were still unresolved issues between them but at this very moment, while she was in his arms, nothing mattered but them being together this way. What was important was that when it came to passion and desire they were in accord.

Passion and desire.

Edgar's words rang loudly in Tag's ears. He thought of all the other women he'd ever dated, some as stunning as a woman could get, but there was something about Renee that was different. She was as beautiful as the rest but there was this ingrained, unadulterated sense of kindness and decency that pulled him to her each and every time.

"Tag?" she whispered moments later, the warmth of her breath splaying against his cheek.

"Mmm?"

"Are we going to stand here like this all night?"

His lips parted in a smile. Only Renee could ask such a question at a time like this. Instead of answering her, he bent and swept her into his arms at the exact moment his mouth settled hungrily over hers. It was by no means a gentle kiss and was intended to let her know just how much he desired her.

She moaned and the sound intensified the deep-rooted longing within him. He pulled his mouth away briefly to ask, "Which way to the bedroom?"

"Down the hall then to your right."

Holding her tight against him, he moved in that direction. When they reached the bedroom doorway he resumed kissing her, letting his tongue explore and devour every inch of her mouth. Somehow, with their lips locked, they made it to the bed. He was grateful she had left a lamp on in the room.

She gave a nervous laugh and pulled him down on the soft mattress with her. He tilted his head back and looked at her, thinking that he'd never wanted a woman as much as he wanted Renee. Anticipation filled his entire being as he slipped off the bed to remove his clothes.

He watched her watch him remove his shirt then he reached his hand out and pulled her off the bed to him. After removing her shoes he turned her around to work at the zipper on her dress. He liked her dress, a silky-looking A-line blue dress that showed off her shapely figure. He had definitely liked seeing her in it, but would enjoy seeing her out of it even more.

"I've wanted you from that first day I walked into your office," he whispered, placing a wet kiss on her shoulder. He felt a shudder race through her body and gloried in the fact that he had been the one to make it happen.

"You did?"

"Yes, and it shook me up some because I've never wanted a woman that much before."

He slid the zipper down and then pushed the garment off her shoulders. All it took was for Renee to do one sensuous shimmy of her hips and the dress fell in a heap at her feet. Next, on one bended knee, he removed her panty hose, leaving her clad in the sexiest bra and panty set he'd ever seen. Simply seeing the baby-blue lace against her dark skin made his loins tighten. Added to that were her gorgeous legs and bright red painted toenails that matched the color of her fingernails. He was of the opinion that for all intents and purposes, she took the word *sexy* to a whole new level. She was the epitome of every male fantasy, definitely his own. His mind began spinning, blood pumped hot and heavy through his veins as he unbuckled his belt and began removing his pants.

From their first kiss he had been fighting the need to make love to her. She was constantly in his thoughts, even when he hadn't wanted her there. Fantasizing about her had become his favorite pastime.

He tossed his pants aside and stood before her wearing only his briefs, and suddenly felt a jolt of desire when she reached out and slid her hand down his chest, letting her fingers slowly work their way beneath the waistband of his underwear to curl around his rock-hard erection. And when she began stroking him, he thought he was going to lose it. He *knew* he was going to lose it if she didn't stop.

"Renee…"

"Yes?"

Her response was as innocent as it could get and he quickly decided that two could definitely play her game. And in this case, two definitely would. He sat down on the edge of the bed and gently pulled her to him to strad-dle his hips. His hands spanned her waist just before they began kneading her buttocks. He liked the feel of her soft skin and the scent of her as well. Damn, she smelled good.

And when she leaned forward and began nuzzling his jaw with her lips and running her hands over his shoul-der and chest, he inhaled sharply, gripping her hips and pushing upward, wanting her to feel just what she was doing to him, how deeply aroused he was.

His mouth captured hers as he lay back, bringing her atop him in the process, the softness of her flesh sink-ing into him. Moments later she lifted her mouth and stared down at him. "We still have some clothes on," she whispered in the silence of the room.

He shifted his body, placed her beneath him and then leaned up and began removing her bra. The moment he uncovered her breasts, his senses jolted and desire slammed into him. They were high, sensuously shaped with protruding dark-tipped nipples that seemed to beg for his tongue. There was no way he could resist.

He cupped a breast in his hand as his mouth greedily latched onto it and began devouring it with deep male appreciation and far-reaching primitive hunger, trying to pull all the sweetness out of it. A rapturous gasp tore from deep within her throat, and moments later, when she shuddered and cried out his name, he was amazed that she had climaxed just from him kissing her breasts.

Good. It would make what he intended to do next even more enjoyable for the both of them. He pulled back slightly, ran his hands down her thighs, fingering the edge of her lace panties. He touched her there in the center and found the fabric damp. He was definitely grateful for that.

Without wasting any time, he removed her panties and then just as quickly he leaned back and removed his own underwear. He looked at her and immediately thought of a chocolate sundae, his favorite treat. He leaned forward and began nuzzling the soft skin of her flat stomach, licking the area around her navel. Her feminine scent surrounded him, making his body harden even more.

"Tag, what are you doing?" she asked, barely able to get the words out.

He lifted his mouth long enough to say, "I'm about to eat you alive, sweetheart. You look beautiful, sexy and delicious." As soon as those words left his mouth he eased his head between her open legs and captured her with his mouth, kissing her there.

"Tag!"

He didn't let up and when she began squirming beneath his mouth, he gripped her hips to keep her still as his tongue continued to devour her in this very intimate way. The succulent taste of her pushed him over the edge and made him even greedier, as desire rocketed through his veins, making him growl low in his throat.

He felt her feminine muscles suddenly clench beneath his mouth and then she came and his tongue savored each and every orgasmic vibration that filled him with more of her taste. She rocked her pelvis upward at the same time as she screamed out his name again.

Before she could catch her next breath, he quickly put on a condom and then eased his body over hers, positioning his erection right smack against her satiny flesh, settling his hips in the cradle between her thighs.

"Open your eyes and look at me, Renee."

Their eyes met and the glaze of stark passion he saw there filled him with male satisfaction. "Don't see color when you look at me," he whispered huskily as he began easing inside of her. "Don't think of social status when you feel me inside of you," he continued, his voice rough and low. "Think of passion, desire. Think of me…the man who wants you."

He continued going deeper into her, holding her gaze. "Say my name, baby."

Renee bit her lip, trying to stop the fears of the future from overtaking her mind. She knew if she said his name now, when they were like this, it would become embedded in her soul forever. He had already found a way into her heart, but to take part of her soul…

"Say it."

Tag tilted his head up and stared down at her. He was

buried deeply inside of her, to the hilt. He hadn't wanted to hurt her but she had been so tight and entering her hadn't been easy. He held still, refusing to move his hips until she acknowledged that what they were sharing was passion between a man and a woman, and color and social status had nothing to do with it. On this point he was determined to be of one accord with her. In a voice that was lower still, he whispered, "Speak my name."

Renee dug her fingers into his back, unable to fight it any longer. He was so intensely male that she knew who he was and what he was to her, whether she wanted to admit it or not. She would admit it but on her own terms. "Speak mine," she countered.

He stared at her and smiled and brushed his fingertips against her cheek. "Renee," he said huskily.

The caress was so tender that she fell deeper in love with him at that precise moment. "Tag." And as every cell in her body vibrated in response to his touch, she said his name again. "Tag."

He leaned down and buried his face in the curve of her neck, holding her close to him. Now that they had put things into prospective, at least for the time being, Tag began moving inside of her, mating with her in a way he'd never done with another woman. He felt the quivering deep in her womb with each and every push and pull. He feasted on her mouth, on her breasts while he increased the pressure, multiplied the thrusts and enhanced their bodies' rhythm.

Moments later when she flew apart, he was flying right along with her. A release, of a magnitude he had never before experienced, ripped from him, shattering him to a degree that made his thighs quake. The low, guttural sound from his throat was necessary to keep the veins from popping in his neck when he threw his head back. He was worshipping her body, claiming her as his.

And he knew when another climax suddenly rammed through him, to piggyback with the first, that no matter what protests Renee might continue to make about them pursuing a relationship, there was no way he could ever let her go.

"I don't want to leave you tonight," Tag's dark-velvet voice murmured softly against Renee's ear, bringing her awake.

She opened her eyes and gazed up into his deep-blue ones and gave him a sleepy smile as she thought of all they had done together for the past few hours. "Then don't."

"Is that an invitation?" he asked, leaning down and kissing her jaw, savoring the line around her lips with his tongue.

Renee's senses immediately responded. "Yes," she purred against his lips. "That's an invitation."

She wrapped her arms around his neck and parted her mouth to welcome his strong, hot tongue that started seducing her all over again, sucking her very breath. At the same time his hand traveled down her naked body to the apex of her thighs. Within minutes he had her writhing and moaning into his mouth.

He slowly lifted his lips from hers and his gaze roamed over her face as he pulled a shuddering breath into his lungs. "I can't get enough of you, Renee. It's like you're entrenched within every pore in my body."

She watched as he stood to pull another condom from his wallet and swiftly roll it into place. When he returned to the bed she held his gaze as he slid his body over hers once more, her thighs automatically opening for him. Like dry tinder, her body ignited when joined to his, and she could feel the tension building inside of her as she raced forward, fast and furious, toward the release he was driving her to.

Moments later she screamed his name, as she felt herself shattering into a thousand pieces. He continued his intimate strokes, withholding his release with iron-clad control while pushing deeper and deeper still. Ecstasy seized her once again and a sensuous cry tore from her lips at the same time she felt him buck and call out her name.

Tag continued to murmur her name repeatedly and it sounded like music to her ears. She slid her hands up over the tense muscles of his back, kneading them as she savored the slow aftermath of what they were sharing. A part of her knew it was time to start pulling back. She was falling in love with him even more and was beginning to need him too desperately.

She knew if she didn't start thinking straight that she would find herself in deep trouble, but at that moment the only thing she wanted to think about was Teagan Elliott, what he meant to her and how he was making her feel.

Seven

Tag slowly began waking just as the first light of morning shone into the room. He breathed in deeply as Renee's sensuous, womanly scent was drawn into his nostrils.

Shifting his body, he glanced over at the empty spot in the bed but relaxed at the sound of the shower. He looked at the clock. It was a little past six. He sprawled on his back and threw one arm across his face to ward off the daylight that was coming through the window blinds. Instinctively, he ran a tongue over his top lip and discovered the taste of Renee was still there, and without any control he released a groan of pleasure at the memory.

Last night had been special to him in many ways and even now his body was exhausted, drained from spent passion. But if she were to walk out of the bathroom, he would be revived and want her all over again.

But by no means, regardless of how sexually compatible they were, did he think what they were sharing was all about sex and nothing more. He had been there with other women, but this thing with Renee was different. He sighed as an unexplainable sensation began developing deep within his chest and a breath he hadn't realized he'd been holding forced its way from his lungs. He wasn't sure what any of this meant but he did know that no matter what problems she thought they had, they would work them out because he had never wanted a woman like he wanted Renee.

With that thought in mind he shifted back on his stomach, buried his head into the pillow and slowly drifted off to sleep again.

Renee adjusted the shower cap on her head as she stood beneath the spray of water. The soreness in her thighs and the area between her legs were a blatant reminder of how long it had been since she had made love to a man, and never with the intensity of what she had shared with Tag.

She had lost count of the number of times they had come together during the night, but each time the pleasure had intensified even more. She had slept with only two other men in her lifetime, a guy she'd dated in college and Dionne. Neither had had the time or the inclination to prolong their lovemaking, and would never have considered withholding their own pleasure to make sure that she soared to the highest peak.

But Tag had.

He had proven there wasn't a selfish bone in his body when it had come to pleasuring her, and no woman could ask for more than that. The thought of everything he'd done made her quiver, deep down in her womb.

She sighed deeply. It was a new day and with it came all the insecurities of yesterday. Nothing had changed. He was white and she was black; he was rich and she was a working girl. But none of that could stop her from thinking about how right he had looked in her bed when she'd slipped out of it, being careful not to wake him. Although it was Friday, it was a busy workday for her, but Tag had a position within his family's company where he could make his own hours, and since he hadn't gotten much sleep last night, there was no telling when he would wake up.

Turning off the water, she stepped out of the shower. She had meetings most of the day and couldn't afford to be late. She would be as quiet as she could while dressing for work. She wasn't used to having a houseguest, especially one like Tag.

Tag awoke with a jolt at the sound of a car backfiring. He sat up and glanced at the empty spot in the bed beside him and saw the note pinned to the pillow.

I had to leave for work. Thanks for everything last night. Renee.

A smile touched his lips. She was always thanking him whether he wanted her to or not. But in this case it should be him thanking her. Everything they had shared had been special and he had gotten the best sleep he had in a long time, ever since that outrageous feud between the magazines and his mother's bout with cancer.

Last night he and Renee had shared a night of passion but he wondered what her thoughts were today. Would she allow their relationship to move to the next level without making a big deal out of things? Maybe it was pure possessiveness on his part, but he didn't intend to wait around for her to call the shots. He wanted to be with her, to continue to share this special relationship with her and he refused to let her end things between them before they got started. Somehow he had to show her that with them, color and social status didn't matter. And he intended to start doing so today.

Getting out of bed, he crossed the room to dig his cell phone out of his pants pocket. Within minutes he had his secretary on the line. "Joanne, clear my calendar of any appointments and meetings this morning. I won't be coming in before noon. And tell Gannon to call me the minute he gets back from his meeting with Rick Howard."

He then placed a call to his father to check on his mother. The news wasn't too uplifting. His mother was still withdrawn, not very talkative and still wasn't ready to see her children.

Sighing deeply, he then placed a call to a florist and ordered a dozen red roses to be delivered to Renee. And last but not least, he dialed the phone number for his good friend Alton Malone.

"Hey, Al, this is Tag. That painting you had displayed at Hollis on Saturday, I want it."

He smiled when his friend joked about Tag having enough of his paintings already. "It's not for me but for someone I've met. Someone special."

Tag laughed when he heard Alton pretend to be gasping for breath. Like Tag's siblings, Alton knew how limited his time was when it came to indulging in affairs. "Okay, knock it off, and yes, I think she's special. I think she's very special."

Renee leaned back in her chair and stared at the vase of flowers that had arrived that day. To say they were beautiful would be an understatement, and it didn't take long for word to get around the office that Renee Williams, the quiet, keeps-to-herself social worker who never dated, must have finally found a boyfriend since she had gotten flowers—and a dozen long-stem red roses at that.

She was glad she had taken off the card and inserted it into her desk drawer before Diane had breezed into her office to see the flowers that everyone was whispering about. Diane had looked high and low for the card, evidently feeling she had every right to read it.

But as far as Renee was concerned, it was a card meant for her to read in private, and since she had a few moments alone now, she pulled it out of her desk and reread Tag's words.

Last night meant more to me than you'll ever know. Have dinner with me tonight so I can thank you properly. Tag.

Renee sighed. According to Vicki, Tag had called twice while she had been in meetings. More than likely he wanted to confirm that she would be free to go out to dinner with him tonight.

She stood and went to the window. Although there was no way she would regret what she shared with Tag last night, a part of her knew it may have sent him the wrong message. Her thoughts and feelings on them dating hadn't changed. She wished things could be different but they weren't and she had accepted that. If only he would.

She turned when the phone rang on her desk and quickly crossed the room to pick it up. "Yes, Vicki?"

"Mr. Teagan Elliott is on the line for you."

Renee briefly closed her eyes, inhaled deeply. "All right, please put him through." Her legs felt weak as she eased into the chair behind her desk.

"Renee."

She swallowed upon hearing the sound of her name from Tag's lips, those same lips he had used to make love to her. His skill and virility in the bedroom surpassed anything she'd ever known. "Yes, Tag, it's Renee."

"How are you feeling?"

She knew why he was asking. No woman made love as many times as they had last night without feeling some discomfort. But then a part of her didn't mind the discomfort. The pleasure she had received had made any discomfort well worth it. "I'm feeling okay, and you?"

"I feel better than I've felt in a long time and you're the reason."

She nervously licked her lips as she glanced across

the room at the flowers. "Thanks for the roses. They're beautiful."

"And so are you. I don't think there's an inch on your body that isn't beautiful."

Abruptly she flushed and moved her gaze away from the flowers, remembering just how much of her body he had seen, touched, tasted. Red-hot embers swiftly flickered to life within her, forcing her to remember every moment, every intimate detail. "Tag, I don't think…" Her voice trailed off. The fact of the matter was that at the moment she couldn't think. She could only remember, and the memories were overwhelming her.

"Have dinner with me tonight, Renee. I want to take you someplace special."

She leaned back in the chair and closed her eyes. "Tag, I don't think that's a good idea."

"And I happen to think it's a wonderful idea, unless…"

Involuntarily, she reopened her eyes. "Unless what?"

"Unless you're ashamed to be seen with me."

She sat straight up in her chair. "That's not it and you know it," she defended stubbornly. "I have been seen with you. I was with you last Saturday and again last night."

"But I don't consider those real dates. I want to take you out to dinner and dancing."

"But I've told you that I don't think it's a good idea for us to take things further," she implored, desperately needing for him to understand. Why couldn't he get it that they were from two different worlds in more ways than one?

"Too late, sweetheart. We've already taken things

further. In my book they can't get any further then they got last night. You might chalk it up to merely a night of passion, a night we lost our heads to lust, but I consider it something more solid and substantial. If you don't think so, then I need to convince you otherwise. Don't try to make what we shared last night nothing more than casual and fun. It *was* more and you know it."

Renee bowed her head. Yes, she knew it. She also knew something else that he didn't know. She loved him.

"Have dinner with me tonight, Renee. Please."

Renee lifted her head. What would it hurt if she had dinner with him? Maybe she could use that time to convince him there were too many issues facing them in a relationship. And then there was the fact that she did want to be with him, share time with him, make love to him again, even though she shouldn't.

"All right. I'll have dinner with you."

"Great! I'll make reservations on board the Harbor."

Renee swallowed. The Harbor wasn't just any dinner cruise ship. It was one that sailed down the Hudson River while catering to the affluent. She'd heard that you had to be a member of the private club to even step on deck, and that the prices were so high she'd never go there in her lifetime and definitely not on her budget. "The Harbor? It's still running, even in February?"

"As long as the weather cooperates, it sails. And I'd like you and I to be on it. What do you say?"

Renee exhaled. How could she possibly tell him no? "Okay."

"And I'll pick you up around seven. Is that time all right?"

"Yes, seven is fine."

"Good. I'll see you then."

Moments after hanging up the phone, Renee couldn't help wondering if she had gotten in deeper than she should have. After all, the deeper she got, the harder it would be to eventually walk away.

Tag glanced first at Gannon then back at Marlene Kingston, not knowing exactly what to say. He'd had a hunch that Senator Denton's resignation hadn't been as benign as it seemed. "And you're sure about this, Marlene? Can we trust our sources?" Tag was well aware how the use of anonymous sources by news organizations had been under heightened scrutiny over the past year.

"Yes, more than you can guess. Here's the name," she said, handing him a sheet of paper.

Tag took the paper and glanced at it, then raised a brow before passing it on to Gannon. After reading it, Gannon whistled. The name on the paper was that of the senator's niece. "This is definitely a strictly confidential source. How did you manage it?"

Marlene smiled. "Jeanette and I attended classes together at Georgetown. Once I started asking questions she broke down and told me everything. She's a highly ethical person and over the years found anomalies in the Senator's behavior that she didn't approve of. She's always felt compelled to keep quiet, but this last thing was the final straw. As you can see, we have a reliable story here, Tag. And what's even more special is that it seems *Time* doesn't even have a clue, which gives us an advantage."

Tag sighed. Marlene's source indicated that Senator Denton had participated in a cover-up in the worse possible way and it was up to *Pulse* to report it. Not only did the American people have a right to know but Tag knew what being the first to print the article would do for sales. It would definitely put *Pulse* ahead in his grandfather's competition game. Big headlines brought in readers, and readers drove the profits up.

Gannon stood and rubbed a hand down his face. "We're going to have to have all our ducks in a row for this one. Senator Denton is well-liked and highly respected, and a cover-up of this magnitude will cause one hell of a scandal. But I want *Pulse* to be the one to expose it."

Tag smiled, feeling the adrenaline rush he'd always experienced when they were on the verge of breaking a story. Top that off with his dinner date tonight with Renee and he felt like a man riding high above the clouds.

"I'll finalize my report and have it on Peter's desk by Monday," Marlene said, interrupting his thoughts.

Tag shook his head. "No. This is going to be your story. You're doing all the digging and the Senator's niece is your contact. You write the article."

Gannon nodded in agreement. "Where the hell is Peter, anyway?"

"He's still at lunch," Marlene said, gathering up all her papers to put in her briefcase.

After Marlene had left, Tag looked over at Gannon and said, "We're going to have to do something about Peter. He knew about this meeting."

Gannon was about to respond when the phone on his desk rang. He quickly picked it up when he saw it was

his private line. Tag, who figured the caller was probably
Erika and didn't want to intrude on his brother's private
conversation, strolled across the room to look out the
window. It was a beautiful day, and seeing all the red paper hearts being displayed in the store window across the
street reminded him that Tuesday was Valentine's Day.

"That was Dad."

Tag turned and met his brother's smiling face. Evidently their father had called with good news. "And?"

Gannon grinned. "He called to say that Erika talked
to Mom and she agreed to help out with the wedding."
Gannon's smile widened even more when he added,
"Dad also wanted me to tell you, Liam and Bridget that
Mom wants to see us on Sunday for dinner."

A smile broke on Tag's face. Although Renee had explained to him what his mother was going through, it
hadn't been easy to be shut out by her. "Hey, that's
great!"

Gannon chuckled. "Yes, it is, and we have Renee to
thank for helping us come up with a plan to boost
Mom's spirit. Thank her when you see her again."

Tag lifted a curious brow. "And what makes you
think I'll see her again?"

Gannon met Tag's stare and grinned. "You will. I saw
the way you were looking at her at dinner the other
night. You are definitely interested in her. I like her and
you're right, she's beautiful."

Tag absently picked up a paper clip on his brother's
desk and said, "I'm taking her out tonight. To the Harbor." He was excited about his and Renee's official date
and didn't mind sharing it with his brother.

Gannon raised a brow as he leaned back in his chair. "The Harbor? So, I'm right in assuming you're interested in her."

Tag moved toward the door and slid his brother a parting glance. "Yes, I'm definitely interested."

From where Renee was standing at her bedroom window she could see a silver-gray Mercedes sports car stop in front of her apartment building. The way her heart began beating she knew it was a different vehicle but the same man.

Tag.

She couldn't help standing there, watching as he exited from the vehicle. He said he would be by to pick her up at seven but for some reason she'd known he would arrive a few minutes early.

She couldn't help but study him as he made his way to her apartment door, his stride long, his steps hurried, unusual for a man who wasn't late getting to where he was going. He wore a black suit and even from where Renee stood she could tell it was made from the highest quality fabric and probably had a designer name attached to it. Tag had Hollywood good looks and watching him was forcing her to participate in one hell of a mind exercise.

Suddenly, as if sensing that he was being watched, Tag glanced up and their eyes connected and Renee felt it, just as surely as if he had been able to defy logic and actually reach up and touch her. He smiled and goose bumps began to rise on her arms, her heart literally skipped a beat, and when he waved up at her, she couldn't do anything but lift her hand and wave back. Turning away from the window, she braced herself for the man who was doing a good job of rocking her world.

Moments later she stood in front of the door, her stomach knotting, her breasts becoming sensitive, a tender ache in certain muscles. Forcing herself to get a grip, she opened the door.

Whatever Renee had expected, it hadn't been Tag sweeping her into his arms and closing the door behind him with the heel of his shoe and then hungrily capturing her mouth, locking it with his as if joining them with some kind of magnetic force, immediately driving her mad with desire. She wrapped her arms around him and whimpered, the sound quickly drowned out by their heavy breathing.

Renee quickly came to the conclusion that she could go without dinner if she could remain here and feast on Tag. When he finally released her mouth and placed her back on her feet, she pressed her face into his chest, thinking that no one had ever kissed her hello quite that way before.

She looked up at him when she felt his hand glide through her hair, and then he was lifting her chin up and leaning down for yet another kiss. There was no way she could not respond to this. To him. Whether she wanted it to or not, loving him was taking her beyond any boundaries she wanted to set. When it came to Tag there were no limitations, but she had a feeling there was unchartered territory that he planned for them to explore. Together.

"I thought of you a lot today," he said, his voice

strained. As he whispered against her ear, his tongue flicked out to taste her skin there.

"And I thought of you a lot today, too," she replied honestly. She hated herself for admitting such a thing but knew she had to admit it anyway.

Slowly, he took a step back and looked at her and then he captured her hand in his, held it above her head and twirled her around, letting the ruffles at the hem of her black dress swirl about her ankles. "You look gorgeous tonight, Renee."

She knew he meant every word and was glad that she had left the office early to do a little shopping. "Thanks."

He took a step closer to her and leaned down and kissed her slowly, thoroughly. Moments later, Renee slipped from his arms. "If we don't leave now we might be late," she said, her pulse racing fast and furiously.

Tag smiled. "You're right. But then I'll have something to look forward to after dinner, won't I?"

Renee swallowed as she nodded. She would have something to look forward to after dinner as well.

The Harbor was a beautiful dinner cruise ship and the moment they stepped on deck via a heated tented walkway, a uniformed waiter escorted them to their table in the Tropicana Room.

Renee glanced around, tempted to pinch herself. This was a new ship and everything looked elegant and expensive, including the marble floors and crown molding. Tag squeezed her hand and smiled down at her. "I hope you like the setting."

She gave him an assuring grin. "Trust me, I do."

They were shown to a white-linen-covered table with a huge glass window that provided a panoramic view of the Hudson. After handing them menus, the waiter left them alone just as the ship began moving. Soft music was playing and not far away a dance floor was set up for dancing later. Muted conversation filled the rooms as hosts and hostesses escorted other arrivals to their tables.

Renee had never been on a cruise before and when she felt the movement of the ship she planted her feet firmly on the floor. "I can't believe we're actually moving," she said nervously.

Tag chuckled. "We are. We'll be out on the Hudson for a couple of hours or so."

She nodded. "You come here often?"

He smiled at her. "I've dined here a number of times with various members of my family." And then, because he wanted her to know just how special tonight was to him, Tag added, "But this is the first time I've ever brought a date here."

Renee opened her mouth, then immediately closed it when nothing came out. The thought that she was the first made her entire body tingle in appreciation, blatantly ignoring the warning signs of what doing so could mean. "Thank you," she said politely.

His smile widened. "You're always thanking me."

"Because you're always doing something nice."

He leaned forward in his chair and whispered, "Can't help it with you. You bring out the best in me."

"And I'm supposed to believe that?" she asked, chuckling.

"I hope you do because it's the truth."

At that moment the waiter returned with a bottle of wine. "I asked for a bottle to be brought out before our meal so we can toast my good news," Tag told her.

Renee lifted a brow. "And what good news is that?" She could tell he'd been in a rather good mood but he hadn't shared the reason for it her during the car ride from her apartment. Instead he had told her how his day had gone at work and she shared tidbits about hers.

"Good news about Mom. Dad called to tell us that she has agreed to help Erika with her wedding and that she also wants to see all of us on Sunday for dinner."

Renee's face beamed with happiness. She knew how much his mother's depression had bothered Tag. "Oh, Tag, that's wonderful! It will take her concentration off her condition and put it on something else. I told you that planning Erika's wedding would do wonders for her."

"Yes, you did tell us, didn't you? And Gannon asked me to thank you for all the advice you gave to us last night. We will be forever in your debt."

For some reason the thought of Tag thinking he owed her something didn't sit well with Renee. "Neither you nor your family owes me anything, Tag. Like I told all of you that night, I like your mother, I think she's a special person and I empathized with all of you. I just wanted to help."

That was exactly what he found so special about Renee. She had such a sweet spirit about her and a passionate spirit as well, judging from last night. The memory of them coming apart in each other's arms was etched deep into his brain.

He had a lot going on in his life with his mother and work, but he couldn't imagine not carving out this time to spend with Renee. "Let's make a toast," he said, lifting his glass. "To my mother's continued good health."

Renee held up her glass to his. "Yes, to Karen's continued good health."

Renee thought that everything about tonight was perfect. The man, the cruise down the Hudson River and the cozy atmosphere. Over dinner they talked more about his mother, his grandfather's outlandish proposal and he provided tidbits on his other family members, especially all the cousins he was close to. It was the information on his grandfather that intrigued her the most.

"Things will work out, Tag, I'm sure of it. From everything you've told me, family means a lot to your grandfather. I can't imagine him doing anything to intentionally destroy that. There must be a reason for what you and your family see as his madness. I've discovered in life that things aren't always as they seem to be."

Tag wondered if she felt that way about them. He clearly remembered what she'd told him that day in her office. Still, she had agreed to go out with him tonight, and he hoped that last night meant as much to her as it did to him. Was she willing for them to give things a try? He was convinced they should continue to see each other, but knew convincing her of that wouldn't be easy. But he would not give up.

"Would you like dessert?" he asked, after the waiter had returned to clear their table. The river was beautiful and the cruise was setting the mood for romance. During several lulls in their conversation, heat and desire had surrounded them. He had felt it and knew that she had felt it, too.

Renee smiled. "No. I doubt that I could eat a single thing more. Everything was delicious, Tag. Thanks for bringing me here."

"It was my pleasure. Would you like to dance?"

Renee heard the soft, slow music and had been noticing several couples move on the dance floor during different times all night. She'd always liked dancing but couldn't remember the last time she'd done so. Dionne had never taken her out dancing. His idea of a good date was her preparing him dinner at her place. Since their breakup she had analyzed their relationship and knew exactly where they had gone wrong. In Dionne's mind he had been the king and she had been his queen who was supposed to cater to his every whim.

"Renee?"

Tag's voice pulled her thoughts from the past. She smiled. "Yes, Tag, I'll dance with you."

Moments later Tag led her out on the dance floor among all the other couples. She could feel a lot of eyes on them but at the moment she didn't care. All she wanted to think about was Tag, and being surrounded by his kindness, his strength and his warmth. And when he gathered her in his arms, every reason she thought they couldn't be together like this floated from her mind. When he pulled her even closer she seemed to melt against him and an involuntary shudder passed through her body.

"You're cold?" he asked, leaning down and whispering the question in her ear.

She shook her head. "No, I'm not cold." There was no way she could tell him that she was just the opposite. Her insides were burning up with a heat that she'd recently discovered only he could generate.

Renee shifted her attention away from Tag to the dining area filled with smartly dressed couples enjoying their meals. Her gaze lit on one couple in particular when the woman leaned over and whispered something in her husband's ear before turning back and staring at Renee and Tag, frowning deeply. She could only imagine what the woman said since her husband was now staring at them with an equally fierce and disapproving look. Evidently they didn't approve of interracial dating.

Not wanting to see their scornful glares anymore, Renee turned and buried her face in Tag's chest and he pulled her tighter to him as the music swirled around them. She refused to let anyone put a damper on things. Tonight was her and Tag's night and she intended to enjoy it.

She sighed contentedly when she felt his warm and tender hands move from around her waist to the center of her back. He leaned down and began humming the tune that the band was playing. She thought he had one hell of a sexy voice.

The ship made its way to shore and after a couple more dances he took her hand in his. He brought it to his lips. "I hope you enjoyed your evening, Renee."

A quiver passed through her. "I did. Everything was perfect."

He smiled. His gaze was intent when he said, "You

were the most perfect thing here tonight and I'm proud that you were with me and no one else."

Renee couldn't help but smile. If he was using all his skill at that moment to set her up for seduction later, he was doing a good job of it. "And I'm glad I'm here tonight with you, as well."

His gaze held hers for a long moment before he took her hand and led her through the crowd. "I want us to be the first ones off this ship," he said, leading her back to the table. "Our night is far from over yet and with tomorrow being Saturday, just imagine all the possibilities."

She did imagine them and doing so only made her fall in love with him that much more.

Eight

Renee sank into the soft leather cushions of Tag's sofa and focused her gaze on him. He was standing across the room in front of a wall-to-wall entertainment system, and the moment he'd pressed a button, soft jazz music filled the air surrounding them.

She glanced around and saw a number of Alton Malone paintings on his wall as well as paintings from other artists. All beautiful. All expensive. But then his condo, being in Tribeca, had to be up there in the high price range. The wine oak furniture was tasteful and blended well with the modern contemporary decor.

Besides the framed Malone paintings, the living room was decorated with several Asian figurines. Tag had indicated they had been gifts from the Watari Museum in Tokyo after he had done an article about it in *Pulse* a few years ago.

Tag had given her a brief tour of the downstairs but hadn't bothered showing her where his bedroom was. She was rather anxious to see it but when the time was right tonight, there was no doubt in her mind that she would.

Given the heat that had generated off them, between them and with them all evening, a visit to his bedroom was inevitable. After what they had shared last night, she was looking forward to it.

When he had whisked her away from the docks and into his car he had asked if she would like to spend a little time over at his place. She had come close to refusing, remembering the cold, disapproving look the couple had given them on board the ship, but then had decided that tonight she wanted to spend as much time with Tag as possible, and when he took her home later she would explain to him why they couldn't see each other again.

"Would you like something to drink?"

He reclaimed her attention and she met his gaze. Her breath caught. The lamp's light seemed to enhance the vividness of his eyes and the blue was so deep that for a moment it seemed like she was drowning in the ocean. "No, I don't want anything to drink."

"And what do you want?"

Renee was silent. There wasn't an answer she felt comfortable in saying out loud. The silence that drifted between them was tangible, as potent and hot as the very air they were breathing. It didn't take much to recall last night and the way his body had taken hers, had gone deep inside of her, thrusting in and out. Then there was his mouth that had acquainted her with a warm, succulent sweetness that would have her licking her lips for days, nights. And last but not least was the memory of his hands and the way they had glided over her skin, touching places that made ripples of sensation start deep in her abdomen and spread to other parts of her body.

"Renee?"

She continued to hold his gaze, hearing the sound of his voice, strained, husky and filled with something else. Urgency. Need. "Why don't you find out what I want," she said softly, invitingly. She then deliberately took the tip of her tongue and traced her lips, knowing what watching her was doing to him.

She licked steadily as she stared into his tense face. Blatant need shone in the depths of his eyes. Her gaze moved lower, past his tightly muscled stomach to the crotch of his pants, and she saw the erection that strained against the zipper. She suddenly felt hot, and the ventilation from the air conditioning was doing nothing to cool off her heated flesh.

"I think I will."

She shifted her gaze back up to his face as he slowly moved toward her with a smile that sent her pulse racing. "You will what? Find out what I want?"

"No, seduce you into telling me."

Instead of joining her on the sofa he pulled her up and settled her body against his, to feel his hardness. Eyes locked to hers, he whispered huskily, "I want you, Renee."

"And I want you, too, Tag."

As if her words were the go-ahead he had been waiting for, he leaned down and his mouth covered hers in a hungry, desperate, ravenous kiss that had Renee moaning in need when he abruptly ended it.

Questioning eyes met his and he smiled and reached out and tenderly caressed her cheek. "I want you to tell me what you want, sweetheart. Your wish will be my command."

Renee drew in a ragged breath, not being able to imagine such a thing. She'd never had anyone cater exclusively to her needs while they made love. She'd never met anyone like Tag before. Telling him what she wanted and him actually carrying out each and every fantasy she had was an incredibly erotic thought.

"Tell me," he repeated.

She met his gaze and said, "For starters, take me to your bedroom and undress me."

Renee saw his blue eyes go hot just seconds before he bent and gathered her into his arms to carry her up the stairs. Her stomach quivered with the excitement of what would happen when they got to his bedroom. Even now, while they were in motion, she caught his scent. Masculine. Robust. Sexy.

When they entered his bedroom she glanced around. His bed, king-sized with a black platinum steel frame, sat in the center of the room with matching nightstands on each side. A dresser and chest were on the other side of the room. The bedroom reminded her of Tag. Neat, manly and with everything in order.

"Now to remove this dress."

He lowered her down his body and immediately went to work at removing her dress, easing down the zipper as his fingers grazed the warm flesh of her bare back. She wasn't wearing a bra. He moved the soft fabric down her shoulders to drop in a heap at her feet, his gaze locked on the breasts he had grown quite fond of the night before.

"Taste them again, Tag."

She didn't have to ask twice. His tongue flicked out and captured a budding nipple into his mouth. When he heard her moan and felt her knees weaken, he reached out and caught her by the waist. He remembered the orgasm she had the last time he had made love to her breasts, but this time he wanted to prolong her enjoyment, make her want him as much as he wanted her.

He gathered her into his arms and carried her over to the bed and placed her on her back, then lifted her hips to slide the panty hose and thong off of her. Driven by a desire whose depth he couldn't understand, he felt compelled to touch her and instinctively his fingers went to the damp curls between her legs.

She closed her eyes as he focused his concentration on pleasuring her with fingers that stroked her mercilessly. He watched as her lips parted slightly and she moaned out her gratification, while her heavy breathing pleaded with him to quench her desire.

"Too soon, sweetheart," he said, pulling back to remove his own clothes.

When she opened her eyes to watch him they were hot, dark and dilated. He didn't waste time as he tore off his shirt and eased his pants down his legs. With his gaze still locked with hers, he began removing his briefs and once he stood naked in front of the bed, her concentration shifted from his face down to his erection.

"Tell me what you want now," he said, his control almost shot to hell. Anticipation was killing him but he was determined to give her everything she wanted.

"I want you inside of me," she whispered before lying back on his thick bedspread.

The darkness of her skin was a stark contrast to the beige coverlet and he thought it was a breathtaking sight. Not wanting to waste any more time, he quickly pulled a condom out of his nightstand drawer. He kept them there although he'd never used them since Renee was the first woman he'd ever brought home with him. Before, it had been his companion's place or no place. He always considered his condo private and never wanted the memory of a woman's presence there. But with Renee he felt differently. He wanted her memory. He wanted her presence. Point-blank, he wanted her.

He knelt beside her on the bed, eager to join their bodies. He took her mouth again in a deep, hungry kiss, the only kind he shared with her. He knew he had to make love to her right then and pulled back to position his body over hers, and just like the contrast of her skin with his bedspread, he noted the same distinction with his skin. The only word he could think to describe the difference in their coloring was *beautiful.*

He broke off the kiss and looked down into her dark brown eyes. "Ready, sweetheart?"

She smiled up at him. "Only for you."

Her words, whispered seductively, released a surge of heat within him, and clenching his teeth he entered her in one smooth thrust. He breathed in deeply, inhaling her body's sensuous scent, and she arched her back, taking him deeper still, clutching him tightly with her womanly muscles, just as she'd done the last time. And just as before, he could only take so much of her agonizing torture.

Tag felt himself on the brink of tumbling over the edge and knew he had to move. He began setting a rhythm, first by starting a slow rocking motion and then thrusting in and out of her, glorying in the perfect fit they made. With each surge into her body he stoked the fires blazing between them and with each retreat he rekindled them all over again. All he could concentrate on was the woman beneath him, how they seemed made for each other. He called out her name each and every time her muscles clenched pleasure out of him, demanding he give more.

And he did.

An orgasm so intense that it shook his entire body tore through him the exact moment she screamed his name and her body bucked beneath him. He suddenly lost awareness of everything except Renee.

With one last hard thrust, he groaned as he felt her shudder beneath him.

As ecstasy slowly gave way to sweet contentment, he shifted his body, but remained buried deep inside of her, not ready to sever their intimate connection. They faced each other, gazed into each other's eyes as each of their limbs slowly became warm, heavy, pleasured.

Tag looked at her in amazement, thinking that Renee Williams was definitely what dreams were made of. He leaned closer and gently kissed her, needing to taste her, to absorb her, to appreciate her. And to thank the powers that had brought this beautiful woman into his life.

After Tag finished getting dressed he turned to watch Renee slip back into her dress. He stared at her for a long, thoughtful moment and a feeling he had never experienced before tugged at his heart, kicking his pulse into high gear.

The passion between them was fiery, breathtaking, but he didn't just want her sexually. He also enjoyed doing things with her, spending time with her, taking her places and sharing his thoughts with her. Tonight over dinner he had told her about his work and the challenges he, his father and brother at *Pulse* were facing trying to compete against the other three magazines. She had listened, hung on to his every word and then she had made several comments that had made him think.

Renee had pointed out that if his grandfather's challenge was making them tense, then imagine what it was doing to the people who worked for them. Were they worried about what would happen to their jobs if the magazine they worked for didn't make a good enough profit? And what changes in the corporate structure would the new CEO make? Changes in corporate dynamics could send workers into a panic and could result in a serious employer-employee relationship problem.

He knew her comments had only been the result of her innate concern for people. She was a person who cared about how people were treated, how a person felt and what a person thought. The latter, he sighed deeply, was the root of their problem, and the very reason she continued to put a roadblock in the way of a developing relationship between them. Tension rippled off him in acknowledging how far apart they still were on the issue of them getting together. They needed to talk.

He leaned against his dresser and watched as she struggled with the zipper on her dress. He liked her outfit. The sexy black dress fit her as if it had been made for her body alone, and the ruffles at the hem showed off a pair of truly gorgeous legs. He felt as though he could stand there and stare at her forever. "Need help?" he finally asked when her attempts at the zipper proved futile.

She shot him a look over her shoulder and smiled. "Only if you'll help me get it up."

He chuckled as he crossed the room to her. "Oh, I think that can be arranged." He easily slid up her zipper then reached around and wrapped his arms around her waist, pulling her back to him, liking the feel of her butt resting against his groin.

"Are you sure I can't convince you to spend the night?" he leaned down and prodded softly in her ear. "I promise to make it worth your while."

Renee sighed deeply and leaned back farther against Tag, luxuriating in the feel of his arms around her. More than anything she wanted to spend the night, to wake up beside him in the morning, like they had the previous night. But she knew that doing so would only make it that much harder to walk away and not look back.

"No, Tag, I don't think my spending the night here will be wise," she said with a shake of her head.

"Why?" he asked, turning her around to face him, although he already knew her argument. But tonight he was ready for it. His gaze locked with hers. "Explain to me why you won't spend the night."

She raised her eyes to the ceiling. "What will your neighbors think when they see me?"

"That I'm one hell of a lucky man."

Renee sighed. Everything about tonight had been beautiful and she didn't want to shatter the enchanted moments, but she had to make him understand. "Not everyone will think that, Tag. There will be some who will not like the fact we're dating."

He frowned and crossed his arms over his chest. "Then I'd say it's their problem and not ours."

Renee shook her head. "What about your family?"

He remembered she had brought up his family before. "I thought I had made things perfectly clear about my family. They don't and won't dictate who I see."

Renee crossed her arms over her own chest and lifted her chin. "No, but they would be concerned. I can't see the public-conscious Elliotts welcoming an African-American into their fold. You even said tonight how your grandfather has always drilled into all of your heads never to do anything unsavory regarding your family name."

Tag's frown deepened. "And you see our dating as unsavory?"

"I don't but there are others who would." She could clearly remember what had happened the last time her name was linked to gossip. It hadn't been a good feeling knowing she was the hot topic of everyone's conversations.

Frustrated, Tag rubbed his hand against the back of his neck. "Don't you think you're blowing this out of proportion, Renee? Almost everywhere you go these days you encounter mixed-race couples. This is New York, for heaven's sake. How about stepping back into the real world and looking around you? Notice the social trend that's evolving. The mainstream of American society isn't concerned about mixed couples anymore. They have a lot more to worry about, like the economy, making sure our country is kept safe, healthy and free. That's what's on their minds, Renee, and not who's crossing racial lines."

"For your information, Teagan Elliott, there are many people in the real world who do care about who's crossing racial lines."

"And you want to give in to them?"

Renee drew her head back and glared up at Tag. "It's not giving in to them."

"Then what do you call it? I like you. You like me. Yet you don't want to date me because of what people might think or say? I call that giving in to a segment of society who can't move on and accept people as people and not attach a color to them."

"Maybe one day things will be different but—"

"I don't want to wait for one day, Renee. The only thing I want is today, this moment. I don't give a damn that your skin is darker than mine. What's important is that I care for you. I want to be with you, get to know you better, spend time with you. And I want you to get to know me. And the more you get to know me the more you'll see that I am my own man. I make my own decisions. I choose my own woman."

He reached out his hand to her. "Will you give me a chance? Will you give *us* a chance?" A smile touched the corners of his lips. "You're a very beautiful woman and personally, I don't think I'm such a bad catch. What do you think?"

At that moment Renee thought her heart would swell over with the love she felt for this man standing before her. She stared into his blue eyes and saw the sincerity shining in their depths. "I think," she said in a somewhat shaky voice as she took the hand he offered, "that you've presented a very good argument."

"And?" he asked, drawing her closer to him. She came to him willingly, which to Tag was a good sign. She smiled while placing her palms against his chest, which, in his book, was another good sign. His heart rate increased and he felt his blood thicken in his veins.

"And," she said, taking another step closer to him, molding her body against his and igniting an inferno within him, "I think that we'll try things your way and see what happens."

"I can tell you what's going to happen," he said in a quiet voice, lowering his head toward hers.

"And just what do you predict?" she asked, rising on tiptoes to meet him.

"I predict that one day we're going to wonder why we even had this argument."

Renee opened her mouth to disagree, but his mouth

came down on hers, effectively kissing away any words she was about to say. Sensation ripped through her when he parted her lips with his tongue and claimed the depths of what awaited him inside.

Moments later he tore his mouth free of hers just long enough to whisper, "Will you stay the night with me?"

"Yes," she murmured through kiss-swollen lips. "I'll stay."

He smiled and kissed her again as his hands eased around to her back and slowly began unzipping the dress that he had zipped up earlier.

Nine

Gannon snapped his fingers in front of Tag's face. "Hey, Tag, are you with us?"

Tag snapped out of his reverie and blinked. He looked first at Gannon and then at Erika, Liam and Bridget. All four had silly grins on their faces at having caught the ever-alert Teagan Elliott daydreaming.

They were sitting in the living room in The Tides, his grandparents' primary place of residence, and where his mother was currently convalescing. As a child he'd loved visiting his grandparents here. Situated on five acres on a bluff above the Atlantic Ocean, the Elliotts' compound had its own private, guarded road. On the estate was the house, a large pool, the pool house, a beautiful English rose garden and a helicopter landing pad. The feature he loved the most was the hand-carved stone staircase that led down the bluff to a private beach with a boat dock. It was from that dock that his father and grandfather had taught him how to sail.

"Tag?"

Hearing his brother speak to him a second time, Tag thought he'd better respond. "Yes, I'm with you guys, although I'm getting bored to tears," he said, smiling. "Talk about something that won't put me to sleep, will you?"

Bridget made a face. "Um, how about if we discuss the fact that you were seen at a Broadway play on Saturday night," she said, tipping a glass of wine to her lips.

Tag rolled his eyes, knowing his sister had gotten her information from Caroline Dutton, a high school friend of hers who was known for her loose lips. Everyone knew Caroline was a chip off the old block since her mother, Lila Dutton, was one of the worst gossips anyone could have the misfortune of knowing. He had run into Caroline at the play on Saturday, and if Bridget knew he had gone to the play then she also knew the person he had taken with him.

"Don't hold your breath for that one." Tag leaned back in his chair and smiled. Waking up beside Renee had been a wonderful experience on Saturday morning. After making love again, they had showered together and then he had taken her home to change clothes.

He had talked her into going to see the *Lion King* and they both enjoyed it immensely. Afterwards, he had taken her back to her place and he had spent the night.

"Your smile is downright sickening, Tag."

His smile widened as he glanced over at Liam. "Is it? Sorry." He knew everyone was curious but he had no intention of sharing the reason for his blissful contentment with anyone.

"Dinner is ready to be served."

Tag stood, grateful for Olive's timely announcement. Olive and her husband, Benjamin, had worked for his grandparents for years as The Tides' main caretakers. Olive, at fifty-five, was the housekeeper and Ben, at fifty-seven, was the groundskeeper. Both ran their own staffs and kept things orderly.

"When will Mother be coming down?" he hung back and asked when the others had left the room.

"She's on her way now," Olive said, smiling brightly. "Whoever's idea it was for her to help with Gannon and Erika's wedding definitely had the right idea. Her mood has improved dramatically."

Tag was glad to hear that. He had been worried that at some point she might start withdrawing again. "I'm anxious to see her." He hadn't seen her since before she'd been released from the hospital.

"And I know she's anxious to see all of you as well. The last few weeks have been difficult for her."

Tag shook his head. "When do you expect my grandparents to return?" He knew they had taken a pleasure trip to Florida to meet with other couples that belonged to the Irish American Historical Society.

"By the end of next week, in time for Gannon's wedding and to get things ready for their anniversary dinner. They call every day to check how your mom is doing and be sure she gets all the rest she needs before she begins her chemotherapy treatments."

Tag sighed and traced his hand down his face. He

tried not to think about that additional phase in his mother's recovery. When he heard voices he walked out into the foyer and glanced in the direction of the staircase. His parents were standing together on the top stair and whatever his father had told his mother had made her smile.

Although she looked somewhat pale and exhausted, there was a part of her fighting for the sparkle and glow to come through. He'd noticed more than once that his father had the ability to bring out that sparkle by coaxing her into a smile with whatever private words he would tell her.

A part of Tag admired what his parents had shared for over thirty years and for the first time in his life he knew that one day he wanted that same thing for himself. The chance to share his life with someone who would not only be his spouse, but his lover and best friend, as well.

"Come on to the kitchen and leave them alone for a little while longer," Olive whispered in his ear.

Tag nodded and followed Olive into the kitchen.

Tag could only be grateful that his mother was doing as well as she was. In a way, dinner was just like old times when they would all share a meal together. But the one thing that was different was that his father hadn't rushed out in the middle of it, thinking there was something at the office he just had to do. Another thing was that after dinner everyone lingered, not in a hurry to leave, and most importantly, his mother was the center of all their attention and concern.

"So how are things going with you, Tag?" his moth-

er asked, sending him a fond smile as they walked together outside on the grounds, her hand firmly anchored
to his sleeve, her steps slower than usual.

He looked down at her and smiled. "I'm doing better
now that I see that you're doing well." His siblings had
left moments earlier and he had remained, needing this
time alone with his mother. The two of them had always
had a rather close relationship. As a child he'd thought
she was beautiful. He still did. And he'd also been convinced that she was the smartest person in the world
since any advice she'd always given him had been
timely and needed—whether he'd wanted to receive it
or not.

"How are things at the office?" she inquired, evidently feeling the need to break her question down further.

Tag let his lips curve, recognizing her strategy. "Work
is kind of crazy right now and a part of me is angry at
Granddad because of the way things are. Over the years
I've felt more than once that some of the decisions he has
made were based more on keeping up appearances than
putting his family first, but I think this recent antic of his
is a real doozy. I can't imagine what he was thinking. Dad
is the eldest, so when Granddad retires, he should right-
fully become CEO. Everyone expected it, so I just don't
get it."

Karen nodded in understanding. "At the moment
none of us do, Tag. I think Patrick's decision hurt
Michael somewhat, but you know your father. He will
abide by your grandfather's wishes."

Karen stopped walking for a moment and looked up

at Tag, fixing her dark eyes on his. "So now, tell me, how are things going in your personal life?"

Tag was acutely aware that his mother, in her own way, was probing. And although she'd always been curious about his personal life, she'd kept the pointed questions to a minimum. For some reason he felt she was asking out of more than polite curiosity and quickly wondered if someone had mentioned something to her. One of his siblings? His father?

He couldn't help but recall that day in the hospital waiting room when he had referred to Renee by her first name and his father had given him that surprised look. One thing Tag had discovered while growing up was that Michael Elliott was not slow. He caught on quickly. Dismissing the thought that the informant was one of his siblings, Tag concluded his father had said something.

He met his mother's gaze and smiled, deciding to be completely honest, the only way he could be with her. "My personal life is going great, although I was having problems with this certain young lady not taking me seriously, but I've finally convinced her otherwise."

"Is it Renee?"

Tag lifted a brow, knowing it was as he'd suspected. His father *had* told her. His smile widened as he answered, deciding not to question how she knew. It was enough that she did. "Yes, it's Renee. We're seeing each other."

Karen smiled. "She's a beautiful girl and I know firsthand how genuinely caring she is. She helped me through a difficult time and for that I'm most grateful.

There's something so uniquely elegant about her and I can't help but notice how she goes out of her way to help someone. I think she's good for you and that the two of you would make a beautiful couple."

After a brief moment of silence, she said, "Earlier, you mentioned something about Renee not taking you seriously. Does that mean she's not fully accepting of sharing a relationship with you?"

Tag chuckled, thinking that was one way to put it. "She was pretty reluctant at first but she's slowly beginning to thaw. I've gotten her to at least agree to give us a chance to see where things will go. Because we're an interracial couple she's concerned about what people will say."

"The family?"

"Yes, among others. We've garnered our share of frowns and stares whenever we're seen together. I can ignore them a lot better than she can."

Karen nodded. "As far as the family's acceptance, I don't think you'll have any problems, however, you know your grandfather. He can take protecting the family's name to uncompromising heights."

Tag frowned, controlling the quick surge of anger that consumed him at the mere thought. "Yes, and when the time comes I will deal with him about this if I have to. Under no circumstances will I let him, or anyone, dictate how I spend my life and with whom."

Karen looked at her son, feeling his resentment. "I'd like to offer some words of advice, if I may."

"Certainly." Although she had asked, Tag knew she would give her advice anyway.

"Since finding out about my cancer I've discovered just how little time we have on this earth to do the things we want to do, to be with the person or people we want to be with. It's made me realize one very important thing and that is nothing, and I mean nothing—not prestige, power or pride—is worth sacrificing the things that you truly want, the things that you truly love.

"Don't be afraid to take time and smell the roses. Don't hesitate in seeking out those things you hold dear. Seeking them out and holding on to them. And don't ever cease standing up for what you believe in, and fighting for those things that you want. Life is too short. Do what makes you happy, regardless of how others might feel. Do what makes Tag happy."

Tag sighed deeply. He smiled, thinking his mother was still the smart woman he'd always thought her to be. He lifted her hand to his lips. "Thanks for the advice. I intend to take it."

"So, how was your mom?" Renee asked as she sank onto the edge of her sofa. As soon as the phone rang she had gotten this excited feeling in the pit of her stomach. For some reason she had known it would be Tag.

"Considering all she's been through I think her spirits are rather high. Her health seems to be improving each day and she's getting around a lot better."

"That's good."

"And she's excited about the plans for Gannon and Erika's wedding, although she understands they want it to be a small affair with just family. Dad says Mom has been busy on the phone with caterers and florists, and

I can tell just from talking to her that she's really enjoying it."

There was a pause, and then he said, "Mom and I got a chance to spend some time alone and I told her that you and I were seeing each other."

An uneasy shiver crept up Renee's spine. "You did?"

"Yes."

"And what did she say?" she asked, trying to keep her voice even.

"She smiled and said she thought we made a nice couple."

Renee arched her brow. "Was that the only thing she said?"

"No. She also told me how much she liked you and how much you had helped her through a difficult time. She actually thinks you're good for me."

A jitter of happiness shot through Renee. She couldn't help but smile. "Did she really say that?"

"Yes, and those were her exact words."

Renee sighed. "Thanks for sharing that with me."

"I'd like to share a whole lot more."

She shook her head, grinning as she thought of all they'd shared that weekend, especially the intensity with which he had made love to her. "Haven't you shared enough?"

"You haven't seen anything yet. I'd like to make plans for us for this Tuesday night. Would you go out with me?"

"Tuesday?"

"Yes, it's Valentine's Day."

"Oh." She hadn't had a reason to celebrate Valentine's Day in so long that she'd forgotten. "And you want to take me out?"

"Of course. I want to plan a special evening just for you."

Renee shifted her body on the cushions of her sofa. "Are you sure?"

Tag laughed. "Of course I'm sure. There's no one else I'd rather spend such a special day with. Will it be okay to pick you up around seven?"

She sighed deeply, remembering the decision they had made. "Yes, seven will be fine. Any particular way I should dress?"

"It's a semiformal affair. One of my mother's favorite charities, the Heart Association, is holding its annual Heart to Heart Ball."

Renee swallowed. That meant a lot of people would be attending. She was just coming to terms with her decision that she and Tag give things a try. She wasn't sure if she was ready to handle something of this magnitude. Panic rose within her. The last thing she wanted to do was to give people something to talk about. "Tag?"

"Yes, sweetheart?"

His endearment caused a sudden calming effect to settle over her. She would do as she promised and give them a chance. "Nothing. I'll see you on Tuesday."

"I can't wait."

She smiled. "Neither can I. Good-night."

As soon as she ended their call she placed her arms across her stomach when it began to feel tense. No, she wouldn't give in to any panic attacks. For now she would follow her heart and see where it led.

* * *

"So what do you think, Erika?" Tag asked.

Erika pursed her lips and sighed. She glanced across the *Pulse* conference room at Gannon, Tag and Marlene Kingston, then leaned back in her chair and smiled. "I think an excellent job was done with this article and that we should definitely make it our cover story."

Gannon lifted a brow. "In next month's issue?"

Erika shook her head. "No. I suggest we go to a special edition. If we sit on this story we run the risk of *Time* doing it first. You can't convince me that sooner or later someone won't get suspicious about Senator Denton's resignation like we did and start digging."

Tag nodded. "Okay then, we're in agreement," he said excitedly. He turned to Marlene. "And I'll add my kudos to Erika's for a well-written story."

"Thanks," Marlene said beaming. "I appreciate you giving me the opportunity to do it."

After Marlene left, Erika lifted an eyebrow and asked, "Where's Peter?"

Gannon sighed. "I don't know. This is another important meeting that he's missed." No one said anything, but Tag knew his brother was being forced to deal with an issue that he'd been avoiding. Peter Weston was simply not pulling his weight.

Tag stood. "All right then, it's all settled," he said excitedly. "Let the presses roll and let's watch the sales flow in."

Later that evening Tag joined Liam, Bridget and his cousin Scarlet at Une Nuit. Despite everyone's smiles he could feel tension at the table the moment he sat down. "What's going on?"

Releasing an affronted sigh his sister said, "Nothing, other than that earlier today I saw Cullen at the office and asked him how things were going at *Snap* and he almost bit my head off. You would have thought I was asking him for some deep, dark secret."

"Personally, I think Grandfather's challenge has got all of you on guard," Bryan said, in defense of his younger brother as he pulled up a chair and joined them. "That's why I'm glad I got out of the family business and started this place. Even then there was too much pressure at EPH. I don't want to think how crazy things are now."

Tag nodded. "Bryan is right. Granddad's challenge has all of us tense. We've always worked together for the good of the company as a whole and have never been pitted against each other like this before. But we can't lose sight that no matter what, we're family."

Liam took a sip of his drink. "I agree with Tag."

Scarlet rolled her eyes, grinning. "You would, since your job as financial operating officer doesn't align you with any particular magazine."

Liam frowned. "Yes, but it doesn't make my job easier when I have to do damage control with all four. Try doing my job."

"No, brother dear, you can keep your job," Bridget said. "I don't know of anyone who could do it better. It's just that things are getting crazy already, just like Bryan said, and it's only the second month. I don't want to think what the summer will bring when things really begin to heat up."

Bridget then glanced over at Scarlet. "And speaking of Summer...where is she?" she asked Scarlet regarding the whereabouts of her identical twin.

Scarlet took a sip of her drink before saying, "Summer's excited about John returning to town in time for the ball tomorrow night and decided to go shopping for something to wear."

Bridget smiled. "I'm glad that I'm not the only one who's looking forward to the ball tomorrow night."

Tag leaned back in his chair and thought of the evening he had planned with Renee and said, "I'm looking forward to the ball tomorrow night, as well."

Renee looked in the full-length mirror that was on the back of her bathroom door, not believing the transformation a visit to the hair salon and an exclusive dress boutique could make. But she wanted to look as special as Tag had promised the night would be.

The day had started off promisingly when a prettily wrapped cookie bouquet was delivered to her at work. She had gotten a curious stare from Vicki, but as usual, her secretary had respected her privacy by not asking any questions. Tag's card had simply said, *Be My Valentine.*

Then when she'd gotten home there had been the delivery of the Malone painting she had fallen in love with that Saturday she and Tag had spent together in Greenwich Village. She didn't want to think how much Tag had paid for the painting and her first reaction was that there was no way she could accept it. But when she'd finally reached him on his cell he'd told her there was no way she could return the painting; it was hers to keep. He then bid her goodbye, promising to see her at seven.

She chuckled as she tossed her hair from her face. Instead of the straight strands she usually wore, her hair was a silken mass of curls that framed her face and tumbled around her shoulders.

She stepped back to study the effect of the semi-formal dress she had purchased to wear. Made of red velvet, it looked sophisticated, chic, tailored to fit. Matte sequins dotted the v-neck that emphasized her high, full breasts, accentuated even more by delicate spaghetti straps. The soft fluttery hemline stopped just above her knees.

The way the dress flowed over her body elegantly displayed every feminine curve she possessed, and the glamorous matching red velvet cape, lined with white satin, was a plus to keep the tonight's chill at bay. She wished that her friend Debbie were here to give her a thumbs-up, but Debbie wouldn't be back in New York until Saturday.

When the doorbell sounded, Renee's pulse jumped before she took a quick glance at her watch. It was precisely seven o'clock.

The lady in red...

Tag's gaze moved with deep male appreciation over Renee's stunning features. In the gorgeous gown she was wearing, she was definitely making a statement tonight, and he was glad he was the man whose arm she would be on.

"You are beautiful," he said, stepping inside her apartment and handing her a single red rose.

"Thank you." Renee brought the rose to her nose and inhaled softly. She then took in the man standing in front of her. There was just something about a good-looking man in formal attire. Tag was elegantly dressed in a black tux that fit his tall, muscular frame as if it had been specifically tailored just for him. She smiled thinking that it probably had been. The white shirt and formal black bow tie added the finishing touches. "I think you are beautiful, too," she said, meaning every word of it.

A slow smile spread across his features. "I don't think I've ever been told that I'm beautiful."

"Well, I'm telling you," she said, bringing the rose to her nose once again. The blue eyes holding hers were igniting a slow burn inside of her. She had a feeling if they didn't leave now they would arrive at the ball inappropriately late.

"Ready to leave?" she decided to ask.

A grin touched the corners of his mouth and she had a feeling he had read her every thought. "Yes, I think we'd better."

The first thing Renee noted when they arrived at the Rockefeller Center was that the main entrance was surrounded by the media. Television cameras, newspaper reporters and photographers were positioned close to the main entrance, which was lined with red carpet.

"Because of the importance of this event, a number

of celebrities will be in attendance," Tag whispered in her ear just moments before she saw John Travolta and his wife entering the establishment as flashbulbs exploded everywhere.

Renee nodded, already feeling nervous. She had never been to a ball before, nor could she recall ever having been in a limo. Tag had surprised her when he'd shown up at her apartment in a limousine, giving her neighbors a reason to raise their blinds in the evening.

When the limo came to a stop in front of Rockefeller Center, a uniformed doorman stepped forward and opened the door for them. The moment they exited the vehicle, flashbulbs went off. Evidently, someone had assumed they were celebrities. Renee felt good knowing that once it was discovered they weren't anyone famous, the photos would be disposed of. She smiled up at Tag when he took her arm, and together they walked into the building.

The first people she recognized upon entering the ballroom were Gannon and Erika. For some reason, the couple didn't appear surprised that she was Tag's date tonight.

"Doesn't this place look fabulous?" Erika said. "Whoever was responsible for the decorating did a wonderful job."

Renee nodded. She had to agree. With Valentine colors of red and white, everything was reminiscent of love and romance. It was there in the red and white carnations that seemed to be practically everywhere and in the red heart-shaped ceramic centerpieces that adorned the tables that were draped in red and white linen tablecloths. Then there were the bright chandeliers overhead as well as the love song being played by the live orchestra. There was no doubt in her mind there would be dancing later, and a part of her was looking forward to dancing with Tag.

For the next hour or so Renee and Tag walked around, socializing. He kept a hand on her arm, keeping her close by his side as they moved around the room, while introducing her to people he knew. And it seemed that just about everyone knew him as an Elliott and immediately inquired about his mother's health and his grandparents' whereabouts. He answered by saying his mother was recuperating nicely and his grandparents hadn't returned yet from their trip to South Florida.

Dinner was extravagant as well as delicious and Renee was extremely grateful they had been seated at the table with Gannon and Erika as well as with Tag's cousin Cullen and his date. When they had spent the weekend together, Tag had told her a little bit about each of his siblings and cousins and she distinctively remembered him saying that Cullen, at twenty-seven, was the playboy in the family. With his dark, good looks she could tell why. But then, she thought, glancing over at her date, no one was more handsome than Tag.

"Dance with me," Tag whispered in her ear once the dance floor opened. She nodded, and without any hesitation she let him lead her to the dance floor.

He slid his arms around her waist, bringing her closer to the fit of him, and she went willingly, deciding that so far tonight everything had been perfect. There were even enough celebrities in attendance to take everyone's attention off her and Tag.

"Thanks for coming with me tonight," he said softly, leaning down as his warm lips gently touched her ear.

His amorous caress sent chills of desire escalating through her body. "Thank you for inviting me."

He chuckled quietly. "There we go again, thanking each other like broken records. If we were alone I would take the time to thank you properly."

She glanced up at him and gave him a jaunty grin. "And which way is that?"

He leaned closer and whispered, telling her of his fondest desire for later. Renee chuckled softly and said, "It's a good thing I don't embarrass easily."

"Yes, it is a good thing."

After the dance was over he was leading her back to their table when someone called out his name.

They turned just in time for a woman to fling herself into Tag's arms and kiss him on the mouth with a familiarity that made Renee blink. "Where on earth have you been keeping yourself, Tag? I haven't seen you for months."

"Hello, Pamela," he said with a dry smile. Reaching out, he pulled Renee closer to his side. "Renee, I'd like you to meet Pamela Hoover, an old friend," Tag said as a way of introduction.

"Hello," the woman said coldly, then turned her full attention back to Tag. Dismissing Renee completely, she said, "What are you doing Friday night? I have tickets to—"

Tag interrupted her. "Sorry, but Renee and I have plans for Friday night."

Although Renee knew that she and Tag really didn't have a date Friday night, she decided not to mention that fact.

"Oh." The woman then gave Renee an unfriendly glance before turning back to Tag. "Then perhaps we can get together another day, for old times' sake. You know my number." She then walked off.

Evidently, Tag felt the need to explain. "Pamela and I dated over a year ago. When she didn't like competing against my work, we decided things weren't working out and went our separate ways."

"Oh, I see." Renee decided not to tell him that what she saw was someone very much interested in rekindling what they once had.

"There're a few people I know over there. Let's go over and say hello," Tag said, leading her across the room.

Moments later Renee found herself surrounded by a number of famous people, most of whose movies she enjoyed watching on the big screen. And Tag was on a first-name basis with each and every one of them. She ignored the feeling of being way out of her league since everyone appeared to be genuinely friendly.

"I figured I would see you here tonight," said a man who walked up behind Tag.

Tag turned at the sound of the voice and smiled. "And I was hoping I'd see you." He pulled Renee closer to his side to make introductions. "Renee, this is a good friend of mine, Alton Malone."

Renee smiled as she presented the man her hand.

"Mr. Malone, Tag never mentioned that you were a good friend of his."

Alton laughed, shaking his head. "Then I will definitely take him to task for that, Renee. I understand you like my work."

"Yes, I do, and I was happy to receive a special painting of yours today as a gift."

"Then I hope you can come to the private art exhibit I have planned this Friday night at a museum in Harlem."

Renee glanced over at Tag, wondering if this was the date he'd earlier insinuated they had. His mischievous smile let her know it was. She nodded her head, grinning. "Thanks, Alton, and I think I will."

A half hour later Renee excused herself from Tag's side to go to the ladies' room. She was about to enter when a very distinct voice from the inside stopped her.

"Can you believe the nerve of Tag coming here with her?" Pamela asked her unseen companion. "What on earth could he be thinking?"

Another woman laughed. "Yes, I saw them the moment they walked in together. I couldn't believe it."

"Me neither," Pamela tacked on. "I looked for Tag's grandfather to see his reaction and someone mentioned that he's out of town. He's going to croak when he finds out that Tag is dating a black woman. Just think of the talk it's going to cause. The one thing Patrick Elliott detests is his family name being connected to any type of scandal."

Renee stiffened and backed slowly away from the door. Deciding she didn't have an urgent need to use the bathroom after all, she returned to the ballroom.

It didn't take long to find Tag. His tall, elegantly attired form was standing across the room talking to his brother and his cousin, Cullen. And then, as if he were in tune with her very presence, he glanced up and met her eyes.

He made the mistake of letting his gaze linger on her too long. The longer he looked at her, the more she could feel the wanting and desire radiating from the very depths of him. Love for him took over her mind, erasing Pamela Hoover's cutting and spiteful words, and filling Renee's mind with one thought: just how much she loved him.

She watched as he excused himself from the group and without looking around and making conversation with anyone, he strolled over to her as if she was the only person who had his complete attention. She wondered if he was aware of how he stood out—tall, dashing, handsome—and she continued to stare at him. Out of breath. Out of her mind.

When he came to a stop in front of her, she wet her lips, knowing the provocative and sensuous gesture would send him a silent message.

It did.

He slid his arms around her waist and leaned closer, and, not caring who was looking, he placed an affectionate kiss on her lips. "Are you ready to leave now?" he whispered.

She liked the feel of being in his arms, being pressed so close to him. She liked having his attention. "Only if you are."

"I am."

And without any more words, he took her hand and led her toward the coat check to get her cape.

Renee remembered very little of the limo ride back to her apartment. Nor could she recall the moments she and Tag shared as they walked hand in hand to her door. But she did remember when that same door closed behind them and he whispered her name just moments before pulling her into his arms.

And she did commit to memory how he had gently carried her to her bedroom, placed her on the bed and tenderly undressed her before turning his attention to himself.

She would never forget how she watched as he shoved his pants to the floor and stepped out of them, confident in his sexuality. And when he got in the bed with her, knelt before her, spread her legs, lowered his head and flicked his tongue across her womanly core, she thought that she had died and gone to heaven.

By the time he had raised his head, she had had not one orgasm but two and he'd given her a look that let her know that before the night was over there would be a third and a fourth.

"Careful," she whispered, after he sheathed a condom in place and moved his body into position over hers. "You're becoming habit-forming."

He smiled down at her. "I'm glad. I want to get into your system, Renee. I want to get into it real bad."

She reached out and caressed the side of his face. "Why?" she asked, desperately needing to know.

"Because," he said, as he slowly entered her, "you're already in mine."

"Maybe. But not enough."

At that moment she didn't know what was driving her but she wanted to be the only woman Tag thought about tonight, tomorrow, possibly for the rest of his life. Maybe it had something to do with the words Pamela Hoover had spoken, suggesting that once Patrick Elliott got wind of her and Tag's relationship it would all be over. Renee wouldn't subject him to any sort of rift with his family and she knew what she had to do if that became a possibility. But tonight, tomorrow, just for a little while longer, she wanted this. She needed him.

She wrapped her legs securely around him and then she began trailing her fingers down his chest, initiating a slow, seductive massage before coming to a stop on one taut nipple.

"What are you doing?" he asked, his voice hitched to a feverous pitch from her touch.

"I'm trying to see just how deep into your system I can get," she said, stroking the nipple slowly, sensuously.

"Take my word," he said through clenched teeth. "You're already in there pretty good."

"But I want to make sure."

"You know what they say about payback," he said, sucking in a deep breath.

"No, I don't know what they say, but tonight I've decided that I'm not going to worry about what anyone says. The only thing I want on my mind is us and what we're doing right now."

Laughing, she shifted her body and after a quick ma-

neuver Tag found himself on his back with her strad-
dling him.

He looked up at her through deeply glazed eyes. "Oh,
you're asking for it."

"From the feel of things it seems like you're the one
asking for it, Mr. Elliott, and I intend to give you everything you want."

And then she began to move on top of him.

It suddenly happened, as soon as she felt his body ex-
plode beneath her. With his last hard thrust she screamed
his name and shattered into a thousand pieces before
collapsing on him, burying her head in the hollow of his
shoulder.

Moments later, he kissed her deeply, thoroughly and
completely, and at that moment Renee knew that instead
of her getting deeper into his system he had gotten totally entrenched into hers.

Contentment surged through every part of Tag's body
as he stood at the foot of the bed and drank in the sight
of Renee lying there asleep atop the covers. Even now,
aftershocks of pleasure rushed through his veins, keeping him hard. The intimacy they always shared was unlike anything he'd ever known. She brought out the
sexual hunger in him, his wanting and desire were driv-
en to extreme points, and unleashed within him was
something so elemental and profound that it took his
breath away just thinking about it.

He started to get dressed as he continued to look at
her. The woman was something else—stubborn, proud,
beautiful and sexy all rolled into one. She matched him

on every level. Surpassed him on some. And pleased him with a magnitude that could leave him gasping.

He sighed deeply as he buttoned his shirt. More than anything he wanted to get back in bed and be there when Renee woke up in the morning, but he couldn't. *Pulse*'s special edition would hit the stands tomorrow morning and there was a lot to do. For the next forty-eight hours the majority of his time would be spent at the office. Once the magazine hit the street he would then have to be on hand to field inquiries from those questioning the story's legitimacy.

Wanting to clear his mind of work, he looked back at Renee and did something he had never done before. He began imagining. How would it feel to have this every day, the chance to sleep with her, wake up with her, spend all the time that he wanted with her?

An emotion he had never felt before suddenly gripped him and the one thing he could not imagine was a life without her. He sucked in a sharp breath when he was filled with a deep longing, a profound sense of need. He'd known that he cared, but until now he hadn't realized how much.

He was in love with Renee.

The thought, the blatant realization didn't make him feel uncomfortable. It sent a warmth through all parts of his body, swelling his heart with love even more. Now he imagined other things. Sharing his entire life with her. Marrying her and making her his wife. The mother of his children.

He wanted to wake her up and tell her how he felt but knew that he couldn't. There were still issues they were working out and although she had agreed to give them a chance, he could still sense her wariness, her uncertainty. The best thing for him to do would be to continue on their present path. He had to prove to her that things between them could work out and there was nothing that existed in this world that could keep them apart.

After getting completely dressed he returned to her, leaned down and nibbled her neck. He couldn't leave without telling her goodbye. "I'm getting ready to leave, sweetheart."

She slowly opened her eyes and drew a long, heavy breath before saying, "How? The limo is—"

"I called for a car." EPH had its own private transportation. "It'll be here in a few moments." As he continued to look at her, he realized this woman held his heart and she didn't even know it. He leaned down and kissed her, tenderly yet thoroughly.

With his lips still locked to hers he slipped his hand beneath her knees and picked her up. He then sat on the edge of the bed with her in his lap. He needed the connection. He needed this. The exquisite sensations that only she could force through his body, an unrestrained surrender that only she had been able to seize.

He reluctantly lifted his mouth sometime later, only after he was thoroughly satisfied that he had given her something to think about for the next few days when he would be so busy with the magazine.

"That special edition comes out tomorrow," he said hoarsely, placing small kisses around her lips. "I need to be in place."

"I know," she said quietly.

"I'm going to be busy over the next couple of days. I probably won't get a chance to see you until Friday night."

She slid her hand up his shirt, straightened his bow tie and whispered, "I understand."

"I'm going to miss you."

She smiled up at him. "I'm going to miss you, too."

Taking advantage of her parted lips, he slipped his tongue back inside her mouth for one last, sweet, mind-stirring taste. Moments later, with a low groan, he pulled back, stood and placed her back in bed. "If I don't leave now, I won't."

"I know that as well."

He held her gaze for a moment, and then took his cell phone out of the pocket of his pants. Somehow in the midst of his whirling senses he was able to press a few buttons, and when the dispatcher came on the line, he said tensely, "Delay that pickup in Morningside Heights for another couple of hours." He clicked off the phone and placed it aside, then began removing his clothes.

Unrestrained. Uncontrolled. He was a man very much in love and once again he wanted the woman, the object of his desire, the person who held his heart. He wanted to make love to her with the knowledge that love was guiding his thoughts, his actions and his words.

When he was completely naked, he joined Renee in bed, knowing that at that moment, this was where he wanted to be.

Ten

When Renee walked through the doors of Manhattan University Hospital that morning she had the eerie feeling of being watched. It seemed that everyone's eyes were on her, and a number of speculative faces turned to stare at her when she made her usual trek across the lobby before stepping into the elevator.

Hoping that that she was imagining things, she walked out onto her floor moments later only to see Vicki look up from her desk and stare at her as well. "Okay, I give up," Renee said, after hanging up her coat and walking over to Vicki's desk. "What's going on?"

"I take it you haven't seen this morning's paper," her secretary said, easing the tabloid across the desk to her.

Renee lifted a brow before glancing down at the paper. Her heart nearly stopped. There, plastered on the front page, were pictures from the ball, and dead center were two pictures of her and Tag. The first was a photograph of them getting out of the limo together, making all of New York aware of the fact that she had been his date. The other photo was taken when he had leaned down to kiss her—the moment right before they had left the ball. Beneath the pictures the caption asked, Has the Elusive Teagan Elliott Finally Been Caught?

Renee swallowed. She hadn't wanted her relationship with Tag exposed to the world this way, especially while it wasn't yet on solid ground. "With all the other stuff going on in this country, I wouldn't think the ball warranted front page," she said, not knowing at the moment what else to say.

Vicki shrugged. "Yes, you would think not." She then added, "I might as well warn you that Diane Carter has called three times this morning. I told her you were coming in late and I didn't expect you before ten. Brace yourself. I have a feeling she'll be calling back, or better yet, she'll be coming up here the first chance she gets."

"Thanks for the warning."

Renee was about to go into her office when Vicki asked, "Did you enjoy yourself last night?"

Renee met the woman's gaze. She saw genuine concern and interest in the eyes staring back at her. Nothing judgmental and no censorship. "Yes, I had a wonderful time."

Vicki smiled. "I'm glad. You're a beautiful woman, Renee, and a nice person. You should get out more and enjoy yourself."

Renee lifted a brow. "And Teagan Elliott?"

Vicki shrugged. "I don't know him personally, but he seems like a nice young man." She glanced back down at the newspaper that was still spread open on her desk. "And no matter how anyone else might feel, I personally think the two of you look wonderful together."

Renee smiled, not realizing she'd been holding her breath. One thing she knew about Vicki was that she was sincere and forthright. "Thanks, Vicki." She then walked into her office and closed the door.

It was sometime after the lunch hour when Diane burst into Renee's office. "Vicki wasn't out front so I just came on in. This is the first chance I've had to sneak away since seeing today's paper. What on earth were you thinking about by going out with Teagan Elliott? That was definitely not a smart move, Renee."

Renee leaned back in her chair, deciding to give Diane credit. The woman definitely didn't have a problem expressing the way she felt. "And why would you think that?"

Diane frowned. "Surely you're joking. Come on, Renee, walk back into the real world. People like the Elliotts don't become involved with people like us. We're not on their social level and with you it's even more serious. There's the issue of—"

"Race?" She preempted Diane's comment.

"Yes, that's it." Diane smiled apologetically. "Face it. You're probably a novelty to him, something new and different. I hope you aren't taking things seriously because if you are you're setting yourself up to get hurt."

"Thanks for the warning, Diane, but I'm a big girl and I can take care of myself." She reached for a file on her desk, hoping Diane would take the hint.

Diane's smile slipped. "I hope so because you'll need to be strong when he loses interest and drops you like a hot potato. If I were you that would be something I'd definitely be thinking about."

Without saying anything else, Diane turned and walked out of Renee's office.

Renee stood at the window and looked down at the busy streets below. The lunch hour had ended a while ago but the sidewalks were still crowded.

Preferring to have lunch alone in her office, Renee had eaten a sandwich her secretary had brought up from the cafeteria.

She sighed deeply. She hadn't wanted to fall in love with Tag for several reasons, and this was one of them. She hated being the center of attention, detested her name being linked to office gossip. It brought back so many painful memories of when Dionne had humiliated her in the worst possible way.

She tried convincing herself that the talk about her and Tag wasn't the same, but in her mind, talk was talk, and she'd rather not have her name linked to any of it.

She tensed when she heard the phone ring and hoped it wasn't Tag. She hadn't heard from him all day and wondered if he had seen the pictures.

She crossed the room and picked up the phone. "Yes, Vicki?"

"Ms. Elliott is on the line for you."

Renee raised a brow. "Ms. Elliott?"

"Yes, Ms. Bridget Elliott."

Renee swallowed. Tag's siblings had been friendly to her last night but she couldn't help wondering if they saw the photographs in today's paper as damaging to their family name. "Please put her through, Vicki."

For the next minute Renee exchanged pleasantries with Tag's sister. Then Bridget surprised her by asking, "I was wondering if we could have lunch tomorrow?"

"Lunch?"

"Yes, tomorrow. We could meet somewhere near the hospital. How about Carmine's, that Italian restaurant on Broadway? Say noon?"

Renee took a step around her desk to quickly check her calendar. Finding the time open, she said, "Noon will be fine."

Once Renee ended the call she slumped down in her chair. Was Bridget inviting her to lunch to tell her that she thought Renee seeing Tag was a bad idea? The last thing she needed was another person criticizing her relationship with Tag.

Tag gazed at the special edition of *Pulse*. On the front cover was the silhouette of Senator Denton highlighted by the words—emblazoned in bold, black letters—"Silence is Not Always Golden".

Tag rubbed his hand down his face. *Pulse* had obtained undisputed proof that one of the military guards at Abu Ghraib Prison had written the Senator and had sent photographs about the abuse going on, but Senator Denton had failed to do anything about it, and had gone so far as to stage a cover-up by having the informer transferred to a military outfit in the heart of the Iraqi fighting. That same individual had gotten killed within days of being put on the front line.

Although the incident at Abu Ghraib had eventually been brought to light, Senator Denton's actions had not. The plan had been for him to quietly resign from office before anyone could discover the truth. Luckily, his niece had overheard him giving orders to one of his staffers to destroy the letters and photographs, and before anyone could do so, she'd read them. Horrified, she'd decided to expose her uncle for the dishonest person that he was. The loss of that young marine's life couldn't be forgiven.

Tag glanced down at his watch. It was close to 10 p.m. He'd been in the office since nine that morning, after finally forcing himself from Renee's bed and going home to shower and change.

Leaning back in his chair, he threw down the magazine and picked up that day's newspaper, a copy of which Gannon had placed on his desk first thing that morning. Tag had smiled when he'd seen the pictures of him and Renee, thinking how good they looked together. He had reached for the phone several times to call her to make sure she'd known about the photographs, but each time he'd gotten interrupted.

It was probably too late to call her now but he'd speak to her tomorrow. In the midst of everything that was going on, he needed to hear her voice and to know that the pictures hadn't bothered her.

He gazed at the photographs and could distinctly remember when they had gotten out of the limo together, as well as the exact moment he had placed a kiss on her lips at the ball. He hadn't been aware that the latter was being captured on film but a part of him didn't care. There was nothing wrong with a man displaying affection for the woman he loved.

The woman he loved.

Thinking it, realizing it and accepting it was easier than he'd ever imagined. He loved her and more than anything he wanted to find a way to make her love him as well, and believe that things between them would work out.

"I can't believe she actually thinks Teagan Elliott is remotely interested in her."

"Hey, isn't that hilarious? I heard that Diane Carter tried to warn her but she refused to listen. She's going to wish she had when she gets dumped. It won't be anyone's fault but her own."

Renee kept walking, refusing to look over her shoulder to see who was speaking. A part of her wanted to turn around and tell whoever they were just where they could go, but she was too professional. Besides, it would be a waste of time since the remarks were bits and pieces of what she'd heard all day, thanks to Diane's handiwork. She sighed, thinking that the one thing she had hoped would never happen to her again was happening. Once again, she was the topic of everyone's conversations.

She stepped into the elevator, glad she was leaving the building even if it was only for a little while. She hoped she didn't later regret agreeing to meet Tag's sister for lunch. Although Tag had told her that he'd be too tied up at the office to call, a part of her wished he had so she'd know what he thought of the pictures.

She'd contemplated calling him but knew how busy he was. She, like everyone else, had seen the special edition of *Pulse*, and had been shocked to read the article about Senator Denton. It had been the hot topic on the subway that morning.

Her thoughts shifted to her conversation with Diane yesterday. Last night, while lying in bed, she'd been forced to acknowledge that Diane was probably right. Eventually, Tag would lose interest and Renee couldn't help wondering where that would leave her heart. Probably somewhere shattered into a million pieces. Could she handle such heartbreak?

As she stepped outside onto the sidewalk she tightened her coat around her. No, she wasn't a glutton for pain, and if she didn't make decisions about their relationship before Tag eventually did, pain would be just what she got.

When Renee walked into Carmine's, she was surprised to not only see Bridget but Tag's identical twin cousins, Summer and Scarlet, as well. She had met the two women at the Valentine's Day ball. She nervously gripped the straps of her purse as the host led her across the room to join them.

"Thanks for inviting me to lunch," Renee said with the first real smile she'd managed in a couple of days, after being greeted with genuine friendliness by the three women.

Bridget grinned. "It was supposed to be the two of us, but then I ran into Summer and Scarlet at the office and invited them along. I hope you don't mind, but Summer has a good reason for us to celebrate," Bridget said, picking up her wineglass.

Renee glanced over at Summer and quickly saw the reason. A beautiful engagement ring adorned the fourth finger of her left hand. "Congratulations! It's a beautiful ring."

Summer returned Renee's smile. "Thanks. John proposed to me on Valentine's Day. We only made a brief appearance at the ball since he'd made dinner reservations elsewhere. That's when he popped the question."

"Have you set a date?" Renee asked, lifting her own glass of wine after the waiter came and filled it.

She wondered then if she was the only one who noted how Summer's shoulders had tensed at that question.

"No, a date hasn't been set yet," the bride-to-be replied.

Renee nodded and took a sip of wine, thinking Summer didn't appear to be as pleased with her engagement as a future bride should be. She set down her wineglass, deciding to leave Summer's issue alone since Renee had a huge one of her own. Tag. She wondered how long it would take before Bridget brought him up.

An hour later they had eaten their meal, and still Tag's sister hadn't mentioned him. Instead, she talked about how improved her mother's condition was and had asked questions as to what to expect during Karen's chemotherapy treatment. Tag's name never came up. Instead, Renee spent an enjoyable lunch getting to know his sister and cousins.

It was only when they were leaving the restaurant that Bridget leaned over, smiled and whispered to Renee, "Oh, and by the way, I thought you and Tag looked great together at the ball as well as in yesterday's paper."

Eleven

The following day Renee walked into her apartment not in the best of moods. The stares and negative comments at work had been worse than ever today and she wasn't sure tonight would be a good time to go out with Tag. She had spoken to him briefly that day before he'd gotten interrupted by someone coming into his office.

On the subway ride home she had replayed everything she'd had to endure for the past two days. She had been so concerned about what everyone was saying and thinking that she hadn't been able to function at work. That kind of worry and aggravation would definitely put a strain on an already difficult relationship and she was beginning to feel it.

More than ever she was convinced that their differences would always be an issue with them.

She glanced at her watch. Tag was to pick her up at seven, and knowing him, he would be punctual. If she was going to cancel their date, now was the time to do so. She picked up the phone, deciding to call him at the office in case he was still there. The familiar voice of his secretary answered after the first couple of rings. "Teagan Elliott's office."

"Yes, may I speak with Mr. Elliott?"

"He's in a meeting right now. Would you like to leave a message?"

"Yes. Please let him know that Renee Williams called and—"

"Hold on, Ms. Williams. I was given explicit instructions to put you through to Mr. Elliott if you were to call. Just a moment, please."

Renee leaned back against the kitchen counter, waiting to be connected to Tag. A few seconds later, he was on the line. "Renee?"

She sucked in a sharp breath. Just hearing him say her name did things to her. She could vividly remember how he'd woken her a couple of mornings ago, kissing her and whispering her name over and over. Before she'd even opened her eyes, he'd drawn her into his warm embrace, waking her senses up to him and the strong evidence of his desire for her.

Could Diane be right? Was she just a novelty to him? Something different? Someone he would eventually lose interest in when the novelty wore off? And what if she did mean something to him? Would he go against his family's wishes if they decided they didn't want her to be a part of it? Could there ever be a chance of a happy ending for them?

"Renee?"

She breathed in deeply. "Yes, it's me. I called to let you know I don't think it's a good idea for us to go out tonight. And maybe it's a good idea if we cool things between us."

"What are you talking about, Renee? What happened?"

"Nothing happened, Tag. I—I just can't handle the talk, the negativity. Look, I know you're busy so I'll let you go. Goodbye."

She hung up the phone and wrapped her arms around her stomach, swallowing her tears, telling herself that she wouldn't fall apart. But when the tears continued coming nonstop, she knew she was doing that exact thing.

Tag held the phone in his hand as he hung his head, frowning. What the hell had happened? He breathed in deeply, knowing whatever it was had to be connected to the pictures that had appeared in the newspaper a few days ago.

"Is everything all right, Tag?"

He glanced up and met Gannon's concerned gaze. Only then did he hang up the phone. Already, he was moving toward the coatrack for his jacket. "No, everything isn't all right. It's Renee and she's having second thoughts about us again." Last night while the two of them were stuck late at the office, Tag had had a heart-to-heart talk to Gannon about Renee, and had even admitted to his brother that he loved her.

"Maybe it's time for you to erase those thoughts from her mind forever or they're going to just keep coming back."

Tag sighed disgustedly. "And how am I supposed to

do that if she keeps letting what people say come between us?"

"Then it's up to you to convince her it doesn't matter. If you love her as much as you say you do, then
you'll find a way to convince her."

Tag nodded. "I hate to run out on you like this but I
need to go see Renee."

"By all means, go and do whatever it takes to win
your lady's heart."

Tag was grateful for his brother's support. "If anything further develops with the Denton story, call me on
my cell phone," he said, rushing toward the door while
slipping on his jacket. "I'll talk with you later."

Renee should have assumed Tag would show up, and
if she'd been in her right frame of mind, she would
have. But she wasn't, so when the doorbell sounded
she fought to get her tears under control. Wiping the evidence off her cheeks, she took a deep breath before
crossing the room to answer the door.

She immediately met Tag's gaze and saw the anger
in the depths of his eyes, which she tried meeting with
complete serenity in hers, knowing she was failing.
There was no way he wouldn't know she'd been crying.

"May I come in?"

Instead of answering, she took a step back and
watched as he crossed the threshold then closed the
door behind him. "We need to talk, Renee," he said
softly, slipping a hand under her chin to stare into her
puffy eyes.

The tears she was holding back threatened to fall

with his sudden shift from anger to tenderness. "There's nothing to say, Tag," she said simply. "We gave it a try and it didn't work."

"No, you gave up too soon."

Fire suddenly sparked in Renee at his accusation. She stiffened. "I'm sorry you feel that way but people are talking about us and I don't appreciate being the topic of gossip at work. They're probably taking bets like the last time."

"I don't give a damn what people are—" He suddenly stopped talking and lifted a brow. "What do you mean they're probably taking bets like the last time? What last time?"

Renee could have kicked herself for letting that comment slip out. "Nothing."

He gazed at her with intensity. "No, I think it *is* something, so tell me."

Renee looked away from his face. Maybe she needed to do what he was asking and tell him about Dionne and why she had moved from Atlanta. Only then would he understand why being in the midst of a scandal bothered her so much. "Let's sit down. You're right. It is time I tell you."

When he started to sit beside her on the sofa she quickly said, "No. Please sit over there." She indicated the chair across from the sofa. She wasn't certain of her control and needed space from Tag. She couldn't handle things if he were to sit beside her, touch her, breathe on her.

He stared at her for a few moments before doing as she asked. As soon as he was settled he met her gaze and waited for her to speak.

She curled up on the sofa, tucking her feet under her. "Before I came to New York I worked at a hospital in Atlanta and dated this doctor for almost a year before finding out he was also dating a nurse who worked the midnight shift. She didn't know about me like I didn't know about her but some of the other doctors knew and were taking bets as to when I would find out. Eventually I did and it was the talk of the hospital. It seemed everywhere I went there were whispers, looks of pity, even laughter. The embarrassment was humiliating. When I came here I promised myself that I would never get involved in any situation where I was the center of attention again. But it seems, once again, that I am."

Tag didn't say anything but stared at her, and Renee knew he was trying to formulate in his mind just what to say. "I regret what your ex-boyfriend did to you, Renee, but I'm not him," he said in a quiet voice. "I am not involved with anyone but you."

She sighed slowly. "That's not why people are talking and you know it."

"Okay, then, let's discuss why people are talking."

"No," she said softly, knotting her hands together in her lap. "We already have, numerous times, and you won't accept how it makes me feel."

He leaned forward and held her gaze. "Then maybe we need to discuss why the talk makes you feel that way in the first place," he said calmly. "Why you can't get beyond the color of my skin and the amount of money in my bank account." He continued speaking in a calm voice. "And before you answer, I want you to know how I feel about you, Renee. I love you. I think I fell in love with you that first day in your office. I want a future with you. A very happy future."

With his admission of love, tears Renee couldn't hold back any longer began flowing down her cheeks. Fighting for composure, she spoke straight from her heart. "And I love you, too, Tag. I didn't want to fall in love with you but I did that very same day as well. But that's just it. We can't have the happy future you want. All I can see is a future filled with the strain of proving our love to the world, constantly defending it, working harder than most couples just to preserve it. Then what if we want children? What will they have to go through?"

Tag got to his feet and crossed to the sofa. He reached out and took Renee's hand and gently pulled her up. "So what if our challenges will be greater than most? Our love will be there to sustain us. And as far as children are concerned, they'll grow up proud of what they are and who they are. Times have changed, Renee. And they are still changing. There will always be people who are bitterly opposed to interracial marriages, but then you'll find there's an even larger number of people who see such unions as an indicator of what life will be like in an even more diverse twenty-first century."

"Dammit, Tag, I can't bank on an unknown future. I can only go by what's in the real world, now."

Both fury and pain flashed in Tag's eyes. "So you're saying that you can't accept me or my love because it will be a problem for others to accept it? Are you saying that you're willing to give up what we can have together because of how others think and feel? What about how we feel, Renee? Is that not equally important?"

"Yes, it's important, but can't you understand that I'm trying to protect you, as well? I heard whispers at the ball of how your grandfather would be against anything developing between us, and I refuse to be the cause of any rift between you and your family."

His face hardened. "I told you that how my family might feel about us didn't matter to me, so don't go there, Renee. Don't look for excuses."

He released her and took a step back. "I don't know what else I can say. I love you. I want to marry you. I want a future with you," he said quietly, feeling the strain of heartbreak and disappointment. "That is what you have to believe and what you have to accept. My wanting those things means nothing unless you want them as well. All I'm asking is for us to put our love to the test and tell anyone who can find any reason for us not to be together to go straight to hell and stay there."

"Tag, I don't think—"

"No," he said, cutting her off, struggling to contain his anger. "The bottom line is whether you're strong enough to step out on faith and love. A week from today is my brother's wedding at The Tides as well as my grandparents' anniversary celebration. I want you to go there with me, not to seek any type of approval from my family but as two individuals who are very much in love and who have committed their lives to each other, and who are ready to make an announcement regarding their future together."

Renee shook her head sadly as tears once again filled

her eyes. In a voice filled with frustration, she said, "I can't do that, Tag. I'm sorry, but I can't."

And before he could say anything else, she rushed to her bedroom and slammed the door.

Twelve

Renee whirled around. Her face was streaked with tears, her eyes swollen and tormented. "What do you mean you think I'm making a mistake?"

Debbie Massey met her best friend's glare as she handed her a wet washcloth. "Renee, you know me well enough to know I don't sugarcoat anything. You asked for my honest opinion so I gave it to you."

Debbie, who'd been out of the country on assignment, had shown up at Renee's place over an hour ago and found Renee still torn up over her dealings with Tag the night before. With a bossiness that Renee doubted she would ever get used to, Debbie had quickly taken charge and rushed Renee off to the bathroom, made her wash her face while she'd told Debbie everything.

"Didn't you hear anything I said regarding all the

problems Tag and I would be facing as an interracial couple? How can you say I'm making a mistake?"

"The same way you did when I broke things off with Alan last year. I didn't follow my heart and I've regretted it every day since."

Renee nodded. Alan Harris, a colleague of Debbie's, was fifteen years her senior. Concerned about what others would say about her dating a much older man, Debbie had ended their relationship after a brief affair. That had been over a year ago and this was the first time Renee had heard Debbie admit that maybe she'd made a mistake in letting Alan go.

Before she could ask questions, Debbie continued. "At some point in your life you have to do what makes *you* happy and not worry about how others may feel about it. You've admitted you're in love with Teagan Elliott and he has admitted that he's in love with you. He's a man— a wealthy one, I might add—who wants to marry you and make you happy. If only the rest of us could be so lucky."

Renee dropped into a chair at the kitchen table, struggling to control the tears that threatened to fall again. "But you weren't around to hear what everyone was saying once they saw those pictures of us."

Debbie frowned. "And it's a good thing I wasn't. People need to get their own lives and not worry about what's going on in other people's lives. It's time you stopped caring about what people are saying and thinking. No matter what, you won't be able to change their opinion about anything, so why bother? They are either accepting or they aren't."

Debbie then tossed the braids out of her face and

peered at Renee over her glasses. "But none of what I'm telling you means a thing if you don't love Tag Elliott as much as you claim you do."

"I do love him," Renee said fiercely. "I love him with all my heart."

"Then act like it. There was a time you used to fight for what you wanted, what you believed in. I remember that day in college when Professor Downey gave you a B and you felt that you deserved an A. Where I would have taken the B and been giddy about it—being that it was a physics class—you didn't give the man a day's rest until he recalculated your scores to discover he'd made a mistake. You got your A and proved your point. Maybe it's time for you to prove another point, Renee. You, and only you, can decide your destiny."

Renee sipped her coffee as she thought about Debbie's words. She then asked, "Have you decided on your destiny, Debbie?"

Her friend smiled. "I think I have. It just so happens that Alan was in London while I was there. The moment I saw him I knew I still loved him. We were able to spend some time together and I've decided that I'm not going to let what others think stand in the way of my happiness. Maybe you ought to be making the same decision."

"Hey, you okay?"

Tag glanced up from his coffee cup and met Gannon's concerned gaze. It was Saturday morning and they had come into the office to take a conference call from Senator Denton's office. There would be a press conference from the Senator's home at noon where he would admit that *Pulse*'s allegations were true.

The special edition of *Pulse* had flown off the magazine stands and already there had been another printing, so there was indeed a reason to celebrate. Both their father and grandfather—who'd returned to town that morning—had called to congratulate them on a job well done. The only sad note was that Gannon had to advise Peter that he would no longer be associated with the company. After all the man's years of dedicated service the decision had been hard, but necessary.

"Yes, I'm all right," Tag replied, running a hand down his face. Next week was his brother's wedding and the last thing he wanted Gannon to worry about was him. "Are you nervous about the wedding next week?" he decided to ask.

Gannon chuckled. "No, just anxious. I can hardly wait."

Tag nodded. "And have you decided where you're going on your honeymoon yet?"

"Yes, but I'm keeping it as a surprise to Erika. I'm taking her to Paris."

"That's going to be some surprise."

Gannon calmly sipped his coffee and after a few moments of silence he said over the rim of his mug, "I didn't ask how things went with you and Renee last night but I get the feeling they didn't go as you wanted. Let me give you a word of advice, kiddo. No matter what, don't let her go without a fight. If you love her as much as I think you do, you'll be making a big mistake if you give up on her."

Tag dragged a hand through his hair. "It's not me giv-

ing up on her, Gannon. It's Renee giving up on me. She
knows that I love her. It will be up to her to decide if
my love is worth all the challenges we might face in the
future." He let out a long breath and added, "And it's my
most fervent hope that she does."

By Wednesday, Renee was still trying to get her life
back in order. So far, work had gone smoothly. Instead
of whispering about her and Tag, everyone focused on
the scandal involving Senator Denton and the press conference he'd held that weekend where he'd admitted all
of *Pulse*'s allegations.

She sighed as she caught the elevator to the tenth floor
to visit with one of her patients. For the past five days she
had replayed in her mind, over and over, her conversation with Debbie, and it didn't help matters that she was
missing Tag like crazy. She thought of him all the time
and missed the good times they had shared together.

She let out a long breath. Nobody could make her see
the errors of her ways more thoroughly than Debbie and
she appreciated her friend for doing that. Since their
talk, she'd been thinking of how a future with Tag would
be versus one without him, and each time the thought
of a life without him was too heart wrenching to imagine. She refused to let what others thought make her lose
the best thing that had ever happened to her. She loved
Tag and he loved her and together they would be able
to handle anything. She smiled to herself, thinking that
later tonight she planned to pay him a visit and let him
know just how she felt.

Renee had stepped off the elevator and was about to

round the corner when she heard the sound of Diane's voice. "Yes, she's been hiding out in her office, totally embarrassed. I would be embarrassed, too, if I had thrown myself at Teagan Elliott of all people. Maybe now she's learned to stay in her place. The nerve of her thinking she could cross over to the other side, and not just with anyone but with a member of one of the wealthiest families in New York. Can you imagine anyone being that stupid?"

Anger consumed Renee and she squared her shoulders and continued walking, remembering her last conversation with Tag and some of the advice he'd given her. Diane's back was to Renee, and the other nurse with whom Diane had been conversing saw Renee over Diane's shoulders. The nurse quickly made an excuse and hurried off, leaving Diane alone.

"Diane?"

The woman whirled around, surprised to find Renee standing there. She raised a brow. "Yes?"

"Do me a favor."

Diane relaxed and had the audacity to smile. "Sure, Renee, what do you need?"

"For you to go straight to hell and stay there."

Renee moved past the woman and then thought of something else, and turned around and added, "And the only stupid thing I've done was not accept Tag's marriage proposal."

Satisfied with the shocked look on Diane's face, Renee turned and resumed walking with her head held high. She couldn't go around telling everyone to go to hell like Tag had suggested, but she felt good about telling Diane to.

* * *

Tag rose from the sofa to turn off the television. It didn't matter that the Knicks were on a winning streak, even the basketball game wasn't holding his interest. The only thing consuming his mind were thoughts of Renee.

Renee.

More than once he had wondered if there was anything else he could have said to make her accept the love he was offering. He needed her in his life like he needed to breathe, and the pain of her willingness to give up and walk away was killing him.

He glanced around when the doorbell sounded, thinking it was probably Liam dropping by. As much as he loved his brother, Tag wasn't in the mood for company.

Opening the door he said, "Liam, I don't think—"

The words died on his lips when he saw it wasn't Liam like he'd assumed, but it was Renee.

"Hi," she said, smiling tentatively at him. "May I come in?"

A part of Tag was so glad to see her that he wanted to reach out and pull her into his arms but he knew he couldn't. He wasn't sure why she'd come but he did know there were still unresolved issues between them and until they worked them out, they were still at odds with each other.

"Sure, you can come in," he said, taking a step back to let her inside. He closed the door behind her. "May I take your coat?"

"Yes, thanks."

He watched her slide the leather coat from her body

to reveal a beautiful turquoise sweater and a pair of black slacks. Both looked good on her. "Can I get you something to drink?" he asked, taking the coat she handed him.

"No, I'm fine."

He nodded and walked over to the coat closet to hang up her coat. He could feel the tension in the air and could tell that her nerves were jumping just as high as his. "It's good seeing you, Renee," he said when he walked back over to her.

"Thanks, and it's good seeing you, too. I was wondering if we could talk."

He nodded. "Sure, let's sit in the living room."

He waited until she sat down on the sofa and then, remembering her request the last time they'd talked, he took the chair opposite her.

Renee crossed her legs, feeling Tag's penetrating stare. Over the past five days she had done a lot of soul-searching and had made a lot of decisions, and she wanted to share them with him.

"Are you sure I can't get you anything to drink?"

"No, I'm fine." Then a few moments later she said, "No, that's a lie and I'm not fine." She stood and slowly began pacing the room. Tag said nothing as he watched her and she knew he was giving her time to collect her thoughts.

"I don't know where to begin," she finally said, coming to a stop not far from where he sat and meeting his concentrated gaze.

"I know one place you can start," he said calmly, soothingly and in a low voice. "You can start off by assuring me that you meant what you said Friday night. The part about being in love with me."

His words were spoken with such tenderness that Renee's lips began trembling. How could she not love such a man as this? And that was only one of the things she intended to reassure him about. "Yes, I meant what I said, Tag. I do love you and I will always love you… which leads me to the reason I'm here."

She took a step back, needing to say what she had to say without being tempted to lean down and kiss him like she wanted to do. That would come later if he still wanted her. "I thought about everything you said that night and I've made some decisions."

"You have?"

"Yes."

"And what decisions have you made?" he quietly probed.

She met his gaze. "If you still want me, if you still love me, then I'm willing to do whatever it takes to make a future work with you, Tag. I'm no longer worried or concerned about what others might say. All I care about is what my heart is saying, and right now it's telling me that you're the best thing to ever happen to me and that you are the one person I need in my life. Now and forever."

She reclaimed the step she'd taken earlier to stand in front of him. She reached out, grabbed his hands and gently pulled him from his chair. "I know things won't always be easy. I know there will be those not happy with us being together, but as long as we have each other, then it won't matter. Our love will be strong enough to handle anything. I truly believe that now. I want to marry you, Tag. I want to have a future with you. I want to have your babies. I want it all."

Tag smiled, let out a relieved sigh and pulled Renee into his arms. "Thank you for reaching that decision. And yes, I still want you and I love you. I will always love you, Renee. And I want to marry you, have a future with you, have babies with you to grow and nurture in our love. I—"

Renee smiled and instead of letting him speak, she stood on tiptoe and touched her mouth to his. Tag, needing the kiss as much as she did, began hungrily devouring her mouth the moment they connected. He reached out, gathered her closer and molded her body to his, desperately needing the feel of her in his arms, close to his heart.

She slid a hand to his shoulder, holding on, fighting for control of the emotions he was stirring to life inside of her. Renee groaned as his tongue relentlessly mated with hers, claiming, absorbing everything about him.

And when the kiss grew more heated and demanding, he lifted her into his arms and whispered, "I want to make love to you."

The kiss had aroused her, too, and thoughts of being naked in bed with him, joining her body with his and sealing their love once and for all had her whispering back, "I want to make love to you, too."

Tag headed for the bedroom and within minutes her wish came true. They were naked in bed, and Tag was staring at her with love shining in the depths of his eyes. When he reached into the drawer to get a condom, she stopped him. "There's no need unless you want to do that. I've been on the pill for a couple of years to regulate my periods."

He met her gaze and tossed the packet back in the drawer. "I've never made love to a woman without using a condom," he decided to admit to her. "But I'm aching to do so with you. And just so you know, I'm safe. Because it's one of EPH's policies, I take physicals on a regular basis."

Returning to the bed, he whispered, "I love you with all my heart," just moments before leaning down, moving his body in place over hers and taking her lips in a slow, sensuous exchange, deliberately stimulating her senses as he slowly entered her, merging their bodies into one, flesh to flesh.

Tag's presence back inside her body evoked such pleasure in Renee that she lifted her hips and wrapped her legs around his waist, not wanting him to go anyplace but here, locked to her. Desire as powerful as anything she could imagine began consuming her, filling her mind with all kinds of sensations, and of their own accord, her eyes drifted close.

"Open your eyes, sweetheart," Tag urged in a low, raspy voice. "Look at me and tell me what you see."

Renee complied with his request and looked up at him, taking in his handsome face, the majestic blue of his eyes and the long lashes covering them. Her inner muscles quaked just from looking at him.

She reached up and skimmed a fingertip along his lips, taking in the mouth that could drive her out of her mind. "What I see when I look at you," she whispered, "is a man who is my soul mate, my fantasy come true, the only man I love and want to spend the rest of my life with, the future father of my babies."

Tag's breath caught with Renee's words. She was so beautiful, captivating…and she was his. "I love you so much," he murmured, before capturing her mouth. He began moving the lower part of his body, feeling the hardened tips of her breasts against his chest.

He established a rhythm and began moving inside her to a beat only the two of them could hear. And then it happened. He threw his head back as a release of gigantic proportions tore out of him. He screamed her name as he relinquished his entire being to passion of the richest and most intense kind. And to the woman he loved.

As if the feel of him coming apart, exploding inside of her, was what she wanted, she followed him over the edge. "I don't believe this," she sighed at the peak of her pleasure. She cried out his name and bucked upward, tightening her legs around him.

"Believe it, baby," he whispered. "This is just the beginning of the rest of our lives together. Forever."

As more sensations tore into Renee's body, the only thing she could do was meet his gaze and agree. "Yes. Forever."

Epilogue

"**R**enee, I'm glad you came," Karen Elliott said, smiling, grasping Renee's hand in hers.

Renee returned the woman's smile. "I'm glad I came, too." She glanced around. It seemed Gannon and Erika's wedding, although it had been done on a small scale, still had numerous invited guests. Everything had been beautiful; especially the bride, and tears had touched Renee's eyes when she'd seen the depth of love shining in Gannon's gaze for Erika.

She glanced up at Tag. They had decided to marry next year on Valentine's Day since that day was so special to them. It was almost a year away but it would be worth the wait. They had decided to announce their intentions to only his parents and grandparents tonight since it was Gannon and Erika's day. But when the couple returned from their honeymoon, Tag and Renee planned to make an official announcement to everyone.

"Where have Dad and Granddad run off to?" Tag inquired of his mother. He had remained at Renee's side throughout the entire wedding, always touching her in some way, making it known, just in case anyone had any doubt, that she was special to him.

Karen glanced around. "Probably in the library. Why?"

"I need to speak with them and I want you and Grandmother included in the conversation."

Karen's smile widened. "All right, let me go get Maeve and we'll meet you there in a few minutes."

When Karen walked off, the smile Tag gave Renee was reassuring, absolute. "You okay?" he asked, meeting her gaze, detecting some nervousness there.

She smiled back at him. "Yes, how can I not be? I'm in love with a wonderfully amazing man and what's so truly magnificent is that he loves me, too."

"Always," Tag whispered, taking her hand and lifting it to his lips. "Let's go congratulate Gannon and Erika in case we don't get a chance to do so later."

Renee nodded. What Tag wasn't saying and what she knew nonetheless, was that after telling his grandparents and parents about their plans, if anyone seemed the least bit not pleased, he intended to leave. He had meant what he'd said about not tolerating anything but total acceptance from his grandfather regarding their future marriage.

A part of Renee wasn't sure they would get it. She had seen the look in Patrick Elliott's eyes the moment Tag had walked into the room with her. Tag's grandmother had displayed a genuine open friendliness when introductions had been made moments before the start of the wedding. But Patrick Elliott had been standoff-ish. Tag had gotten the same vibes and had placed a protective hand around her waist, reiterating silently that he didn't need, nor was he seeking, his grandfather's approval.

Tag and Renee walked into the library sometime later. A Victorian-style chandelier hung from the ceiling, illuminating the elegance of the stylish room. Tag had told her when they'd pulled into the estate from the private road that the entire house had been lovingly decorated by his grandmother.

"I understand you wanted to speak with us, Tag," Patrick Elliott said in a deep, gruff voice. Renee studied him. Tall, distinguished-looking, with a medium build, he actually looked at least ten years younger than the age Tag had claimed his grandfather to be. His hair was completely gray and his eyes were the same shade of blue as Tag's. And the one thing she noted was that there wasn't a hint of a smile on his face.

"Yes, I have an announcement to make," Tag said, holding Renee's hand and closing the door behind them. His parents were sitting on a gray sofa and looked at them expectantly. Tag's grandmother was sitting in a chair within a few feet of where Patrick stood with one elbow resting on the mantel of a massive fireplace.

"And just what is this announcement?" Patrick asked.

Tag met Renee's eyes and smiled. "I just wanted all of you to know that I love Renee very much and I've asked her to marry me, and she has agreed to do so next year on Valentine's Day."

Tag's parents, as well as his grandmother, immediately hugged the couple and offered words of congratulations. However, a quick glance at Patrick indicated he hadn't moved an inch and there was a stunned, frozen look etched on his features. "Marriage?" he finally asked, his deep voice drowning out everyone else's. "Are the two of you sure that is what you want to do?"

Tag's hand tightened around Renee's waist. "Yes. Marriage is precisely what we want and what we plan to do," he said, meeting his grandfather's gaze.

It was quite obvious that Patrick wasn't ecstatic with the news, and it was just as apparent that Tag wasn't letting his grandfather's lack of joy influence him in any way.

"I'll be telling the rest of the family when Gannon and Erika return from their honeymoon, but I wanted the four of you to know now."

It was Tag's grandmother, who knew her husband better than anyone, who decided the best thing to do was to make sure Patrick gave his blessing. She went to her husband. "Aye, 'tis a night to celebrate. On our anniversary day one of our grandsons got married and another announced his engagement to a very beautiful young woman. 'Tis a bit special, don't you think, Patrick?"

Patrick met his wife's gaze and everyone knew the woman that he loved more than anything was daring him to contradict her. He only hesitated for a brief moment before lifting her hand to his lips and saying. "Yes, darling, it is special."

Leaving his wife's side, he went to stand before the

couple. "I wish the two of you the best," he said, shaking Tag's hand and then pulling Renee to him in a hug.

"Welcome to the family, Renee," he said in a voice that was still somewhat gruff. "And after this wedding takes place I fully expect you and Tag to start working on some great-grandchildren for me and Maeve to enjoy while we still can."

He took a step back. "Now we need to return to the wedding reception, which will be followed by Maeve's and my anniversary party." Without saying anything else, he walked out of the room.

Later than night Renee lay in Tag's arms, their limbs tangled, their bodies naked, after having just made love. She sighed with pleasure as well as contentment. Gannon and Erika's wedding had been beautiful and the anniversary party that followed for Tag's grandparents had been nothing short of exquisite.

"Are you sure you want us to wait until next February?" Tag asked, leaning over and nibbling at her ear. "That's a long time from now."

Renee smiled as she tilted her head back. "It's less than a year, but I'll find a way to keep you busy until then…not like you don't already have enough to do at work. At least by our wedding the feud between the different magazines will be over and behind everyone."

Tag nodded, looking forward to that day. "How about a big wedding at The Tides?"

Renee grinned. The suggestion definitely appealed to her. She had fallen in love with his grandparents' home. "I think that's a wonderful idea," she said, leaning up and touching her lips to his. "And of course we'll let your mother plan everything."

Tag chuckled. "Of course."

Renee's smile faded somewhat when she said, "Your grandfather hasn't accepted the idea of our marriage one hundred percent, Tag."

Tag met her gaze. "No, but that's his problem and not ours," he said fiercely. "However, I have a feeling that by the day of our wedding he will have come around. And if not, then oh, well. Nothing, and I mean nothing, is going to stop me from making you an Elliott a year from now."

With a smile, Renee leaned up and kissed him. "I like your determination."

"You do?" he asked. "And what else do you like?"

She reached down and her fingers found him hard, large and ready again. "Um, I definitely like the way you go about taking care of business," she said, shifting her body to let him know what she wanted and needed.

He leaned down and kissed her, and responding to him was so natural she took everything he was offering and more. And when he straddled her body and slowly eased inside of her, her mind went blank except for one thought. Yes, she definitely liked the way he was taking care of business.

* * * * *

Don't miss the next exciting titles in
THE ELLIOTTS.
Pick up Cause for Scandal *by Anna DePalo and* The Forbidden Twin *by Susan Crosby, available in March 2007.*

ENGAGEMENT BETWEEN ENEMIES
by Kathie DeNosky
(The Illegitimate Heirs)

After a scandalous rumour erupted, honourable tycoon Caleb Walker made employee Alyssa Merrick an offer she couldn't refuse...

TYCOON TAKES REVENGE by Anna DePalo

Infamous playboy Noah Whittaker gives gossip columnist Kayla Jones a taste of her own medicine, but finds that love is far sweeter than revenge.

THE MAN MEANS BUSINESS by Annette Broadrick

Business was millionaire Dean Logan's only thought until his loyal assistant, Jodie Cameron, accompanied him on a passionate Hawaiian vacation and put marriage on the agenda!

DEVLIN AND THE DEEP BLUE SEA
by Merline Lovelace
(Code Name: Danger)

Helicopter pilot Elizabeth Moore thought sexy stranger Joe Devlin was a mystery to solve—and if she hadn't just been jilted, she might have made an effort to uncover *all* his secrets!

BABY, I'M YOURS by Catherine Mann

Three months after their whirlwind affair, Claire McDermott discovered she was carrying Vic Jansen's child and that she wanted more than just an honourable offer of marriage...

HER HIGH-STAKES AFFAIR by Katherine Garbera

An affair between them was strictly forbidden, but when passion struck Raine Montgomery and rich, sexy Scott Rivers under the bright lights of Las Vegas, it was on the cards!

On sale from 19th January 2007

Visit our website at www.silhouette.co.uk

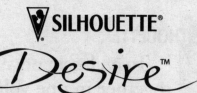

SILHOUETTE®

Desire™

Dynasties:

THE ELLIOTTS

Mixing business with pleasure

January 2007
BILLIONAIRE PROPOSITION *Leanne Banks*
TAKING CARE OF BUSINESS *Brenda Jackson*

March 2007
CAUSE FOR SCANDAL *Anna DePalo*
THE FORBIDDEN TWIN *Susan Crosby*

May 2007
MR AND MISTRESS *Heidi Betts*
HEIRESS BEWARE *Charlene Sands*

July 2007
UNDER DEEPEST COVER *Kara Lennox*
MARRIAGE TERMS *Barbara Dunlop*

September 2007
THE INTERN AFFAIR *Roxanne St Claire*
FORBIDDEN MERGER *Emilie Rose*

November 2007
THE EXPECTANT EXECUTIVE *Kathie DeNosky*
BEYOND THE BOARDROOM *Maureen Child*

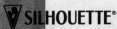

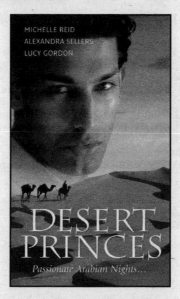

2 FREE

BOOKS AND A SURPRISE GIFT!

We would like to take this opportunity to thank you for reading this Silhouette® book by offering you the chance to take TWO more specially selected titles from the Desire™ series absolutely FREE! We're also making this offer to introduce you to the benefits of the Mills & Boon® Reader Service™—

- ★ FREE home delivery
- ★ FREE gifts and competitions
- ★ FREE monthly Newsletter
- ★ Exclusive Reader Service offers
- ★ Books available before they're in the shops

Accepting these FREE books and gift places you under no obligation to buy, you may cancel at any time, even after receiving your free shipment. Simply complete your details below and return the entire page to the address below. You don't even need a stamp!

YES! Please send me 2 free Desire volumes and a surprise gift. I understand that unless you hear from me, I will receive 3 superb new titles every month for just £4.99 each, postage and packing free. I am under no obligation to purchase any books and may cancel my subscription at any time. The free books and gift will be mine to keep in any case.

D7ZED

Ms/Mrs/Miss/Mr ....Initials ....

BLOCK CAPITALS PLEASE

Surname ....

Address ....

....

....Postcode..............................

Send this whole page to:
UK: FREEPOST CN81, Croydon, CR9 3WZ